Uturax[1] ~ Ixta's and Nacon's Story

Cover Designers: BetiBup33 and Hamza Nadeem

Cerritos Books

Foreword

Dedico este libro a mi viejo, es decir, a mi esposo
muy querido, a todos mis hijos y nietos porque
siempre me han inspirado.

To my husband, kids and grandkids, thanks. JJ
Dayton

Any similarities in names, people and places are
purely coincidental.

TABLE of CONTENTS

Prologue

Today: day 6 of the calendar cycle Martius

Ixta woke, feeling feverish and disoriented, before any of the rest of the ship's crew stirred. She alternated between chills and fever, dripping in sweat one moment and then five minutes later, shivering with chills. The immediacy of her discomfort made her focus on all her symptoms to try to figure out why she felt so wretched. Her cold, clammy t-shirt and boxer shorts, already damp from her fever phase, chilled her even more. She rubbed her arms when the goose bumps rose as a new chills phase began.

She swung her legs off her narrow bed and put her feet on the floor. Her cabin was a standard, tiny six-by nine space. Her sleeping cot lined one wall and on the other side of the very narrow aisle was a tiny desk and RV size bathroom. Given her rank as lead anthropologist, she had private quarters, however small, that afforded her a place to escape from the proximity of the rest of the crew. While the accommodation was nothing to brag about, they were private and for that, she was grateful.

Ixta was a tall, red-headed Terran female with a few freckles on her fair skinned face. Her long hair was in a sleep-mussed braid that hung at her waist. Nearing thirty, she looked all those years and more today as she glanced at herself in the mirror inside her narrow closet door and reached for some dry clothes to replace her sweat-soaked boxer bottoms and t-shirt. Looking at the wall clock beside her bunk, she saw that it was 4:30 a.m., not time to get up yet. It would be another hour and a half before the rest of the crew started stirring.

Suddenly, a recollection of last night came back to her as she remembered some of the evening's events. They started to come rushing back to her, causing a sickening feeling as bile rose in her throat. It was the feeling of totally screwing up, making some super *grande* (big) mistake that was unfixable. She had clearly crossed an unwritten line last night with Nacón, one of the Uturaxan people, one of the emissaries who had greeted their expedition when they had landed months before. But what, specifically, had she done? Her foggy brain refused to concentrate other than giving her the feeling that she had made a grave error, that she had done something that would be called unacceptable by her captain and crew and would change her life forever. Not knowing what she had done was certainly worse than anything she could have done. Wasn't it?

Chapter 1: First Contact (Five Months Previously)

They were fresh off their ship after the long voyage. For some, it was their first trip. Ixta had been on two previous trips but was still enthusiastic about the discoveries she hoped to make on this new planet, Uturax. Sometimes crew members became cynical, jaded by their voyages, unable to see things with a fresh set of eyes. For them, the constant thing was that everything would always be different and as such lost interest for them. As the person in charge of collecting information on flora and fauna on this planet as well as any archeological artifacts, she knew she had more work to do today. She would use native animals, reptiles, insects, and plants along with any artifacts and buildings to construct a profile of this planet and its inhabitants to record in the ship's log to be sent back to Earth and catalogued in the archives along with all the other known planets in the galaxy that Terran explorers had already visited.

As an anthropologist, she was usually in the first encounter group that made official first contact with any indigenous inhabitants on the planet and this trip was seemingly no different as she'd gotten no contradicting orders from the captain. Though she didn't really expect this to be a first contact in the strict sense of the term, she was looking forward to being part of the team that made this ship's first meeting with the alien planet.

Oddly, this planet had no real information about it in the database and certainly nothing negative to indicate that it was hostile. For some reason, traders and other ships had avoided this planet for years. It was unusual at this stage of space exploration and trade, with numerous routes that had been long established, to find a planet about which nothing was written or recorded. That raised many questions in Ixta's mind. Something wasn't right, but at this point, she didn't know why she felt that way. It seemed impossible that this planet was undiscovered and theirs was the first ship to visit it in all these years. It wasn't remote enough to have been bypassed by all explorational voyages before now. Perhaps they would get lucky and truly be making a first contact here on this planet.

There had been no hostile weapons fire aimed at them when they had landed, and they had spent several hours now on the ground setting up a base with no hostile attacks. Their experience had been that if a planet was going to act war-like, it occurred upon entry to the atmosphere or touching down on the surface. Of course, they wouldn't rule out the possibility that an attack could still occur. Until they learned more about the inhabitants, they would proceed with caution.

It was customary to wear dress uniforms in case there was a political hierarchy that cared about details like that and enjoyed a formal greeting. Where there was a royal family, many planets had an elaborate ceremonial manner of greeting. Captain John Paul Wells, first officer Justin Daniels, Ixta Tikal and Ethan Baker, the lead biologists for today, all gathered at the hatchway similarly dressed. Wells had assembled the crew several hours before touchdown for a brief recap of first contact protocol and given them all a copy of the fleet's regulations on their tablets to reread before they landed.

Now that the ship was settled and landing procedures had been completed, Wells was anxious to get things started on the planet's surface. Captain Wells nodded to his first officer to open the hatch, and they looked out. Just inside the door, the captain had a team of armed soldiers ready to spring into action if this alien greeting party changed its demeanor. Each of the first encounter team wore pistols under their dress uniform jackets along with armor-cloth vests just in case they should have to defend themselves from attack. Science personnel had taken readings that determined that the atmosphere had acceptable oxygen levels to breathe without breathing apparatuses. Thus, no headgear and oxygen packs were required, which made communication easier for all involved.

Near the bottom of the ramp, they saw a delegation of exceedingly tall, hairy humanoids waiting for them in the clearing near the end of the boarding ramp. It was a group of male aliens only and they all had at least shoulder length hair or longer pulled back into ponytails. Their coloring was medium toned, and their hair colors ranged from dark blonde to almost black. They were dressed in four colors among their group and the person at the front of the phalanx stepped forward with his hands open, waist high. Wells and his crew took that as a sign that they had no weapons, and it would be safe to proceed. Wells and his first officer noted the precision with which the group moved as one which bespoke training in maneuvers for war. There appeared to be a chief and another male of social standing near his side, perhaps another in the royal family, a very tall alien who could be related to one of the leaders, though they were not able to determine much about relationships among the inhabitants at this point. Perhaps it was a president and his cabinet.

They were not human but were mammals and did have characteristics of both human and animal. The ceremonial headdress and gem encrusted staff carried by the male in front made him look more like a chieftain than a president, however. They noted that all the males wore some type of large gemstones either in armbands or around their necks. The crew's delegation would just have to wait and see and gather more data before learning the lead male's true rank and position.

The usually unflappable Captain Wells lost his train of thought as he looked up at the imposing, glowering aliens literally towering over him and then awkwardly offered his hand to shake with the nearest alien. Snapping back to reality and his composure at the collective gasp he heard from his crew, he now hesitated because of his breach of first contact protocol. But the alien leader ignored his hand anyway after first closely assessing Wells to try to determine his motives for such an unusual, inappropriate act. Diplomatic crisis averted because the alien chose to ignore the captain's error, the indigenous leader folded his hands over his chest after handing his staff to a member of his party behind him. He seemed to be waiting, willing to take his cues from the newcomers. Ixta and the rest of the first contact team just stared at Wells, shocked by the faux pas.

First mate Daniels reached over to touch Wells on the arm, clearly appalled at Wells' gaffe. What was going on here? Wells never screwed up like he had just done. *'Oh hell, what a way to get off to a bad start. Wells must be crazy or under the influence of something today to do what he just did,'* Ixta thought, not knowing that Ethan and Justin were sharing that same thought. *'They must think we're really stupid assholes right now to have screwed up this meeting before it even got started. I just hope that these aliens don't understand drug use and being high or we're really screwed.'* Ixta's idle musings made her think further, *'Oh, no. Hell no. That can't be what just happened. Can it?'*

Regardless of the rebuffed handshake, which was not a well-thought-out gesture now that he'd regained his composure and thought more about it, at least there hadn't been a hostile reaction, Wells reflected as he thought about his next move. However, Wells feared his inappropriate action didn't set the stage for a good beginning to their relationship. Wells was usually the master at these first encounters. All he could think to himself was that the extreme height and forbidding countenances of this alien group had rattled him. Nevertheless, the captain took it as a positive sign that the aliens were still there and willing to see what would come next.

Captain Wells opened his hands and next withdrew a translator from his pocket, showed it to the delegation, and then looked questioningly at their obvious leader. Finally, the alien nodded, an uncertain look on his face, and Wells punched some buttons and spoke into the translator. It crackled and then came out with a language none from the ship were familiar with. From the look on the faces of those in the delegation, neither were they. Wells punched in some more codes, tried again with the same results and then and third and a fourth time. Still no response, just puzzled looks and a growing irritation. Moving quietly to step beside the captain, Ixta made a suggestion softly and Wells just looked at her, irritated at the interruption. Ixta suppressed a gasp as she looked into his eyes and saw his dilated pupils. *'Shit! Not now! I was just runnin' my mouth to myself about this a minute ago. I never really thought he'd fuck us all like this with his drug problem.'*

It had been rumored that Wells had had drug issues in the past but was supposed to have recovered after a lengthy stint in rehab. At least that was the gossip on the ship. Of course, none of the crew had been privy to this information prior to committing to this voyage, but there had been whispers of his recently sketchy past. The crew had not known anything concrete about his problems, only about his extensive experience in interstellar travel.

Apparently, he'd fallen off the wagon. Wells tried again with a new code based on her suggestion. This time, the translator produced some sounds that the planet's natives responded to.

Seeing this, Wells barked, "Well, I'll be damned. That's an old universal generic trader lingo. Not expected in someplace this remote. At least we can communicate now." Ixta got no thanks for her suggestion which solved the problem, but she didn't expect anything positive from Wells who wasn't known for being especially friendly or positive with anyone on the crew except for Daniels, his first mate whom he'd crewed with for a number of years. Seeing that he was strung out on some drug made her more certain he wouldn't acknowledge her help or probably even remember it later.

Ixta suppressed a sigh and brought her mind back to the moment to concentrate on what was being said. While the conversation was finally getting started, her eyes roamed the area noting the lush vegetation that was the backdrop to the clearing with tall mountains beyond. Tall, feathery branches were reaching up toward the sky, a striking green, with plentiful and healthy leaves. They looked like regular trees with a tropical twist. Clearly, this planet was a hospitable environment to at least some vegetation. Her eyes continued their sweep upward to the sky which consisted of vibrant hues of purples and pinks as a backdrop to the twin suns. Her mind wandering, Ixta forced herself back to the conversation to see if any information of value was being exchanged.

Using the translator, Wells explained, "We are from the planet Earth, and we are called Terrans by those we meet on other planets."

By talking through the translator, Wells was able
to exchange other small details of information about
their origin and get the point across that they meant
no harm and were just here to study, make new
friends and perhaps establish a new trade route if that
was acceptable to the Uturaxans.

After listening to Captain Wells, finally the
Uturaxan leader, grabbed the translator awkwardly
and said, "Welcome to our world of Uturax."

Seeing the leader's words as a good sign, Ixta and
Ethan, one of the ship's biologists, were both eager to
get permission to explore and get samples to take
back to Earth. Wells and Chaac, the Uturaxan leader,
discussed this and a few other details. It was agreed
that the next day, Nacón, the tall younger male who
seemed to be an important member of the group
because the apparent leader spoke primarily to him as
they had waited for the ship's occupants to walk
down the ramp, would meet Ethan and Ixta at the
ramp after first light for a tour of the planet.

It seemed that Nacón shared a closer relationship
with Chaac, but their translator hadn't come up with
a word for it when they discussed his role in the
exploration tomorrow. Ixta hoped to figure that out,
among other things, during the next few months that
they were docked here. She was glad that she would
have more time with the tall alien obviously in his
prime because he was good looking, if a little furry.
For now, the crew felt this was a good beginning,
finally after a rocky start and they said goodbye for
the day and returned to the ship, surprised when they
got inside that so much time had transpired. It had
felt like they were out there only a matter of ten to

fifteen minutes but learned from the crew inside that nearly an hour had passed while they were communicating with the delegation.

The next morning, Ethan and Ixta met at the hatch door a good thirty minutes before dawn really arrived. Neither one wanted to miss a minute of this opportunity to make what they thought could be their first real contact with these people. In these days, true first contacts with new alien races don't happen very often as trade routes had been established for years. For both, this opportunity was an unexpected one that they both looked forward to. Yesterday didn't count for much in their scientific judgment because not much had really been learned about the alien culture other than they had graciously overlooked the captain's stupid gaffe by offering a handshake. Rather than acting offended, the aliens had ignored the breach of standard protocol among all first contacts.

The crew members present knew they would have been written up if any of them had done something so stupid. The aliens looked remarkably humanoid in many ways, except, of course, for that fur over their bodies. Ixta idly wondered if a famous Earth classic film series that portrayed a tall, hairy alien as a main character in several of the films in the series had been a relative of this group of humanoids, but quickly dismissed that, knowing that the creator of an ancient earth classic film series about science fiction couldn't have made it to this primitive place for ideas.

These humanoids with their kilt-like garments looked like the Scottish highlanders of many, many centuries ago who had fought to protect their lands.

She hoped that the Uturaxans never got angry with them as they were massive and powerful. They looked to be in excellent physical condition, trained athletes or warriors perhaps. Surely the rest of the inhabitants here couldn't be as big as those in the delegation. Perhaps they had sent their tallest males to be intimidating to the newcomers, the uninvited guests to their planet.

Well, their intimidation tactic, if that was the intent, worked. The captain had uncharacteristically been rattled. Ixta could only guess that their expressions that were certainly unfriendly, coupled with their extreme height and imposing physicality had gotten the captain distracted and off track in his drugged state. They had looked huge and imposing to all the Terrans.

"Well, what do you want to do first?" Ethan asked Ixta with excitement and enthusiasm.

'Caray, (Geez) this kid makes me feel old,' Ixta thought but answered, "I expect we'll do and go wherever they take us. Initially, till we gain their trust, I doubt we'll have much say over where we go and what we see. Let's just wait and see and let them take the lead. I don't want us to offend anyone with being 'pushy'. We didn't get off on the best foot with them yesterday, thanks to Captain Wells, so let's not compound that problem and further complicate and degrade the less than stellar impression they have of us."

Privately, Ixta was wondering if Ethan was going to be a problem on this outing. He was known for his over-enthusiastic approach to almost everything. She could understand his excitement at learning new

things, but politics were part of this outing, and she
was concerned that Ethan didn't really understand the
importance of establishing positive relations with the
aliens on this planet, especially after their captain's
inept performance in yesterday's first contact, Ixta
felt she and Ethan needed to mend fences and present
a much more favorable impression of the crew for the
Uturaxans if this relationship was going to develop
along positive lines. She knew that she and Ethan
would be on parade today for the Uturaxans to judge
their behavior. She wanted to do all she could to
ensure that their assessment of her team was positive
and did something to eradicate yesterday's awkward
introduction to the aliens. Ethan's tendency to talk
before thinking could be a problem, but he was an
excellent biologist, and she wanted to see if she could
control his mouth to have the benefit of his
knowledge for the expedition today.

"Yes, of course. That makes sense. I just wanted
to make a mental wish list of things to see," Ethan
said, his excitement deflating as the reality of her
words set in. Why would the Uturaxans take them all
over their planet when they didn't know yet how
much the Terrans could be trusted?

Though they looked to have a simple,
uncomplicated culture, they might not be that naïve.
Impulsiveness aside, Ethan was smart and quickly
assessed the complexity of the situation once
prompted by Ixta's words. He knew that Ixta had
reservations about trusting him at this stage of the
mission when relationships with the aliens were
being built. It was a step up for him to be allowed on
the planet this early in the relationship-building

process. Usually, he had to wait till relationships were somewhat determined and could not be undermined by his occasional reckless lack of judgment.

He had come to realize recently that the crew's opinion of him wasn't complimentary and was a handicap he'd created for himself. He hoped to show Ixta on this trip that her trust in him wasn't misplaced. He was lucky that his name came up on the rotation today from the team of biologists and he knew he had to try to be more circumspect than usual. She had the option of skipping over his name in the rotation, but since she hadn't, he didn't want to let her down. He knew he needed to work on his impulsiveness which made the rest of the crew regard him as the kid on the crew. He had sat out more than one mission because other crew members felt they couldn't really count on him to think clearly and analyze before acting.

"Well, we're about to find out just what we'll do. No more anticipation. I see the one they called Nacón yesterday. He's here along with about a half dozen more."

"How can you tell them apart? They all look the same to me," Ethan interjected.

Ignoring his comment, Ixta continued, "If you don't mind, I'd like to take the lead in talking with the group meeting us. Take your cues from me. Do you have a problem with that?" Ixta asked, hoping that Ethan would have no objections as exchanging angry words with him wasn't the way she wanted to start the day. She hated to pull rank unless necessary but would do so if needed. It would just be simpler if he agreed, and they could move forward.

"No, you're the senior officer in this duo and as you know, I tend to speak before I think."

Relieved that the details had been worked out so easily, Ixta turned and opened the door so they could leave. While Ixta was senior, most patrols were run in a democratic manner with both members taking the lead as necessary. Had yesterday gone better initially, Ixta might not have felt the need to be so careful in this meeting and exploratory outing.

They both looked out at the clearing near where the ship's ramp ended as Nacón and his entourage arrived. The jungle vegetation was the backdrop for their tour guides who stood lined up in formation behind their apparent leader. The trees looked different from any they'd encountered yet on this voyage on the few planets that did have growing plant life. They were tall and had distinctive leafy foliage.

Glancing back at the humanoids, Ixta noted that no one looked especially happy to be there, and several looked downright unhappy and sullen. She also noted that they wore different shades of colors of clothing, but more of the earthy, rust color prevailed. Additionally, they all casually wore some type of amulets with roughly faceted jewels on them. To a man, they all wore their long hair pulled back into a ponytail and they all looked serious and forbidding. *'Jeez, their hair's almost as long as mine. Interesting. Are all the males on the planet this good looking? Surely, they didn't find just the handsome ones to work with us. They all look great and Nacón is the best of the lot. Focus, Ixta. Focus. Fantasizing about the alien greeting party today won't help me to be careful about the impression we are going to be making. A lot is riding on today's encounter.'*

Using the Universal Translator, Ixta said, "Good morning. We are incredibly happy that you have agreed to help us learn about your planet. I am Ixta and this is Ethan."

Nacón acknowledged her by nodding his head and the six males moved beside him, three on each side, and nodded in unison.

"Um, well, how about we get started?" Ixta asked, hoping that the Uturaxan group wasn't really as reluctant as they looked right now, their faces set in very serious expressions.

The Uturaxan males looked at each other and then at Nacón for orders. They all just stood there, looking forbidding.

Finally, Ixta said, "Is something wrong? Did I misunderstand what Chaac said, last night?"

Ethan added, "Have we offended you in some way? That was not our intent."

Nacón shook his head slightly and said, "No. You have offended no one."

Ethan muttered to Ixta, "Well, you could have fooled me. This may be going nowhere fast. This greeting party of dog giants doesn't give a shit about helping us."

Nacón's eyes went to Ethan quickly, a frown moving across his face, his jaw clenching, and just as quickly disappearing. Ixta asked herself if he could have understood Ethan because that's what it seemed like had just happened. No, it had to be Ethan's tone as he was clearly not happy with the turn of events, his enthusiasm of a few minutes gone. Being confronted with the aliens' sour attitudes about this tour had made this seem like work rather than an exciting, exploratory mission he had hoped for.

Ixta turned to Ethan and said, "Shut the fuck up, asshole!" under her breath, certainly loud enough for Ethan to hear, but she hoped that her voice would not carry to the aliens in front of them. But it did carry to Nacón who silently approved her chastisement of the overeager younger man who seemed to have prejudices against his people.

"Well, then could we get started? We'd like to learn about plants and animals native to your planet as well as any cultural artifacts. If you would permit us to do so, we'd also like to gather a few plant samples to take back to our planet. We have a museum with these kinds of samples from other planets and would like to include samples from your home here. We would, of course, not remove any artifacts or animals and would only take plant samples that you approved beforehand. Of the artifacts and animals, we would just like to take photographs for our archives," Ixta said brightly, determined to try to put a positive spin on the moment and just forge ahead though she felt flustered in this alien male's presence.

It was a new, unfamiliar feeling to Ixta who had sworn off the opposite sex after her last relationship. Her body and feelings had been in stasis as far as she was concerned, and they could stay that way. But there was something that inexplicably drew her to the tall male in command of the alien group. Fur aside, he was good looking and had a compelling personality. *'If he weren't such a grouch and intent on showing off how intimidating they all are, he'd be someone I'd like to get to know better.'*

Nacón just looked intently at her, said something under his breath to his companions that she could clearly hear but not understand and then turned suddenly to the right and broke into a brisk trot. *'Let's show them how vulnerable they are to our whims. Keeping them off guard will reveal how they deal with uncertain situations,'* Nacón thought to himself as he and his entourage set a fast pace without turning to see if the Terrans followed. *'Maybe they won't even follow and then our obligations to them for today will be over.'*

Not going to accept being left behind while their Uturaxan guides left them in the dust, Ethan and Ixta turned as one and ran after the indigenous group trying to catch up with them. Quickly, they left the clearing and entered the lush jungle growth. They followed a barely visible path and went deeper into the foliage. The fronds of palm-like plants gently flapped on their heads as they made their way through the jungle. Occasionally they would step over a fallen branch on the path. One of the plants was prickly and sticky looking, and they gave it a wide berth, following the lead of the Uturaxan group moving ahead at a good clip. Finally, Nacón looked back and saw the Terrans struggling to keep up, breathing heavily, but gamely following them and he relented. Reluctantly admiring their pluck and deciding that maybe they weren't as bad as their stupid captain yesterday, he raised his hand to call a

halt to his men and turned to the Terrans, took the
translator out of Ixta's hand, and said,

"While you rest a moment, you might as well
know how I feel about this assignment I've been
given. I think it's a waste of my time and my men's.
We'd rather be training or hunting than walking you
Terrans around Uturax. It is beneath our skills. Now
do you feel better for knowing?"

Ethan's face got redder, and he just gasped for
another breath, halting next to the group, and
slumping against a tree trunk next to the trail, but
looking at the brooding Uturaxans with apprehension.
Looking first at Ethan to silence him with a look
before he opened his mouth and said something
imprudent and offensive, Ixta had plenty to say to
Nacón.

Between breaths, she managed to tell Nacón what
she thought, "Well, not especially. How did you think
we'd feel to hear you complain about spending time
with us? It's insulting. Be that as it may, Chaac said
he'd be happy to help us learn more about your
planet. This must not seem like a very important job
for you, but it's very important to us. We really want
to learn about your planet, Nacón. It's a beautiful
place here where you live, and we would be honored
if you would share it with us to learn more about your
planet and your culture. We hope this information
will help us to understand Uturax better and make us
better allies. But if you prefer, we can ask your leader
for a new guide for our work."

"Do not insult *me* by going to my father to tell him
I did not do his bidding," Nacón ground out, looking
even more unwilling and angry than before, if that

was possible. "I will do as he asked, but for a warrior, taking Terrans on a sightseeing trip is not how I would choose to spend my days." Ixta was sure that Nacón grew taller as he spoke, his angry features also augmented by his extreme size.

"My apologies, Nacón. I do not mean to insult you. I can see that this assignment must be boring to you, but it is not to us. It is just so very important. Please, let's put aside our differences, call a truce, if you will, and get started looking at some flora and fauna. All right?" Ixta silently congratulated herself on getting this alien male to clarify his relationship with the leader. He was his son. This was valuable information to share with her captain later today. She just hoped that she hadn't pissed him off to the extent that he would renege on their tour today. If he did, there would be no getting to know him better.

'I must have been crazy thinking how I'd like getting to know this guy better. He's clearly not on that wavelength or he wouldn't be so eager to get rid of us. That'll teach me to look at alien men as people to get to know better or whatever that means. Shit. Like my grandma would say, pretty is as pretty does'. This guy may be good-looking, but his superiority complex stinks.'

Unwillingly, Nacón began to like this Terran female for her words, her lack of fear of him and her seeming understanding. Perhaps she didn't mean what she said, but at least the words were correct, and she had conveyed them in a convincing manner. It *was* boring having to escort these off-worlders around his planet. However, he had been training as a warrior for many years and that did have its boring moments though he loathed to admit it to anyone outside of his immediate friends who were, of course, warriors too. He and his men had practiced against each other for so many years, that they could all anticipate the others' moves when sparring. Consequently, sparring had lost some of its luster to them all.

Maybe talking with these Terrans would provide a distraction for them for a time anyway. At this point, they had no new moves to learn and no new men to train. All the males and females eligible for service in the army were already in service and training, so there would be no more recruits for another four to six years when a new group of adolescents reached their majority. Training did serve to keep them in excellent physical shape should the need arise to defend their planet, but it had become very routine to Nacón and his inner circle lately. It was a job, of sorts, that kept many of the Uturaxan people in their prime occupied for most days. Well, he wasn't about to share that with this Terran group. Let them feel indebted to him and his group for showing them around. You never knew when a sympathetic enemy could come in handy during a skirmish.

Nacón mentally dismissed the Terran man who was looking very fearful and uncomfortable. He clearly was not a person to pay much attention to. It would seem that there would have to be more of these exploratory expeditions into the interior with the ship's crew. Nacón at least hoped he would have more time with this woman who intrigued him. While very different from the women on his planet, she was not unattractive. He wondered if the males on her crew would find her as nice to look at by their standards of beauty as he did. He liked that she was tall and athletic and unafraid of him and his men. He also appreciated her efforts at diplomacy and even liked her threat to go over him to talk to his father. It was a good tactic in war and negotiations. Unlike the male crew member, she'd called 'Ethan,' she seemed fearless and willing to speak up for herself but also willing to accept responsibility and apologize when needed. Another good tactic. *'Point earned, Terran woman.'*

After the rocky start on the first day of initial greetings with the captain and the Uturaxan delegation, Nacón had decided as the day wore on that, unlike the ship's captain, he liked this Terran woman who made him look at his planet differently every time they discovered the oddest, most ordinary things.

Since they seemed destined to spend more time together, he was relieved Ixta wasn't anything like the captain yesterday whose actions kept the council talking for quite a while about his crude, insulting greeting. Additionally, the Uturaxans had noticed that the captain of the Terran vessel seemed to be under the influence of some kind of drug. He must think them stupid to be using drugs before meeting an alien delegation in a first contact. They had, however, noted that the rest of the delegation that came down the ramp to meet them were not on drugs; perhaps that indicated that the captain's drug-induced state was a personal aberration for him. They hoped that would be the case as they discussed what they felt would be appropriate things to show them in the coming visit and those they assumed would follow.

That first day, Nacón and his men led them past an old ruin of one of their first towns and Ixta immediately sat down on the ground and began to carefully and painstakingly sift through the rubble till she found a pottery shard. You'd have thought she'd found the mineral ununtrium or gemstones from her excitement and enthusiasm.

Seeing that the Terrans, at least the two of them represented in this fact-finding duo, seemed genuinely interested in learning, Nacón had a change of heart and decided to take them to a textile operation that had been moved into the village last night for this purpose just in case they needed something else to see and to occupy their visitors with if the morning went well. While he still didn't like the male, who seemed to be prejudiced against the Uturaxan's distinctly alien appearance, he did like the woman and wanted to accommodate her wishes to see more things. The male had made an indelible impression on Nacón and his men with his prejudiced comment, calling them giant dogs. Chaac had anticipated that the off-worlders would want and expect to see more than the jungle near their landing site and by his order, the village had been busy the preceding night moving in some operations to show them without exposing any of their secrets to the Terrans. It was too soon in their relationship to share more than superficial facts and previous visitors had not fared well on Uturax, not having left to spread the word about their planet, once their deceitful intentions had been ascertained by the Uturaxans. No survivors meant no news spread out in the galaxy about Uturax.

After much time had been spent between Ethan and Ixta examining the shard, Nacón decided it was time to move to the next predetermined site. "Come. We have more to show you today. Follow me."

Ixta and Ethan looked up, surprised because they'd been totally involved in the examination and cataloging of the shard. Ethan and Ixta, glancing first at their watches and then up, seeing Nacón and his companions standing by somewhat impatiently, they realized that they wanted to leave now, and that considerable time had been spent looking at their discovery.

Sighing and reluctantly returning the shard to its place on the ground, Ixta said, "All right. Where to next?"

"We are going to visit our clothing huts so you can see how our clothing is made." Nacón responded and then looked at his troupe, indicating that they offer no explanation in addition to his. Varying responses were given by his men from nodding heads to a blink of the eyes, but they all seemed to be giving assent to Nacón.

Seeing the look pass between the men, Ixta wondered what Nacón was up to but had no choice but to get up and follow along with the group that was doubling back along the trail they'd been on previously to bring them to the old camp.

"Did you notice anything strange going on back there?" she asked Ethan under her breath.

"Yeah, I didn't get that look that they shared. You don't think they're planning something against us, do you?" Ethan asked, a worried look on his face, his previous unease still very much present in his mind.

"We'll just have to go along and find out. We're out here all alone with these men with minimal weaponry to help us out if we need it. We're outnumbered and they look strong as hell, so let's just hang tight and see what happens," Ixta responded, all romantic thoughts she might have harbored about getting to know the alien leader's son better vanishing, suddenly wishing she'd paid more attention in her hand-to-hand combat training she had taken as preparation for this last voyage.

Apparently, the alien populations encountered on recent missions by other ships in the IPEC (Interstellar Planetary Exploration Consortium) had had more than the usual hostile receptions, so regulations had changed. Everyone now had to take this additional training in self-defense. Shaken by Ethan's words that changed her line of thinking completely and her realization that they were quite vulnerable here alone in the jungle, Ixta felt scattered in her thinking. Then she remembered that she had done quite well in the training, even taking down some of the stronger male crew members during sparring matches. Of course, none of them towered over her like these alien men did. Instead of being in charge and completely competent to meet any situation, she felt uncertain for the first time in many years. She decided that uncertainty was a feeling she did not like.

"Easy for you to say, Ixta. You were the best in our team during the karate training right before we lifted off Earth. I couldn't even pass all the tests,"

Ethan grumbled, even more uneasy now that Ixta had
voiced some concerns. Ixta excelled at everything,
including hand-to-hand combat, but all he felt he was
good at was lab work where he was a stickler for
details and gave every effort.

Nacón heard Ixta and Ethan muttering under their
breaths but was unable to make out what they were
saying. He couldn't miss their anxious looks,
however, especially the man who looked quite
concerned. Wimpy type, he figured. Not much of a
man. The Uturaxan scientists all served in the army
and while war wasn't their first pursuit, they were all
able to acquit themselves well in combat. Apparently
Terrans didn't place as high a value on combat as did
his planet. Good information. Looking at the two of
them, he figured the woman would be more difficult
than the man to subdue. She looked very fit and
confident. *'I like that in a woman. ¡Carumba! (Darn
it) Am I crazy?'* He knew they must both carry
weapons though they couldn't be too formidable as
they had to be small, concealed handguns. The man
looked incapable of using a gun to defend himself
though. Interesting information. He could see the
wisdom in his father's decision to allow the Terrans
access to the planet. They hoped to learn much about
the off-worlders, and this was the easiest way.

This time, Nacón chose not to run as the Terrans
clearly were in terrible shape by Uturaxan standards,
especially the man. The woman did manage to keep
up with them on the way out through the jungle, but
just barely. Nacón did have to acknowledge that their
legs were shorter and thus they were not built for
speed as were the Uturaxans. Since they were

walking their way back to the village, it took them much longer than the initial trip out. It was hot and the dual suns were high in the sky by the time they reached the village. The humidity caused steam to rise off the damp earthen floor and not a breeze stirred the branches and fronds of the trees.

"Do you wish to return to your ship to eat and drink before we continue, or would you like to share food and drink with us now that we have returned to the village?" Nacón inquired pleasantly, expecting them both to flee as they hadn't recovered their air of confidence that they had started the day with.

Surprised by the offer of hospitality, Ixta looked questioningly at Ethan for his opinion.

"I'd like to go back to the ship, I think," Ethan said, by now thoroughly exhausted and feeling less and less secure with the Uturaxan contingent of men as the day wore on. Rather than loosening up and relaxing, they looked just as vigilant and frankly as terrifying to him as they had at first sight in the morning. Grateful for the offer to leave, he had answered without thinking or consulting Ixta.

"Fine. I'll talk to you later, Ethan. I'm staying here for now," Ixta said to him and turned to Nacón.

Ethan almost said something to Ixta when she announced that she was staying for lunch. Incredulous at her apparent disregard for her safety, he looked at her again, but Ixta had started to leave with Nacón. He hoped she would be all right but didn't know what he could do at that point to see that she would be safe. He was not going to reconsider and stay with these terrifying aliens for a moment longer than he had to. Thankfully, he'd been given the chance to make a graceful exit that he hoped wouldn't offend any of them. Alien exploration wasn't what it was cracked up to be when the aliens were these huge, intimidating warrior types.

Hurrying back to the ship, he worried what he would tell the captain if Ixta didn't return later in the day. Too late; he was starting to feel guilty about leaving her there alone. *I wonder if I'll get in trouble because I left her there. But it was her decision. Surely Wells can't hold that against me. He should be glad that one of us at least had the sense to make the correct decision. I can always say that since she was the senior member of our team, it was her own decision.*

"Thank you for your kind offer of food and drink. I would love to have the opportunity to share food and drink with you. Ethan will return to the ship," Ixta added unnecessarily as Ethan was already scurrying off in a rather undignified manner.

Nacón nodded at Ixta and wondered how a man would leave a woman alone with people he didn't know and who had treated him somewhat cavalierly earlier in the day. Also, what kind of woman had no fear to spend time alone with alien people she knew not at all? Either very brave or very foolish.

They went to the clearing and entered a hut near the center and almost as soon as they were seated, serving women began to bring fresh fruit and grilled vegetables to the table. Another duo of women brought bowls of water and cloths with which to wash their hands to each of them around the table. Others brought pitchers of cool water and filled the cups on the plank table. Leaves resembling Terran banana leaves served as individual plates and there were no eating utensils. A small jug was brought and set in the middle of the table. Another jug was brought with a hot oatmeal-like substance inside that Nacón called *atole (gruel)*. An earthenware dish, clearly hand built pottery, was then set on the table in front of Ixta with a crude spoon that contained a thick light amber liquid.

Nacón said, "If you like a sweet taste, the *miel de agave* (agave honey) is used to sweeten the *atole*. Let it cool for a minute; then you can eat it along with the fruit.

Ixta, seeing that Nacón and his men were already eating, tentatively took a taste of the "oatmeal" with her fingers as she saw the men do. The crudely made wooden cups that had been placed before each of them were filled with what looked like water. It was cold and tasted fresh if slightly citrus. The *atole* was good and she decided she loved the sweetener that was like honey and poured more on the oatmeal. The grilled fruit was fresh and delicious. All in all, a simple meal, but very satisfying.

"This is delicious! I do thank you for bringing me here and offering me this wonderful food. I can't wait to see your clothing facility next. Will that still be convenient for you after we finish our meal?"

Watching Ixta dig right into the food without a moment's hesitation, Nacón admired her boldness and her willingness to try the food of his planet. Not all off-worlders tried to fit in, preferring to keep to themselves. It could have been a trap for her, an attempt to poison her. However, she obviously wasn't feeling threatened and acted like she'd been digging

her fingers into *atole* her whole life. She acted like
one of the guys around the table, comfortable and at
ease. Nacón decided he liked the Terran female's
attitude and comments and responded pleasantly with
"We will go there after we wash. Rosaura, bring us
more wash water."

One of the serving women turned and brought
over several bowls of water and fresh pieces of cloth
to use as towels. Ixta watched as the men shared the
water bowl to wash the *atole* off their hands and did
the same when it was passed to her. She stood when
Nacón stood, smiled, mouthed what looked like the
word 'thanks' and bowed to the serving women in
gratitude and turned to leave.

Nacón noted her courtesy to Nana and Rosaura
who had served them, found it surprising after their
captain's crass behavior yesterday, but pleasing. He
then led the group across the clearing to the far side
of the little village and entered a hut that was at the
edge of the jungle. He opened the door and motioned
for Ixta to go inside. Nacón signaled to his men to
wait for him outside by the door.

Once inside, Ixta was met with the sight of four
looms of varying sizes and two spinning wheels.
Women were weaving and spinning. Ixta saw crudely
woven baskets holding what looked like wool and
cotton. Apparently, they were spinning and weaving
cloth from both. Given the heat today, she could only
guess that the wool must mean that there would be a
change of the seasons to cooler weather at some time
in the future. She made a mental note to herself to tell
the captain about the wool and its implications. The
women were very skillful and chattered softly among

themselves in a language different from any that Ixta had ever heard. Occasionally though, she would hear a word that almost sounded familiar but then as soon as the thought formed, it was gone, like smoke vanishing in the wind. She didn't know what she was hearing, but it seemed odd to her that she could even guess some of the meanings. With no context, she really had no way of knowing if her guesses were accurate. She just assumed they were discussing their work. For all she knew, they could have been planning an attack on the ship, unlikely as that was from this group of artisans.

Looking at Nacón, she asked, "Could I see the wheel where they are working with the wool, please?'

Puzzled, but willing to go along with what Ixta was interested in for the moment, Nacón said something to the woman to his right who nodded in response. Belatedly, he wondered how she knew the name for that piece of equipment or seemed to know the type of material being spun.

'I wonder how she knew what to call the wheel? This is an antique piece of equipment, but she seemed to know what was happening and that they are spinning wool on this wheel.'

"Would she mind if I tried?' Ixta asked after standing and watching a bit.

"No problem," Nacón replied surprised by her request. Spinning was a lost art, and one not seen in many worlds anymore. People were either too primitive and their planets untouched by even primitive machinery or too technological and machines had long taken over work such as this.

The woman stood and moved aside, and Ixta took her place on the stool, tossed her braid back over her shoulder, restarted the single treadle wheel and began to draft the carded fleece to spin it into a yarn of as close to the same diameter as she could. It had been a decade since she had sat beside her grandma and spun yarn, but she felt like it should come back to her. Her hands would remember the rhythms, she hoped. She was right. Her fingers did remember the old rhythms, and she soon settled into them, relaxing and remembering her happy times with her grandmother.

Both Nacón and the women of his tribe were transfixed by the scene, watching the off-worlder spin the yarn as if it were an activity she did every day. She seemed to be enjoying herself and was doing a good job with the yarn. She looked up and smiled at Nacón as she grabbed another rolag (roll of fiber) of wool from the basket to blend in with the one she was finishing, holding it to the other one that was dwindling, watching as it caught and began to wrap around the forming yarn. The other workers in the hut also started watching her with surprise, abandoning their tasks at hand. It was extremely difficult to find people within the Uturaxans with the old skills who could run any of the equipment in this hut today. It was a lost art that the young people, who were enthusiastic about war games and little else, found boring and did their time in the weaving areas reluctantly. While they had weaving technology to produce fabric in large quantities when needed, the clan leaders still favored the soft, finely woven material produced from the handspun yarns.

Looking up at Nacón and the women and seeing the surprise on their faces, Ixta said in explanation, "I learned to do this in summers when I visited my grandma on her farm. She raised alpacas and sheep and loved to spin yarn and knit sweaters. It wasn't about not having the money to buy yarn and sweaters; it was about the satisfaction of creating something you grew and made. I'm glad I can remember how to do this still. Since I'm not shearing the animals, then skirting, washing, dyeing and carding the fiber, but only spinning, I feel like I'm getting off easily. Let's see, did I miss anything in the steps of the preparation process? No, I think I got it all. Just now, I was only embellishing and adding to all the arduous work others have put into this process to get it ready to spin. I feel like I should be more helpful with the rest of the process."

"You surprise me, off-worlder. It is a skill of value that you have. It is a good thing to create something useful of purpose for yourself and others. I had not thought your people would know these old skills," Nacón replied.

Ixta laughed, "Don't get the wrong idea, Nacón. I don't think most Terrans can do this. Not all were lucky to have a grandma who wanted them to learn the old ways of doing and creating. I consider myself fortunate to know some of the old ways. To have wool, you must have sheep or other animals with soft fiber, and you must also grow cotton to produce the fibers being used here on some of the other wheels. Could I see your animals next? Also, I would like to see how you grow your food, too. I learned how to plant a garden and cultivate vegetables for our table from my grandma as well. Perhaps another day you can show me how you produce food to feed your people and the animals that produce this beautiful fiber."

Silently cursing himself for not thinking this through, Nacón saw that he should have realized there was a possibility someone would ask the questions she had about the source of these fibers they were spinning today. When he and Chaac had discussed this spinning facility neither had anticipated that she would know anything about the process as no previous visitors had known anything and only gave a perfunctory glance at the equipment when shown this facility on a tour. They had hardly thought she would not only know something about it but would actually sit down in the spinning hut and join the spinners in their task. She was inexorable in her pursuit of knowledge. She had demonstrated that from the first moment they'd met.

"Yes, perhaps another day. You can see here how we finish the yarns and threads to weave our clothing. We dye the fabric we weave with natural dyes made from plants we find in the jungle. If you do not have any more questions, I will have my men escort you back to your ship." *Clearly this woman was much, much different from the captain. These Terrans would bear watching. They were full of surprises today. Or at least this one Terran woman was.'* Nacón clarified to himself.

The other Terran, the man Ethan, very much reinforced yesterday's negative impression. He wasn't much of a man, and he made many condescending remarks about his people. At least he did till the woman finally shut him up. Her words were strong and good and showed a lack of prejudice. *'I like that. I think I like her. There was much to like in her today.'*

Looking at her watch, Ixta said, "Yes, another day. Thank you very much for your time today. I have learned so much and really enjoyed learning more about Uturax. It has been a long time since I spun yarn, and it brought back many wonderful memories of my grandmother. Thank you again. You have been a most generous host. Please share my gratitude with your father."

'Nice words. Correct words.' Hearing only sincerity, Nacón decided that guiding and wandering around his planet with this female wouldn't be so much work after all. His father had been right about this endeavor. He had learned quite a bit about the Terran culture and more in specific about one Terran female. While her red hair seemed odd to him, he decided that, on her, it was acceptable. He wished he could see it loose from the confining braid and flowing free and unfettered down her back instead. Her strong work ethic and consciousness about political, off-worlder etiquette made him begin to like her, against his previous intent to hate her along with her crewmates. It didn't hurt that she was attractive, he decided. He hoped he was not wrong about her as he didn't like to misjudge people. As a warrior, that could be fatal.

Off-world on a spaceship, watching old Terran science fiction movies was a common form of entertainment, often a cause for laughter as many of the movies were so removed from the reality of space travel that they were comical. As more than half of each crew was usually male and a good portion of the female crew members were soldiers, movies about soldiers, cowboys or science fiction were the most popular. The look of these aliens on their current planetary stop was like some of the characters in old sci fi movies in the ship's library.

The captain was very interested in this planet for its resources and the inhabitants as allies as they were warriors. An alliance with them was advantageous for Earth as new allies always had the potential of bringing respect to the ship among other planets in this part of the galaxy. Though Uturaxans were virtually unknown, what was said during their meeting indicated that they were known as fierce warriors who rarely lost a fight when someone chose to challenge their authority. But it seemed these aliens preferred diplomacy and measured discourse whenever possible and were considered an honorable culture with hopefully strict rules dictating expected behavior. Wells recognized he hadn't handled yesterday's first contact well. The aliens could have become very angry at his fuck up of protocol. *'Shit, I should write myself up for being a stupid asshole!'* They were slow to draw their weapons but when all else failed, they were clearly warriors who looked accustomed to winning every conflict.

Oddly, there was little written about this planet and its people, just innuendos and half truths about both the topography of the planet and its inhabitants in just a few paragraphs. It took quite a bit of digging in the ship's archives to assemble any information at all about Uturuax. What was known was sketchy at best.

This contrasted with many other planetary outposts that had every detail of government, inhabitants, predators, minerals, commerce, and degree of advancement of the civilization well catalogued and on record for most of the known world to see in page after page of details. There were few secrets this far out from the known civilized world.

For some odd reason, this planet was shrouded in secrecy. Given the lack of information about the inhabitants and culture, it was surprising that they were viewed with respect since so little was known. The captain decided he would have the glory and excitement of adding to the annals of Earth's history in exploration by the information his crew would add about Uturax.

Ixta, as the resident anthropologist and the lead crew member assigned to flora and fauna information gathering as well as any signs of native culture, would often meet with Nacón and spend considerable time with him as he helped her find specimens to take back home to Earth during the next weeks.

Wells instructed his most trusted crew members to accompany Ixta and whichever biologist went on the exploratory trips with her once the Uturaxans had accepted the outings as routine. They were to casually look around for the sources of the gems and crystals every Uturaxan wore. However, since the first attempt to accompany her had been rebuffed, Wells had told them to carefully sneak off when no one was looking and to explore sectors where they

knew Ixta and a biologist wouldn't be. There was
more to this planet than they had been permitted to
see thus far. He was certain of that. Ixta was such an
idealist she'd probably think him crass if he told her
of his goal of locating the gems that he decided that
she would not be privy to those conversations with
his crew. He'd keep it between his most trusted men
whom he knew were just as greedy as he was. He
knew that if the Uturaxans casually displayed such
wealth that there had to be more for the taking, and
he was certain he was the man to do so, making
himself and his closest crew members rich in the
process.

Following their first exploration of Uturax, Ixta
was anxious to return to the planet's surface, but the
next days were busy with work on the ship. Ixta,
Ethan, and a bio-assistant were occupied in the lab
setting up the greenhouse and getting vegetables
started and the lights set up along with the watering
system. Ixta was eager to get back to exploring the
planet. She supposed it would have to be with Ethan
as he was still on rotation for the fact-gathering trip.
While Ethan had a bigger, more impressive title than
the bio-assistants, they were all PhD's and experts in
their own right even though they weren't given
corresponding titles which were often in short supply
on voyages such as this one.

Ixta was done listening to Ethan's bigoted
comments, however, and planned to give him an
ultimatum the next time he opened his mouth and
something pejorative came out. She was trying to
hurry Ethan along with the greenhouse set up as fast
as she could, but detail after detail kept coming up

with this project which was ultimately very important for the crew's health and well-being. Finally, all was done, and Ixta got Captain Wells' permission to go with Ethan to the village to see when they could do more exploring along with his admonition to keep her eyes open for weaponry.

Nacón's men brought him word that the Terran male and female who had been looking around with them last week were back and approaching the village. He told them to bring them to him as he quickly finished what he was working on, returned to his hut, and put everything away that would reveal any details about himself and his planet to the approaching Terrans.

"Good morning, Nacón. How are you today? I hope you and your father are both well."

Surprised by her polite inquiry about his health and that of his father, Nacón responded,

"We are both well, thank you."

"Uh, we came to see when it would be convenient with you to take us exploring your planet again, Nacón."

"Tomorrow would be acceptable. We will meet you again at your ship as we did before."

"Excellent. Until tomorrow, then."

As Ixta and Ethan turned to go, Nacón was left wondering what they would put together for them to see tomorrow. A day should be enough to find something for them to see without having to go to too much trouble. Perhaps they could do what they did last time and take them into the jungle for the morning, thus allowing people back in the village

some extra time to prepare what they wanted seen by
the two Terrans.

Oddly, he was looking forward to seeing her
again. *'What's that kind of thinking going to get you?
She's not a woman to you, but a Terran, an off-
worlder and that never goes well even though each
ship comes with promises and initial enthusiasm.
That lasts about as long as it takes them to notice the
gems and crystals we wear on everything and then
that's it for another group. Their greed always
outweighs their ethics. This will be another group
without honor as I'm sure time will tell.'*

The Uturaxan group was waiting when Ixta and
Ethan walked down the ramp from the ship shortly
after dawn the next day. It was a beautiful morning,
and Ixta was looking forward to moving into the
jungle before the heat and humidity got high and
uncomfortable. Nacón and his men took a slower
walk through the jungle this time, having decided he
no longer had to prove a point and that he approved
of this woman and didn't want to wear her out before
they arrived at another set of ruins. If she had become
excited by a pottery shard last time, he felt she would
be ecstatic when she saw the crumbling walls of the
old village just ahead. Rounding the bend in the path,
Nacón heard Ixta's exclamation as the old ruins came
into view. Turning to Nacón, she grabbed his arm in
her excitement, forgetting protocol.

Surprised at her touch, Nacón looked down at his
arm and her hand, deciding that he didn't mind this
woman's touch, however risky it was. She was the
first off-worlder who had ever touched him and lived.
She truly didn't understand what she had done, but

she was a woman, a beautiful woman in his eyes, and
he felt a gut-reaction to her touch, or more exactly, a
sexual response to her touch. He felt the reaction of
his men as he heard their slight intake of breath when
she touched him. Simultaneously, he heard their
swords being pulled from their scabbards. He just
looked over at his men and shook his head slightly,
indicating that nothing was to be done in retaliation.

Looking around, Ixta saw the group of men had
suddenly moved to surround Nacón, having quickly
reformed in a defensive posture, swords drawn. They
looked angry and imposing. Immediately sensitive to
the obvious change in atmosphere, Ixta gasped softly
and wasn't sure what to do about her gaffe, so she
quickly released Nacón's arm, whispering to him,
"Whoa, what just happened? I'm so sorry! I meant no
harm. Please excuse my error," as her lapse in
protocol became evident to her and seeing that attack
didn't appear to be imminent, she then turned and ran
forward with Ethan on her heels. "This is incredible!"

Ethan got out his camera and looked to Nacón for
permission and when he got the nod, began shooting
pictures of the crumbling stone walls. While he took
photos, Ethan asked Ixta, "Why did the dogs get all
hostile back there? His soldiers looked like you were
about to be history back there. Are we still OK with
these aliens? Friendly and helpful were not on their
faces back there."

"Forget it, Ethan. And shut your fucking mouth if
you're going to insult them. I already told you before
not to talk about them like that. This is the last time
you'll go with me on these tours if I hear that shit
from you again. At this point all we need is to get

expelled from this expedition by the indigenous. I
shouldn't have grabbed his arm. I just didn't think
because I was so excited about the possibility of
seeing this old village. I treated him like I would have
treated you or another crewmate. It was a major
mistake to touch him. It was my fault totally. They
were just protecting him. Apparently, he accepted my
apology because we're still standing and not lying in
a bloody heap. Feel better now?"

"Well, I did till you got to the bloody heap part of
it."

"And Ethan, let me be clear: don't you fucking
ever call any of these people dogs around me again or
today will be your last trip with me off the ship. I
mean what I'm saying about this. You can rot in the
lab and input data for all I care. There are plenty of
eager beaver scientists who would love to have your
spot. There is nothing you have to offer if you can't
control your thoughts and your mouth. You are a
fucking racist, and I won't permit that on my team.
Understood?"

"Yes, ma'am," Ethan responded sullenly, knowing
that Ixta would follow through on her threat and her
position and rank on the ship meant she could remove
him with no explanation. It was also true that there
was a line of scientists just waiting for the chance to
spend time on the planet for research purposes. "Shit!
I never thought I'd get told that these fucking alien
dogs matter more than I do to her," Ethan muttered
under his breath.

Nacón had come close enough to hear their
exchange and felt both furious at the bigoted
biologist and pleased by Ixta's words to Ethan.

Apparently, he had correctly judged both, but he felt relief that the woman had measured up to his high expectations because on seeing her again, she was indeed quite attractive. *'What the hell am I thinking? An off-worlder woman and I'm thinking she's pretty. That cannot come to anything, or my father will have something to say. But it doesn't hurt anything to look and appreciate, does it? All that talk I gave her about important warrior work to do and here I am acting like a juvenile again and thinking about a woman that I shouldn't even have an interest in. I'm glad none of my men can read my mind or I know my father would have a serious talk with me to set me straight in my thinking. I feel young and untried again just thinking of what that talk would look and sound like. Not good.'*

Ixta and Ethan both lost themselves in the moment of this discovery. Inside the ruin, there were many utensils around the former fire pits among other things left from many years ago. Finally, Ixta stopped and sat down on what was left of a half wall and just looked, taking it all in, and then turned to Nacón when he appeared in her peripheral vision.

"I'm sure this is nothing new to you. After all, you knew of it to bring us here. It is incredible. I feel lucky to be part of this. Some people wait their whole lives to see something this old and well-preserved as an example of your civilization. I am honored that you have shared this with us."

Nacón looked at Ixta for a moment, trying to determine if she was sincere or just saying polite words to try to make a good impression. Clearly, she wasn't that concerned about an impression, or she wouldn't have grabbed his arm earlier. Surely, she had training in appropriate behavior when dealing with aliens. Many cultures never let an off-worlder explore their planets, let alone come into physical contact. Off-worlders brought new diseases with them oftentimes and it was too familiar a gesture, too forward, a violation of protocol, especially when dealing with the ruler's own son.

Seeing nothing in Ixta's eyes and face other than sincerity, Nacón nodded at her, thinking again that she was very different from most off-worlders he had come in contact with. He had met non-Uturaxan women in first-contact groups before, but none had ever impressed him or gotten his attention like Ixta had. He didn't know what it was about her, but thinking back on it, decided he liked her familiarity with him and her touch. However, he hated to admit that to his men who would be horrified and would undoubtedly share any comment like that with his father. Unfortunately, the whole tribe was watching him, hoping he would choose a mate and carry on with his family line. He knew that his soldiers took bets on whom he would choose every time a new round of women began trying to get his notice. Living life on a stage did have its drawbacks. His people were very involved in everyone's lives since their numbers were small compared to other times in their history when their planet was more densely populated. They no longer had collections of large cities for a person to lose himself in. So, for the moment, Nacón decided to keep his thoughts about Ixta to himself to avoid comments and questions from friends and family.

"Uh, Nacón, I'd like to talk about what happened
back when we first got to the ruins if you don't mind.
"What do you not understand about it?"
"Your men, in seconds, were all grouped around
you, and they looked like they were ready for battle.
Their swords were drawn, and they had a defensive
posture all grouped protectively around you. That's
the part I don't understand. I had no weapon and did
not act threatening, at least I didn't think I did."
"Terran woman, no off-worlder touches any of us,
let alone members of the royal family. My people
show me respect as the king's son and no one of my
own race would come up to me and touch me without
asking my permission first."
Ixta's face went white as the enormity of her faux
pas became clear. She hadn't really thought it out
other than her initial thought that they were really
pissed. She'd forgotten for that moment that Nacón
was royalty here. If he were president on her planet
the Secret Service detachment around him would
have had her in custody by now. "I'm really sorry. I
meant no harm or disrespect to you or your people. I
was just excited by the wonderful ruins you brought
us to and didn't think."
"Ixta. Disrespect is only part of it," Nacón
explained patiently. "Off-worlders can bring disease
to our people. An epidemic could start. You could be
carrying a harmful sickness with you that doesn't
affect your crew but could kill all of us."
Ixta gasped, looked horrified and shaken and
rushed to say, "Oh, Nacón. Shit. I never thought of
that. I'm more than sorry. I'm horrified. I would

never want to make any of you ill. Hell, I can't believe I was that stupid. I am so sorry!"

"What's done is done. My men were only seeking to be prepared to protect me if your intent was to cause harm. I determined that it was not meant to be harmful, just ignorant, and told them to stand down."

Chastened, Ixta agreed, "Yes. It was very ignorant on my part and a serious breach of protocol. I should know better, Nacón. I do know better. We are trained in protocol, and I forgot. There is no excuse. Will my error cause you to suspend our visits and touring of your planet? I hope that we can get beyond this and continue. I really enjoy learning about Uturax."

She added to herself, *'And you're hot and I really like hanging out with you,'* then chastised herself for having those thoughts about an alien male who was a member of the royal family and clearly not available for a casual relationship. She knew she could not think of him as just another male, any male that she'd met on her travels. The males she had met previously on voyages had been open to casual relationships and it wasn't uncommon for romantic attachments to be formed with human people on other planets, but the prince of this planet would definitely not fit in that category for several reasons: being alien and royalty.

Nacón was tempted to give her a hard time about it just to make the point, but he believed her when she said she just hadn't thought. She did seem sorry. "I accept your apology, and your visits and tours may continue." Not knowing that he shared the same thought as she had about the attractiveness of the other, he admitted to himself that there was no way he was not going to see this woman whenever the opportunity presented itself.

For the first time in quite a while, he was interested in getting to know this female, to learn more about her. She intrigued him and attracted him very differently from the women on his planet. He vowed to get to know her better as she truly interested him, and he found that he liked that unique feeling as he hadn't wanted to get to know anyone better in a long time. His only concern was keeping up the façade his people used in dealing with visitors to their planet though watching his speech to avoid revealing their knowledge of this and other languages was going to be tedious. It already was.

Ixta looked up at Nacón's eyes, really looking at them for the first time, deciding they were beautiful. His hair was slightly wavy and fell thickly past his shoulders, shorter tendrils framing his face, much of those having slipped free from his ponytail. His hair was a deep amber color, and his eyes were hazel with long, dark lashes and now sharply focused on her.

Realizing her thoughts were wandering far afield and forcing herself to focus on the issue at hand, Ixta replied, "Um. Well. Thank you, Nacón. I really appreciate your understanding. I would have hated to think that my impulsiveness caused a breach between us and our two cultures."

Nacón felt an awareness for her as a woman that he hadn't really put much thought into before. Thinking back, he had been spending much of his idle time thinking about Ixta, her forthright personality, honesty, and willingness to admit when she was wrong and to apologize for it, if need be, and

. . . her body. He had started to notice and categorize all the details of her body and found them pleasing. *'What am I doing? This is the last thing that my father had in mind when he agreed to these expeditions. I'm sure my being attracted to an off-worlder, a human from Earth, would not give him a good night's sleep if he were to know. I haven't spent time thinking about a woman like this since I first reached my majority. Surely these thoughts aren't befitting a warrior of my age and rank.'*

Nacón didn't know where his thinking would take him, but for now, he enjoyed looking at her and teasing her occasionally as their relationship grew more comfortable and relaxed. He hoped there would be many excursions that would take place on his planet and give him more opportunity to spend time with this woman. While his rational self told him that this attraction could have no purpose and would lead nowhere, he was still attracted to her and wanted to learn more about this human woman.

He would have to be vigilant and careful not to draw attention to his interest in her before his men who might feel compelled to comment on it to Chaac. While they were loyal to him, their allegiance to Chaac came first and the planet's safety would be primary. Nacón thought they might see this woman as a threat to their way of life if he displayed too much interest in her. Also, it was so unlike him to have focused like this on a woman as his relationships in the past had been very superficial and spontaneous. Much like his men, he took advantage of the opportunities to join with women as they presented themselves. There was no planning in any of the very temporary alliances he had formed, at least on his part.

He was not unaware that some of the elders and their daughters had put a lot of thought into creating situations for meetings to occur that had never resulted in their hoped-for marriage alliance. However, he and his men, he would have to admit, did enjoy the attentions of the females on his planet who often behaved like they were important stars of Uturaxan society rather than just a bunch of soldiers. Nacón had no illusions about their motives or about himself being anything other than a regular soldier who happened to be the son of their current ruler.

The pattern of these first two weeks continued with weekly tours of the planet. The only novelty in the pattern had been the day that a larger contingent of crew had shown up with no apparent purpose other than to accompany Ixta and Ethan. When questioned as to their reason for being on the outing, they acted as if they were trying to come up with a real reason. Nacón had looked at Ixta who was looking askance as the men, and she gave her head as slight shake as she looked at his questioning eyes. The new crew members were quickly sent back on the ship. Thwarted in their mission to locate the gem mines, the crew members retreated to the ship and the mess hall, wanting to avoid reporting to Wells about their failure to get on to the planet.

Well, that went well," Nixon said sarcastically. Wells is gonna be pissed as usual. He's right though. Did you see the size of those gems on those dogs' arms?"

"Shit, yeah. They looked like emeralds and rubies. We've gotta be careful not to let Ixta know though. She's such a do-gooder she'd never go for robbing them of all the shit we can get our hands on."

"She's either got a blind spot or just fuckin' stupid not to have picked up on what we do after first contact on all these planets. This isn't the first one we've tried to locate gems and shit to loot," Preston commented.

"Still, she's fine and I'd to get myself some of that pussy," Jimmy said lasciviously.

"Fuck off, asshole. I've got her already picked out for me. Remember that all of you motherfuckers. She's mine." Preston declared, scowling.

"Ha! It would seem that she doesn't know that yet," Nixon laughed as he stood up. "I'll go tell Daniels that we couldn't even get past the end of the ramp today. Wish me luck."

Remembering Ixta's request to learn about their methods of planting and growing, Nacón had arranged a visit to one of the fields. They visited the gardens where crops were just now coming up, promising a bountiful crop if the weather continued to be favorable as it had thus far. Once again, Ixta asked permission to get involved. They were just planting some seedlings and before Nacón knew it and could react, she was down on her knees, digging holes and setting the delicate seedlings in the dirt. She would then carefully pat the dirt up around the plants firmly settling one in the ground before moving on to the next one. She asked her surrounding farm worker companions, using Nacón as a translator, if she should water the seedlings or would that happen when all the seedlings were in the ground. Finding that watering would be done by someone else as soon as they finished planting, she gamely kept on till the wooden tray was empty of plants even though the heat and humidity were climbing. He could see her clothing become stained with her sweat and he watched in fascination as the shorter strands of her hair that had worked loose from her long braid began to curl around her face as it also dampened with sweat. Occasionally, Ixta would stop to wipe the sweat off her forehead, barely missing a beat in her planting rhythm.

"Nacón, is the sky always so beautiful? The pinks and purples are breathtaking as a backdrop for your two suns."

"Er, yes, Ixta. As long as it's summer here, the sky looks like this. Winter, however, is not the same. The cold and the winds leave the sky grey most days and we do not often see our suns."

Nacón decided Ixta was a breath of fresh air, so different from the women of his planet that he had known to date. They had yet to have a conversation about political alliances or how many offspring he hoped to have. Both of those topics usually dominated every conversation with Uturaxan women he used to meet around the campfires at celebrations. It was nice to meet a woman who wasn't afraid of getting dirty and helping. It was a first for him to see a woman work willingly on a task that most would consider beneath them.

Though their military assignments required all to rotate through the more mundane chores on the planet, there were ways that some of the wealthy nobles managed to buy deferments for their pampered children. Most could not avoid combat training, but there were a few loopholes out of physical labor that wasn't deemed an essential combat skill and consequently, some of the rich, pampered youth did not do much that Nacón would call useful. The potential brides that had been paraded in front of him in quick succession did not serve in the military or do much of anything as their wealthy families had bought them exemptions.

Lately, however, Chaac and the council were working to limit these exemptions as they felt that it created a division of classes that was contrary to their core beliefs of equality. There was a duality on their planet that balanced having a royal family and a class of nobles with a very democratic form of government. Somehow, the blending worked. But the potential brides he'd been forced to interact with had all avoided military service up to now. Thus, their lives were very narrow, and they had tunnel vision about most things Uturaxan. Their focus was on the social aspects of life on their planet which didn't provide them with many shared topics for real discussion. Nacón mused that was why he found them all so boring.

Initially, Nacón's and Ixta's communications had been sketchy at best, but as they both learned words from each other's languages, they were able to communicate much better. Ixta's boss, the infamous captain of the ship, had a pair of universal translators that he used to talk with Nacón's father Chaac, but the rest of the crew had to do the best they could with simple hand signs and short words they exchanged on the rare occasions they interacted with the Uturaxans. Consequently, Ixta and Nacón had to limp along without the ease of simple communication since the first days when the captain had relented and let Ixta and Ethan take a translator for their first forays into the jungle.

Several weeks into these visits, the captain had decided that the translator was too valuable to let it off the ship every time Ixta and Ethan left to gather new samples. Thus far, the indigenous had proved harmless, but the captain was ever cautious and wasn't willing to risk losing one of the translators while they discovered more about this planet. It is better to sacrifice a few scientists than an irreplaceable piece of expensive equipment, though he didn't really think he could explain away the loss of any of his crew to his superiors. Equipment or personnel? It's better for him not to lose anything.

But Ixta and Nacón found ways around the lack of words as they became more creative in exchanging ideas. Nacón found he looked forward to Ixta's visits even if she did continue to bring along Ethan for whom he had little regard and respect. Several times, she brought another off-worlder, the ship's doctor, a tall, exotic-looking purple Argentian, along on the explorations. The doctor was pleasant and, being an alien himself, seemed to have no prejudices against the Uturaxans like some of the other crew members obviously did. The ship's crew thought he had not heard them, but Nacón had heard them call him and his men 'dog' and 'Sasquatch.' At first, he hadn't even known what they were talking about but had brought it to his father and the council. Once researched and understood, the Uturaxan council wasn't happy with the Terrans and their obvious prejudice against them. These comments did not advance the credibility of the off-worlders among the Uturaxans as sincere potential trading partners or allies.

Nacón had to point out, in all fairness, that not everyone was calling them pejorative names. Still, that was part of the total picture they were forming of the current off-world visitors. He decided that he did like the big Argentian doctor, however, who was unassuming, uncomplaining, and loved to tell humorous stories. He was much taller than the Terran men and didn't seem to find the Uturaxans size intimidating as he was powerfully built himself and just as tall.

Ixta logged all that she could about the Uturaxans: a handsome race, very humanoid in appearance in terms of arms, legs, body, and face but their bodies were covered in what looked like silky hair, about three or four inches long. Their hair color tones ranged from black to a light brown, honey colored with very few blondes. Their skin tones were harder to tell as they spent their days outside and were tanned from the dual suns that shone relentlessly this time of year. The women were rarely seen and were the size of a tall human woman if generalizations on their size could be made from the few that had been seen. The men were larger and some of them towered over the average-sized human crew. Others on the crew were taller and closer in height to the smaller of the Uturaxan men. Most of the younger men had shoulder length or longer hair that was usually pulled back in a type of ponytail. Among the older men, some wore short hair, and others kept the ubiquitous ponytail. Women, the few that they saw, wore their hair long and either braided or pinned up on top of their heads.

All of the aliens wore what looked like a kilt made of somewhat coarse hand-woven material. She noted that Nacón's seemed to be more intricately woven, to be of a higher quality fabric. Though Ixta had yet to see how these kilts were constructed, the fabric looked as though all the fibers had been hand spun and then woven on looms like the ones she had visited on this planet. They were dyed various colors from vegetation gathered on the planet from what Nacón had told her the day she had visited the looms and spinning wheels. The different groups within their tribe wore different colored garments. That is, the men and women of one group wore rust-colored kilts, another group wore green, another, a dark blue and the final group, a deep golden yellow colored fabric.

She also noted the amulets worn either around their upper arms or around their necks that shone in the sun as the sun's rays bounced off the beautiful jewels. Occasionally, a man or woman would appear wearing a length of cloth over the shoulder, tied with another length of fabric at their waists. There would often be a large brooch holding the shoulder cloth in place. It seemed to be a more ceremonial garment as day-to-day wear just involved the kilt-like garment.

Ixta had classified these groups as clans for lack of a better word. She assumed that more of the women oversaw producing the cloth and making the kilts as all the men seemed to talk about was fighting and training, though her rudimentary Uturaxan language skills made her uncertain of this. Many of the Uturaxan men and women seemed to spend much of each day on drills involving hand-to-hand combat. Ixta had noted that the women often drilled together somewhere else as the few that appeared with the men left carrying small swords, not to return that day. That explained the lack of firepower to shoot at their ship when they arrived. This culture was rather primitive and had no real machinery other than tools and machines made of wood that had been built to aid in harvest and making clothing. Cooking utensils were simple with wooden and ceramic bowls used. Ixta had seen no metal implements except sword edgings. There were crudely fashioned metal edgings to the large wooden swords all the men wore.

The hierarchy of government was tribal with a chief who seemed to make all the major decisions for everyone. There was also a council of elders whom the chief consulted on the bigger issues. The women didn't wear anything to cover the upper half of their bodies and the human crew liked to joke about their breasts and the difference in their appearance from human women. At this point of this voyage, far from the last recreational stop, all the men were making jokes with poorly veiled sexual references. The primary difference between this planet's inhabitants and the humans was the short soft-looking fur covering their faces and bodies. Some of the crew wanted to call them "dogs" or "Sasquatches" as a joke, but the captain overheard and forbade them from making derogatory comments about the indigenous telling them they would derail any hope they had of forming a trade alliance. Some of the crew still called them Sasquatches, a reference to a mythical character in folk tales on Earth from many, many years ago, under their breaths when they were angry. Nacón had finally asked Ixta the meaning of that word. She had been embarrassed to tell him but had finally relented. She couldn't blame him for the hard, angry look that had come on his face when she explained the reference. She had considered not telling him or inventing another meaning but was glad that she had shared the truth.

"Ixta. I thank you for your honesty with me. Even when the information you tell me does not flatter your people, you are honest. I give you thanks for your courage in telling me the truth and for honoring me with your loyalty to the truth. You would make a good warrior."

Ixta blushed, unexpectedly touched by his words, and smiled shyly, looking up at Nacón's face.

"I don't know what you think of me as, Nacón, but I count you as one of my friends now and friends don't lie to each other. They deserve the truth even if it's inconvenient."

Nacón nodded and smiled at Ixta in response.

'Friend. Well, I guess that's progress when a beautiful woman likes you enough to call you friend, though I was thinking other thoughts about her.'

Chapter 2: *Martius* -- early morning

Last night came back even more vividly as Ixta hopped out of bed to run the few steps to her bathroom to throw up in the toilet. She felt stiff and sore along with her nausea and fever. She remembered drinking a cloyingly sweet beverage that Nacón had brought with him. Telling herself that she was gathering information on the planet's fauna, she'd made the decision to go with Nacón to the celebration that he had managed to communicate information about to her. The details weren't clear, however. Not sure, she thought it was to be a celebration of some sort. They had left the space camp compound and had gone to a village outpost close by to celebrate the marriage of one of Nacón's friends. At least that's what Ixta thought they had been celebrating as they all sat around the fire, laughing and drinking. She recognized many of the younger men around the fire and a few of the women sitting a few yards back from the inner circle around the fire, which was rare as the women usually kept to themselves and without exception, did not approach off-worlders. Ixta covertly observed and absorbed every detail of their dress and mannerisms as she'd had almost no opportunity to observe the women even from a distance.

She couldn't fail to notice that many of Nacón's inner circle were there, and they looked at her with surprise. She could see the questioning looks on their faces as their eyes met Nacón's. She noted that none of the women had a welcoming glance for her or even acknowledged her presence. Several men looked disapproving initially, but their faces quickly became devoid of expression once Nacón gave a slight shake of his head. Not sure of how to catalog that reaction, Ixta settled in beside Nacón, prepared to enjoy what the night would bring. This celebration was something new to her that she'd not been permitted to see in the previous months. Any of the gatherings of the people in the village had been structured, even scripted as she thought about it. Tonight was such a contrast to all her previous interactions that she couldn't help but notice how relaxed and festive everyone seemed.

As the night wore on, she noticed some of the women of the tribe quietly coming closer into the circle to sit next to some of the men. The women looked just as fit as the men, their muscles clearly visible in their clothing with their arms and part of their legs exposed though covered with short, furry-looking hair. She had never seen a Uturaxan that wasn't fit if they looked younger than the age of grandparents. The older generation's bodies had gotten soft, but you could tell by looking that they had also been muscular at some time.

As the night progressed and more drinks were consumed, casually, without saying anything to anyone, couples began slipping away in pairs, arm in arm. Soon, the only ones remaining were Ixta, Nacón

and a few old grandfathers who by then were too
drunk to say much of anything. They were snoring as
they leaned over, heads on their knees. No one even
paid them any notice at this point because most were
gone. The couples that were close enough to observe
them were cuddled together kissing and did not care
what the rest of the group was doing. From the way it
looked, Ixta guessed that they would soon leave to
have sex rather than staying near the fire. Sexual
attraction didn't need language skills to translate but
hung in the air as the couples moved away together
for more privacy. Not knowing if that were the case
but feeling shy about asking Nacón what they were
going to do, Ixta just assumed that sex was on their
schedules for the next while.

   As if reading her mind that had strayed to thoughts
of sex, as naturally as if this happened every day
between them, Nacón turned to Ixta and brushed her
lips with his, cupping her face with his hand, stroking
her cheek softly with his fingers. At first, the
sensation was strange as the area around his lips
wasn't covered with the hairy mustache she expected.
Ixta must have decided that it felt fine as it was,
though because she quickly recovered from her initial
surprise, decided she didn't care and welcomed
Nacón's kiss. He softly explored her lips with his,
allowing Ixta to either become more comfortable
with their physical contact or to reject it. When she
showed no signs of rejection, Nacón gently took her
lower lip between his lips and lightly sucked it before
running his tongue along her lips, seeking entrance
into her mouth. Ixta responded with a sigh as she
opened her mouth for him. As he began to explore

her mouth with his tongue, he was rewarded with Ixta's tongue tentatively touching his, as if she was uncertain whether to proceed with this or not. Again, allowing her time to decide, Nacón was rewarded when Ixta touched her tongue to his again, this time with more pressure. Elated by her response, Nacón felt he could safely take their exploration to the next step and deepened his kiss from an exploratory testing of the waters to a serious connection.

Ixta felt his hand reach for her braid and bring it around to the front of her chest front where he gently laid it over her shoulder so that it rested between her breasts. He then took off the tie from the end and began to unravel the braid till her hair was unbound. It felt so sensuous for him to be handling and stroking her hair that Ixta didn't care where this was going but only knew that she wanted it to continue. He put his hands on either side of her head, hesitated for a moment and then threaded his fingers through her hair on both sides. *'If I were a cat, I'd be purring.'* It felt very sensual, and Ixta decided she liked the turn of events. She almost said something to express her disappointment when he removed his hands from her hair, missing that intimate contact.

Next, she could feel as he took a strand of her hair and wrapped it around his finger. While not as intimate as before, Ixta felt that this action indicated that Nacón wasn't finished with touching her. She had recognized an attraction between them for some time, but ship's rules were extremely specific about not fraternizing with the indigenous on the planets they visited. They had an easy, comfortable relationship and acted like old friends and that included occasional flirting on both of their parts. At least, Ixta thought it was flirting on Nacón's part as she was still unsure about most of the nuances of male and female interactions in his culture. Thinking back, she had seen very few Uturaxans unless they were the ones Nacón placed in front of her.

Puzzled by her relationship and interactions with him, Ixta felt he was more human than alien. However, he didn't relate to her in the same way other aliens had that she'd met on previous voyages. There was something different about him. At least she had rationalized her attraction to him as different from a "normal" alien. Notwithstanding her lack of couple's knowledge, Ixta felt excited that she was experiencing something completely new on many levels. She had never seen couples here interact together until tonight, so Ixta could only guess about romantic relationships here. She guessed that they must exist to form family units. Spending the night in the presence of younger Uturaxan couples was a first for her.

All that she was sure of was that Nacón had turned out to be a thoughtful, educated companion once he got past emphasizing his warrior's role in life to her. She was beginning to realize that this culture was not primitive at all in its thinking though she had to admit that Nacón had provided precious few examples of Uturaxan life other than the very mundane. In her many outings with Nacón and his men, she was careful to avoid touching him again lest his guard draw their weapons once again and go into defensive formation, but had noticed that Nacón did occasionally touch her, more of late, when he would

put his hand on her back or hold her elbow to move
her along in the direction he was going.

The scientist in Ixta catalogued this kiss away like
she did everything else she observed, saying to
herself that kissing seemed universal as far as she
was concerned, and that gathering research was
always a good thing. She was sure this encounter was
going to push the boundaries of fraternization as his
unbraiding of her hair had been very sensual and
almost tender. His kissing her had clearly stepped
over a boundary line. Obviously, this was something
that Nacón had done before as he was really
accomplished at kissing from Ixta's point of view.
That told her that kissing was part of sexual play on
this planet rather than something unusual. She
reached up to touch his face, but he grabbed her hand
and wouldn't let her continue. *'Shit, I can't believe I
still can't touch him after he's just kissed me like
that.'*

Nacón broke off the kiss, looked closely at Ixta for
a moment and then gracefully rose, pulling Ixta up to
stand beside him. He looked down at her for assent as
he made to turn away and she nodded though she was
unsure of what she was agreeing to. However, at this
stage, she was slightly drunk from the nectar that
packed a punch as well as feeling the effects of her
physical responses from kissing Nacón, resulting
from a long celibate period in her life. Both were
propelling her forward. She probably would have
agreed to pretty much anything with this alien male
she had come to trust explicitly at this point. She
heard that little warning voice in her head asking her
if she knew what the hell she was doing, reminding

her that overindulgence in alcohol and some serious
kissing did not excuse irresponsible behavior.

She told her inner voice to shut up and they took a
few steps away from the light of the fire and entered
the edge of the vegetation and were quickly hidden
by the lush jungle growth in this area of the planet.
Pulling Ixta to his side, Nacón then took off the kilt-
like garment he wore, spread it on the ground and
then sat down looking up at Ixta with a questioning
look. Though it was dark all around, the fire cast
enough light through the trees and plants so that Ixta
and Nacón could still just see each other. Ixta
remembered noticing that he was wearing a leather
loin cloth under his kilt but said nothing and sank
down to sit on the ground beside him. Nacón again
gave her a questioning look and Ixta smiled at him as
he began to kiss her again, this time with more
intensity than before, apparently finding the answer
he wanted in her expression on her face along with
her willingness to join him on the ground. *'Surely,
she knows something is going to happen between us.
I wonder what she's thinking right now?'*

Nacón wasn't sure where this was going as he'd
never had any kind of romantic attachment or
interaction with an off-worlder before. But Ixta was
different to him as he felt they had formed a
friendship with all their meanderings over the planet
while she did her job. They had even managed to find
a common, if strange, language of communication
that wasn't English or Uturaxan. It sounded stilted
and a little odd to both their ears but did provide them
with a means to share ideas. He didn't want to
frighten her and knew instinctively that the more

physical traditional Uturaxan sexual give and take that his race enjoyed could possibly scare Ixta. Or not. He admitted ruefully to himself that discussions about flora, fauna and ruins left a lot to be desired about human relationships. He felt close to her and was interested in a romantic connection between them but hadn't known how to ask her how she felt about him as neither had the right words to discuss a topic like serious friendship or romance or at least they'd never tried to find those words before. For once, he was impatient with the restrictions Chaac had placed on his people to closely guard their language skills and culture from off-worlders.

He felt like a boy in his teens again, not the seasoned warrior he was. He liked and trusted Ixta and felt an attraction to her that he wasn't sure how to move forward with. Nacón was fascinated by her way of looking at things and welcomed her companionship. He had tired of the Uturaxan women and their pursuit of him for years. They rarely showed any interest in anything of note about him except his rank and their possible political alliance with his family.

Tonight's celebration had provided the perfect set of circumstances to find out how Ixta felt about him. A wedding celebration provided a commonplace event for couples to pair off and join their bodies. Fertility was always celebrated as part of a wedding feast as couples here married to have children. Thinking of children and the family he had always hoped to form, Nacón made a leap in his thinking as he looked at Ixta again and knew that she attracted him like no woman had previously. No Uturaxan woman challenged his thinking like Ixta did. She had no ulterior motives whereas all the Uturaxan women were scheming to have him choose them for his princess to later be queen of Uturax. He'd never really felt a connection to the women he'd been around and joined with before because he couldn't trust their motives. Some were more skilled than others in hiding their true feelings and aspirations, but all had the same motivation that was obvious: wealth and rank.

Talking with Ixta through the few months of their association, he realized that he enjoyed mentally sparring with her on a wide variety of topics. She clearly did not share in the prejudices of some of her crew members towards his race. She always treated him as an equal and even over-stepped the boundaries of protocol at times by not according to him the respect due and required by his proper rank and position. Other than his few closest male friends who were also in line to hold high rank in the Uturaxan tribal government, he had never had discussions like those he had with her, even hampered by her language difficulties. He often talked with his father and their political advisors about many topics and debated with them about the best course of action but never had ventured into conversational topics like those with the women he had previously associated with on the planet. Women did occupy positions of power, but none of them were in his age group and thus never gave him occasion to debate with them. From his experiences with the younger set of Uturaxan women, they didn't

think about anything other than being queen one day
or acquiring jewels to add to their wealth.

His talk with Ulises yesterday came back to him
now in vivid detail. *"Mi príncipe (my prince),* you
spend so much time with this Terran woman, why
don't you just join with her? I can see it in your face.
You are curious about her and want to share sexual
pleasures with her. Am I right?"

"Do the others talk about this behind my back? Do
they see something in my relationship with Ixta that
they are afraid to tell me?" Nacón had shot back at
his friend and captain.

"No, *jefe (boss).* You know my job is to see and
anticipate everything about the circumstances and
situations that surround you. I see desire in your face
when you look at her. It is not specifically forbidden.
Why do you not join with her?"

"I. . .well. . .*La maldita* (the damn) off-worlder
does have my attention, Ulises. I can't think of
anything or anyone else. I just hadn't gotten that far
in my thinking on what to do about it. I don't know. I
just don't know. We'll see."

Ulises just shook his head and smirked at Nacón.

Looking at Ixta again, Nacón's mind was clearly
back in the now. Deciding to just forge ahead to see
where it went, Nacón offered Ixta another drink from
the jug of *pulque* as he took another sip himself,
perhaps for courage. At first, shaking her head, but
then relenting with a "why not?" look on her face,
both shared another swig of the potent drink. Nacón
hoped Ixta would choose to join with him as he
wanted to see this encounter to its natural conclusion
as kissing her made his body want to take this

exploratory physical alliance to the next level. She was different and that was a good thing to him after being pursued by all the eligible women on the planet for so long. Her strongest quality for him was her honesty. Setting the jug down on the ground, Nacón reached again for Ixta, this time wrapping his arms around her to pull her body closer to his as she turned her face to his and then leaned into him, fitting herself under his arm, beneath his shoulder.

Analyzing how she felt when Nacón hugged her, she was wonderfully comfortable and protected and remained relaxed in his arms, snuggling up closer to him. She felt safe with him, trusted him. She knew him better than any man she'd ever spent time with as they'd spent hours just talking about nothing, about everything. Nacón gently turned Ixta's face to his with two of his fingers. He traced her lower lip with his forefinger first and then ran his finger along the top line of her upper lip. He leaned in and gave her a soft, gentle kiss to see how Ixta would react now that they were completely alone together. She didn't pull away or reject him, so he did it again, enjoying the moment of closeness that he'd fantasized about for a long time.

As with his kiss, Ixta initially had strange feelings as the inner surfaces of his arms were not covered in the same kind of soft, short silky fur that she expected. Deciding that the overall feeling wasn't unpleasant at all and didn't really matter, Ixta leaned closer into Nacón as she returned his kiss. The slow, languorous kisses became more intense as Nacón's tongue found hers again. Their mouths were imitating the sexual contact that both began to want as the next step in their first physical and sexual encounter. Soon, they were clutching at each other as their passion grew and Ixta's scientist's mind was saying, 'Well, this isn't really very different from kissing back on Earth.' She felt his hands running up and down her body, exploring. However, when she tried to do the same, he would move back to restrict her hands from exploring his body.

Another warning bell went off in her mind when she felt Nacón unzip her overalls, from the top down, a little at first. This was clearly a time to call a halt to this encounter if there ever was one. Decision time for Ixta. However, the mental warnings didn't tell her to stop him as she was enjoying the sensation of his warm hand as it moved her breast up and out of her bra that sprung apart as he touched the clasp in the center front. Now, he could softly touch her breast. Though bras weren't used on Uturax from what Ixta had seen, Nacón had had no problem figuring out the clasp and opening it quickly. *Men, she wryly noted, are all alike.'*

Ixta knew that the human breast was very different from the Uturaxan breast in that the Uturaxan women she had seen had three sets of breasts to have enough milk for their litters of children from what she had observed of the few women around the camp. She noticed that Nacón seemed fascinated by her breasts and their apparent sexual connection and sensitivity. She had heard from listening to the other soldiers' comments that single births were unheard of on this planet and usually offspring were born as triplets or quadruplets. Also, Uturaxan breasts lacked the perfect round shape of Ixta's. Her right breast, gently cupped in his hand, was soft and fit his big hand perfectly. He noted that it was larger than he had thought once freed from that constraining undergarment she wore. Nacón could tell that Ixta was enjoying his touches as she was sighing softly into his mouth as he continued his exploration with his hand while he continued their kissing. His fingers moved to outline the area around her nipple; then he grasped the nipple and ever so gently gave it a tug. He decided that he liked what he'd learned thus far about Terran lovemaking that didn't seem at all different from what he knew.

Feeling like he might as well capitalize on the situation based on her positive feedback thus far, he freed her other breast from the other half of the garment she wore and cupped both breasts as he continued to kiss her. Not as affected by the *pulque* and the surprise of finding themselves in this situation as Ixta seemed to be, Nacón was seemingly more in charge of his faculties as he continued to learn about human anatomy. He had been thinking about Ixta for quite some time in a way that was not related to planetary research, and he was now doing the things he'd fantasized about with her body.

Thinking again, *'Why not take this to the next level? It seems my decision has been made about what will happen tonight with Ixta.'* Nacón kissed Ixta again on the mouth and then lowered his head to gently lick the nipple of her breast loosely held in his right hand. He was curious as to how she would react and clearly Ixta had enjoyed his playing with her breasts up to this point. Ixta's intake of breath and moaning was all the encouragement needed as he took her entire nipple in his mouth and gave it an exploratory suckle. Ixta grasped his head, pulling it more firmly to her breast as he obligingly continued to suck. His tongue could feel the nipple extending in his mouth and he enjoyed the sensation as much as she seemed to. Already aroused, he felt himself grow harder as he suckled her breasts, first one, then the other.

Foggy as her brain felt, completely caught up in this sensual moment, his kisses to her breasts were so erotic that Ixta could feel them in the core of her body. She felt herself moisten further in anticipation as she felt each pull he made on her breasts with his mouth. The rhythm of it was almost too much. Then he would return to her mouth, his tongue mating with hers in preparation for an even closer connection. Emboldened by his successes thus far, Nacón continued the downward trail of the zipper and helped Ixta out of her jumpsuit overalls as he quickly shed his leather loin cloth.

Ixta's somewhat disconnected brain lazily registered the change in temperature and lack of clothing, but she was so physically turned on by the whole situation and if she were honest with herself, had fantasized about this moment for a while, that she made no effort to call a halt to Nacón's lovemaking. Lust had taken over her decision-making process. In fact, she was trying to determine what to do next to move this forward as she looked down at their now naked bodies. His male anatomy was different from human men in that the fur on his body made it harder to discern individual parts though she did notice something standing erect in between his legs. She barely knew where to start and in her slightly drunk and physically aroused state, didn't really care.

She wasn't that drunk to be unaware of her actions, but it had been so long since she had shared sexual pleasures with anyone that she didn't want to call a halt to the events that were unfolding. She was content to let Nacón lead this experiment, and she would just sit back and see where it took them. It had been many months since Ixta had had a sexual partner, and her body was clearly anticipating this encounter more and more. She could even pretend that she was gathering scientific information though she knew that was a lie. She was just caught up in a pleasurable moment and wasn't willing to stop. The fact that Nacón was an alien was a thought that passed through her mind, quickly, but was replaced just as quickly by the thought that he had become her close and trusted friend. She felt closer to him than anyone on the ship's crew except Dr. T. and couldn't think of him as an alien any longer. Captain Wells and regulations were far from the forefront of her mind at that moment.

Nacón almost lost his perspective when he looked down at the naked Ixta, a vision to him as her body seemed so sleek and well proportioned. The human form before him was hairless except for the area between her thighs and her smaller frame made her look completely different from any woman he'd been with before. Till now, he'd avoided being involved with any off-world women.

Uturaxan culture did not prohibit premarital sex and at times presented situations where consensual sex among non-related adults over eighteen winters was encouraged as a celebration of fertility. Uturaxan culture placed a high value on mated pairs and considered these premarital pairings to be trials for lifelong commitments for the sake of the children that would be born to the union. However, no semen was ever ejaculated into a woman till they were committed to each other through a marriage ceremony. A woman could find sexual release with a man's penetration, but a man's outlet had to be from his own hand or a woman's mouth on him.

Thus, when an Uturaxan man committed to a woman, he was expected to make his life with her and raise a family through carefully planned conceptions. Families could trace their lineage back for generations. Nacón had not committed to any Uturaxan woman yet, though many opportunities had presented themselves to him through the years since he'd achieved his majority. He supposed that every woman he had joined with had hoped that "in the moment" he would make that snap decision to commit to her and share his seed with her. He had to admit that many he had joined with were highly creative in their methods of trying to trick him into losing control. Some wanted to withhold sexual pleasures of any kind and others planned elaborate seduction scenarios involving trying to get him drunk. Some even offered drugs, but Nacón knew that starting down that path just to find pleasure had too many pitfalls. None of his circle of friends had been lured into the drug scene either partly because of his example and intolerance, but as warriors, they had to be prepared for danger.

Readiness for war had kept them safe through the years and Nacón saw no reason to deviate from the path his father had set. Being the chief's son was no small detail in his community. Though Uturaxans were long-lived and Nacón hoped that his turn to lead his people would not arrive for many more winters, he knew that he had to live his life in preparation for that time. He wanted to make his father proud and be a good king as his father had been.

Making a split-second decision to make Ixta his wife if she chose to accept him by joining, Nacón turned to her. He would honor her with his seed and that would show his commitment to her and unite them in his culture's eyes. Perhaps this was a reckless decision on his part, but since he had met Ixta, Nacón could think of no other female and his friends were teasing him about being absentminded lately as he found himself daydreaming about her when they were apart. If they only knew he was daydreaming about a woman, and an off-worlder at that, the teasing would be merciless. They were his band of brothers, not of blood, but of shared experiences and commitment. They wouldn't believe that he had fallen for a woman as he had been so careful of avoiding female entanglements up to now.

Lacking an artificial means of birth control in the early years, the Uturaxan physiology had adapted to the planet's climate and seasonal cycles. Women could only ovulate in the warm weather cycle and then it was only triggered by sexual activity in the release of the male sperm, induced ovulation. Unlike mammals on most other planets, women here didn't have a heat cycle or menses and men were easily capable of and expected to suppress sperm release during joinings, thus eliminating births during the short, but harsh winter weather cycle. Both males and females planned conceptions carefully to safeguard family alliances and relationships and to prevent the loss of infants during the awful arctic cold months. Their bodies had adapted through the years to make this rather primitive birth control method quite effective for them. Whereas this method had long been considered practically useless elsewhere, evolution had shaped the planet's inhabitants' physiology through the years to be effective.

Naked and small by Uturaxan standards notwithstanding, Ixta's form was beautiful to Nacón and aroused him to the point that his body cried out for release. Encouraged by her responses, he reached for the triangle between her thighs and slipped a finger between her folds cautiously, not wanting to make a mistake at this stage. Ixta caught her breath and slightly spread her legs apart to help him with his exploration. Nacón began to stroke her, and Ixta's moans began again, telling him he'd found an area needing more exploration and attention. When he again started to suckle her breasts as an accompaniment to his rubbing and then cautiously inserting several of his fingers inside her, Nacón was convinced that there was no reason to stop as Ixta seemed to enjoy it even more if her moans and openness to him were any indication. As his touching had continued, Ixta had opened her legs further and had continued to hold his head to the breast he was suckling.

Releasing her breast from his mouth, he started to roll her over on her knees to mount her to complete their act of mating, the preliminaries completed in his mind and by his custom. Ixta froze when he stopped kissing her and he tried to roll her over. Though not opposed to a little variety in sex, moving her to change her position suddenly brought Ixta back to the present, out of her fog of sexual pleasure. Resisting, Ixta started to pull away from him. Suddenly this intimate situation didn't feel so comfortable and the right progression of events anymore as she was brought back to reality, almost.

However, the *pulque* and her arousal from their shared kisses both on her lips and her breasts as well as his intimate touch had taken her to a point where she didn't want to stop the events from progressing. Unsure of what Ixta wanted as she clearly didn't want to assume the most common Uturaxan position for mating, Nacón decided that if she wanted to continue, she would show him about Earth customs on her own. He hoped that she wanted to continue because his body was as committed to finishing the ritual of mating as he thought that hers was. Maybe he'd gotten it all wrong though. This was territory that their many hours of conversations had never touched on and he regretted that oversight in this heated moment. *'Vaya.(Well) This is not the time to stop, Terran woman.'*

Ixta looked up at a baffled Nacón, made a snap decision to make him her lover even if just for tonight, turned to face him directly and quickly wrapped her legs around his waist, pulling him closer to her. Nacón interpreted her actions as an open invitation to culminate their physical union and eagerly guided himself inside. Ixta had idly wondered if his private part was also hair covered and thought that sounded gross and problematic but discovered that it wasn't when she felt him easily enter her. She felt his muscular thighs as he slowly pushed himself inside her, comfortably filling her completely. Her body accepted his penetration, accommodating his length and size. She felt filled in such a good way as her body had been devoid of male companionship for so long and her "toys" never completed her like this male did.

Without knowing how it came on her so suddenly, Ixta became desperate to reach a climax; her body that had been denied for so long capitalizing on the engorged male member filling her so nicely. Ixta quickly determined that this would not be a long and slow mating for her and increased her tempo, moving her hips in concert with the thrusts that Nacón began after his initial slow, gentle entry, both increasing the speed and intensity almost immediately. This was not to be a slow, sensual mating but it had the desired result as both shared the same desperation to reach a climax and were able to quickly do so as they frantically mated, thrusting hurriedly and repeatedly, no finesse in the act. She felt Nacón stiffen and then spasm into her as they came together. She could feel his arm muscles tighten by her sides and the muscles in his thighs tighten as well against the back of her legs that she still had wrapped round his hips as he continued to pump his sperm inside of her womb.

Belatedly, Ixta wondered if there would be consequences for his sperm being spilled deep inside her womb. The feeling of him deep inside her assured Ixta that it did indeed reach the opening of her womb. Apparently, this exercise in "information gathering" wasn't destined to be of any great length of time as both had reached fulfillment soon after they began. She could only imagine what a long, slow coupling would have been like with Nacón but still, mating, while it had been frenzied, had left her satisfied and enjoying the afterglow of coming with Nacón.

CHAPTER 3: The Infirmary

Ixta felt that there was more to this story than had just come back to her, but her current discomfort had her mind occupied elsewhere. First things first. She felt like shit and had to see about that before she would worry about what else might have happened between them last night or to recall the sexual pleasure she remembered feeling after they had sex.

The rest of the night and what might have happened next weren't part of her memories at this point as she knelt on the cold floor of the bathroom, fighting the nausea and the headache that threatened to break her skull into pieces. After vomiting the contents of her stomach, Ixta sat back on the floor and wondered why she'd never gotten some sort of rug to cover it. It was colder than hell down on this floor. Deciding that she couldn't continue without some kind of medication to get her to a work-ready state, she pulled on dry boxers and a new tank top and padded out of her cabin toward the infirmary. No one else was awake and she was glad that she didn't have to explain this hangover and shaky state she was in.

Unfortunately, soon after she entered the infirmary, softly closing door behind her and turning on the light, "Joss" (MsgavJosss Tvitmpr, Dr. T.), the crew's doctor, entered by the other door bending his head to avoid hitting it on the top of the door frame, the one that connected with his cabin. His vibrant purple scales shone in the clinic's bright lights. Since his face was also covered with scales, it was impossible to discern if he looked tired or not. She doubted he was upset with her though as they had become friends through the time they'd spent on common issues during the voyage.

"Ixta, what are you doing here? Is something wrong? You look terrible. Here, sit down on the table."

"Aw, Joss, I didn't want to wake you. I feel awful and needed something to get me back in shape for work today."

"Maybe you should tell me first why you feel so bad. I don't mean to imply anything, but if I didn't know better, you look like you have a hangover."

"Well, I guess you're not far off on that one, Joss. You know that drink they make here? It's called *pulque*. I don't even know what time I got home last night 'cause I was so out of it," Ixta said as she shivered violently.

"Er, no, Ixta. You're the only one of us who's really made friends with the indigenous here. None of the rest of us ever hang out with them like you do. I'll have to take your word for it. You've kind of set a new norm by being friends with me. If you haven't noticed, this crew isn't particularly fond of aliens of any kind, friend or foe. They would hardly want to learn more about this race."

"What? Well. Um. That drink *pulque* is very sweet and goes down really easy, but I can't remember much of last night as the night wore on." Part of her

registered that there was a lot of information behind
his comment that she should explore with him. Later.
Much later when she felt like herself again.

"Well, let me start with some blood work because
you shouldn't have chills and fever like you seem to
at the moment from just getting a little, no make that
a lot, drunk."

"OK, Joss. Let's make this quick though," Ixta
said as she held out her arm for Joss to draw blood.
That done, he put the sample into the computer for
analysis. Ixta was completely comfortable with Joss
because in his role as the ship's doctor, he often
collaborated with Ixta and Ethan and other biologists
about what they had found on planetary explorations.
They had developed an easy friendship with their
many planetary ramblings. On all the planets they
visited, the local flora interested him for palliative
care for the crew. "And just for the record, I wasn't
that drunk. I had a little to drink and felt a little buzz.
That's all. You're making this sound like I was
falling down drunk."

Joss just looked at her, nodded and walked back to
his lab.

A few minutes later, Joss was back beside Ixta
who had by then grabbed a blanket and wrapped it
around her shoulders.

"Ixta, this is puzzling. There seems to be only a
slight amount of alcohol in your bloodstream with
quite a few antibodies fighting infection. What else
did you drink and what exactly did you do?"

"The *pulque* was all I drank and I'm having
trouble remembering what else I did other than a

nagging feeling that I stepped over a line of good taste, or policy or something."

As Ixta uttered those words, an image of Nacón on top of her thrusting came into her mind and she said, "Oh no! Oh, Joss, I've screwed up--literally! Captain is going to fire me first and then kill me later!"

"What do you remember now about last night, Ixta?" Joss said, concern in his eyes.

"Don't judge me, Joss. Please, don't judge me." Ixta said in a small voice as her memories came tumbling back into her mind, one after another.

"I remember Nacón on top of me having sex."

"What? Unbelievable! Outrageous! Rape is never going to be tolerated here or on any planet. I never thought he was that kind of guy to force himself on you. That's barbaric! They ARE dogs. The crew wasn't wrong about them being savages. This will not go unpunished."

"Whoa, doc. It wasn't rape. I told you I was slightly drunk and maybe my inhibitions were lowered some by that and it all started out slowly and innocently."

"I don't suppose he used a condom." Joss said quietly, accepting what Ixta was telling him without further comment. Whether he thought she'd lost her mind by breaking this cultural Terran taboo as well as the ship's rules or not was a conversation to be had now but for another day. Now, he just needed to help her through this crisis.

As an alien crew member, he had occasionally contemplated what it would be like to have a relationship with a female crew member, Ixta in particular, but the taboos were too great, and he'd spent too much time on his career to risk it for a little recreational sex. However, he wasn't as repulsed by the idea as he knew the rest of the crew and their captain probably would be. When he'd signed on this ship, he'd noted that interspecies sexual contact was prohibited, one of the endless lists of rules he was required to agree to for his current position as the ship's doctor. Thus, their relationship had settled into an easy friendship. Joss doubted that she even knew he'd had some sexual fantasies about her early on in their relationship as good friends.

He still remembered one of their lunches just to get together earlier on this voyage when they'd both taken a seat at a table to the side of the mess hall. Joss had noticed the hostile looks that the crew members sent his way as they entered the mess hall in groups for lunch. Apparently sitting with Ixta was more than a few could stomach because one particularly obnoxious one had come up to their table and said, "What the fuck's going on here? Ixta have you lost your fuckin' mind sitting here alone with this alien piece of shit?"

Rolling her eyes first at Joss, Ixta had said, "What the fuck's going on with you Preston? I'm just sitting here with one of my friends eating lunch. You'd better remember that you just called the ship's doctor a piece of shit. The next time you need medical care, hope that he doesn't have a good memory for remembering assholes and their bigoted comments. Now leave us the hell alone!"

Preston had been taken aback by Ixta's condemnation and looked back at Joss as if surprised to be reminded of who he was and then grumbling under his breath had left them alone.

"Sorry for that jackass and his stupid comments. Now, what were you telling me about Argentia?"

Joss had not said anything during the entire exchange, but his heart had been warmed by Ixta's response to Preston's bigotry. Joss didn't know if it had more to do with Preston's obvious interest in Ixta or his distaste for seeing her with an alien. That and other indignities he'd endured from this particular crew reinforced his fears for Ixta once the captain found out about her escapade last night.

"Condom? This is a primitive planet Joss and he's an alien. What are you thinking? No, there was just unprotected sex between me and an alien, the chief's son. I don't have an arm implant for birth control anymore because I don't have a boyfriend and the last time I did have both, the boyfriend and the implant, my arm got all red and itchy around it so I had it removed and took monthly injections instead. But I haven't taken any birth control injections for months. I just didn't see the need. Clearly, I didn't plan for last night's activities to transpire as they did."

"Well, then Ixta, I think that your body is reacting to his sperm then. It's too alien for your body to accept its presence without a fight. That would explain the fever and chills and elevated white blood cell count. Maybe even your slight memory loss. We have no way of knowing just what was in the *pulque* or his sperm."

"You say that so calmly, Joss. What am I going to do? I can't miss my shift today and I surely can't tell this one to the captain. You won't either, will you, Joss?" Ixta pleaded, hating the pleading sound of her voice. She thought of herself as strong and capable, but this experience was telling her things about her personality that she wasn't happy to learn. She couldn't remember sounding this puny and incompetent since she was in primary school. She mentally cuffed herself on the side of her head and determined to do better in managing her feelings, which felt like she was on a roller coaster ride.

"Well, Ixta, since this isn't life-threatening, then I don't think I have to say anything just yet. We'll just have to see how you do. Have you thought about what Nacón has told his family and tribe about last night? The captain just may have to deal with this issue after all. He wouldn't like to be blind-sided by a surprise like interplanetary sex if Nacón shares his adventure with his father who then chooses this as a topic for a chat with Captain Wells. Wouldn't that make an interesting casual conversation with the captain?"

"That just sucks, Joss. Very funny. I'll worry about that later, much later. How long do you think I'll feel like this? I have to go to work in a little over half an hour and need to appear normal to do my job. I don't want to have to get into any explanations about why I'm sick with anybody but you."

"Ixta, let me give you something for both fever and nausea and we'll see how you do on that. Have you considered that you could get pregnant?"

"Pregnant! What are you talking about? You're really starting to piss me off!" Ixta shouted.

"You must have missed the birth control talk back in junior high and then again in the Academy," Joss said with a wry smile. "Do you need a refresher course? I would be happy to oblige."

"Ha. Ha. You're hilarious today, Joss. No, I hadn't considered getting pregnant. Obviously."

"This is so unlike you Ixta. You don't have a boyfriend back home that I know of, and you haven't hooked up with any of the crew on this voyage or in any of the outposts we've stopped at. I've seen that you do seem to know people almost everywhere we stop though. You never drink more than a cup at the crew's bar, and I've never seen you drunk. Sometimes you don't even drink a social cup with the crew. You would have been the last one I would have picked to be in this kind of situation."

"Well, Joss. You must need more sleep. I don't know when you've been less helpful in the pep talk area. You're supposed to be making me feel better. Some friend! And yes, I do know people in most ports because I visited places all over the galaxy when I worked on my doctorate. Remember I told you I did one of those accelerated PhD programs. It involved a lot of fieldwork." Ixta said and then she swallowed a sob, the movement making her head split apart again. "I was just gathering information on the fauna here, Joss."

"Now who's being disingenuous? Right. You may try to tell yourself that line, but we both know that's not true. Plus, the captain will never buy that one. You got drunk and then had sex. Both things should never have happened. Since when does gathering native information require drinking to excess and having sex with indigenous people?"

"Back to my comment about my doctor being an ass to me. . ."

"You're right, Ixta. Sorry about that. We'll just take this as it comes. The only documented cases of interplanetary/interspecies sexual contact have been several cases of rape. Really, in all these years of exploration, there have just been very few contacts of this kind. At least very few recorded contacts. I have a hard time believing that there has been no sexual experimentation among the more humanoid species. But with all the regulations against interspecies sex, I doubt that people shared this information if they did experiment.

"Hey, the good news is that none of those rapes resulted in pregnancies. If there were experimentation between species and offspring resulted, I doubt they would never have been able to keep that quiet and there's been nothing written to date. With the rapes, the women's bodies rejected carrying a pregnancy because the species were too different. At least that's the hypothesis, though to me, it's not that clear because "morning after drugs" were given also in almost all the cases. So, more than likely, you don't have to worry about becoming pregnant. Also, not every sexual act results in pregnancy either."

"Great. Just how do you happen to have those details at your fingertips?" I can't imagine you've had this talk with many others before."

"Correct. Never. I've never counseled any of my patients about the results of interspecies sex. This is a first. However, these cases were so unusual that we studied them at medical school and at the Academy when I did my specialty in interplanetary medicine. You tend to remember the unusual," Joss responded, looking thoughtful. "At any rate, the injection I'm going to give you for nausea and fever isn't strong enough to harm a fetus if you turn up pregnant."

"Please, Joss. Don't even say those words. It's way too soon to know about that, isn't it? I want to know. Can you tell me that yet?" Ixta asked, concern all over her face.

"Uh, Ixta. If you are pregnant, I do have some medications that would cause you to abort the fetus," Joss said quietly not wanting to convey an opinion either way about taking the "morning after pill."

"Joss. While I don't hope or want to be pregnant, I would not do anything to get rid of it, OK? I guess that's not exactly current thinking on unwanted pregnancy, but at this point, that's how I feel. How I think I feel. Shit, what am I going to do?"

Joss looked at Ixta and reconsidered what he knew about her. She was clearly much more vulnerable than he had known her to be in their previous dealings. She was nearly three decades of age now and always appeared confident and in charge. Tonight, she sounded like a teenager in trouble. Maybe she was pregnant and hormonal already. He didn't know much about the reproductive cycle of the Uturaxans. He had heard, but didn't really know, that their women weren't pregnant for as long as humans. However, he'd based that observation from precious few sightings of Uturaxan females and random comments he'd heard from Ixta. He would have to find out more. Just because the other interplanetary/interspecies cases of sexual contact hadn't produced any offspring didn't mean that this one wouldn't. Or maybe they had, but no one had wanted to admit such an event because they feared being ostracized by their peers.

The ship's team had noted in their dealings with the indigenous that the Uturaxans were very humanoid in appearance with the only difference being the fine hair covering on their bodies and the three sets of mammary glands on the females. Also, they were exceptionally tall. He hadn't seen any naked males, so he really couldn't form an opinion, but from what Ixta had just told him, the males seemed to function like human males. He wondered if Ixta would remember more details to share with him. From a scientific viewpoint, this was remarkably interesting, though slightly creepy and voyeuristic to want to know sexual details about a woman he'd considered dating and sleeping with himself.

He felt bad for his detachment as this was clearly an emotional crisis for Ixta. He considered her a friend now and the reason he'd thought about asking Ixta out several times was that she didn't seem repulsed by his Argentian scales and vivid purple skin tones like some of the crew. He hadn't felt like that would have violated the edict against interspecies co-mingling which seemed to be specifically aimed at more than platonic relationships as long as their contact was casual. On the occasions that they'd scheduled to meet in the mess hall for lunch together, they'd gotten very negative feedback from their fellow crew members and that had been off-putting to Joss.

However, the time had never seemed right to ask Ixta out on a real date, but they had developed a comfortable friendship during this trip. While theirs was a crew that was "mixed" by design, that didn't ensure that all crew members felt the same about interacting with the aliens in any situations not related directly to their jobs. And even then, Joss had heard some negative comments and had been on the receiving end of some nasty pranks at the beginning of this voyage. Providentially, word of his skills as the ship's doctor had spread and the more negative crew members left him alone, fearing to jeopardize their medical treatment if needed at a later date. Fortunately for Joss, who would never have denied anyone less than his best in medical care, these crew members never knew that their health did not depend on their treatment of him.

"Ixta, would you like me to set up an appointment with Dr. Ferguson for you to talk about this?" Joss asked, referring to the ship's psychologist.

"The ship's shrink? Shit. Oh, no. Hell no. The last thing I want right now is to relive all the details of last night. Not yet. Let me get through feeling like shit first and then I'll see how the rest of today goes. OK? Also, I'd rather talk to you than the shrink. I know you and trust you."

"Whatever you say, Ixta. Thank you for the vote of confidence. Come by later today to see me to give me an update and let me draw another blood sample to analyze. Will you do that for me?" Joss asked, smiling and warmed by her words.

"Yes, sir. I already feel better. I don't know what
you put in that shot, but at least I don't feel like
puking anymore and I've stopped sweating and
shivering. Thanks, and sorry about waking you."

"Don't mention it. For the opportunity to explore
new medical science, I'll wake up in the middle of
the night any time."

"Funny. Aren't you the comedian now?" Ixta said
sarcastically as she got up off the examining table,
sounding and feeling more like herself. Realizing that
the soreness seemed to be localized between her legs,
she now knew the reason for it. She did remember
enough about last night now to remember that Nacón
had felt very big inside her and had filled her
completely. She hadn't felt discomfort though when
he first penetrated her, just a wonderful, sexy
fullness. She did remember that much about last
night's events. Their mating had been pleasurable for
both of them, and they had climaxed together. She
wondered how many times they'd had sex but knew
it had been more than just once. Too bad that she
couldn't remember more about it as what she did
remember had been very erotic and pleasurable.

Just thinking about what she could now recall
made her feel something she hadn't felt in years. In
those moments of sex with Nacón, she felt wanted
and safe. She trusted him and that feeling of trust
made her memories of last night feel good and right.
She hoped that more details would come back as the
day progressed. She did remember how quickly they
had taken up a fast rhythm with her meeting his
thrusts, her hips coming up to meet Nacón's. She also

remembered coming quickly and Nacón's face as he thrust inside her rapidly and then came.

As more details came back to her, she could remember how it felt for him to pump his seed deep into her womb, something she'd rarely experienced in her previous sexual encounters. He had emptied his sperm inside her as he climaxed. She also remembered the look of completion and satisfaction on his face. Apparently, some male reactions were universal. The face of her alien friend had turned into something else in her mind after this encounter. He was very physical anyway and now she would have to say, sexual. In his gentle way, he had certainly taken charge of the moment. For someone purported to be the fiercest warrior on the planet, he had been very gentle and thoughtful with her last night. She had trouble reconciling the two images but was glad that he had been so attentive and caring with her all night long.

While she couldn't really recall other joinings of their bodies, she had the feeling that there had definitely been more than just that first and that he had continued to care for her body and her feelings as the night went on. It was no less than what she expected from the male who had become her best friend in the space of a few months. Cherished was the word she'd use to describe how he'd made her feel last night. That memory stuck with her even if the details of their sexual couplings eluded her other than a few distinct memories of feeling him thrust inside her body and her raising her hips to meet each thrust. There was no doubt a psychological term to describe her feelings for him, one of falling for the subjects of her investigations, but it eluded her and frankly she didn't care. Her feelings were her feelings, and she didn't need or want a scientific label for them. Surprised to feel a tear roll down her cheek, Ixta hastily wiped it away and left the infirmary.

Ixta returned to her cabin, showered, and changed her clothes with moments to spare and made it to the mess hall as the other crew on her shift were just getting their meals and sitting down. She grabbed several pieces of toast and found a 7Up in the refrigerator and took her plate to her usual table. She felt much improved from a few hours ago even though her returning memories from last night haunted her. Her usual table companions all sat down and immediately dug into their breakfasts, ensuring that they had time to eat everything they wanted before the bell rang for their shift to begin. Ixta was glad that conversation was always kept to a minimum at most meals at the beginning and middle of the shift as quickly consuming food for energy was more important to the crew members than making small talk. Chatting up her fellow crew members was the last thing she wanted to do. She didn't know if she would have been able to conceal her turbulent feelings and the last thing she wanted to do just now was reveal her latest exploits. In the back of her mind, she worried that Nacón may have said something to his father who would then share this information of their liaison with the captain. She didn't know how to prepare for that if he had shared their experiences with Chaac. Better to just put that thought aside for now, she decided.

"Hey Ixta, we haven't seen much of you lately. Still spending all your time with those dogs? Is that why you don't have time for us males here on the ship?" Preston asked with a snide look on his face.

"Aw, leave her alone guys. She's just doing her job. Right, Ixta?" Melanie said looking at Preston and at Jimmy to quell any further comments.

Forced to look up and to join in a conversation was the last thing Ixta felt like doing, especially on this topic, but she knew she had to or Preston who'd been trying to get her to sleep with him for much of this voyage would never shut up. She'd never really liked him and today, he was the last person she wanted to talk with.

"Just doin' my job y'all. Just doin' my job. Can we cut the crap and eat so we can get started on time instead of running to our post like some of you usually have to?" Ixta responded looking each of them in the eye.

Preston met her eyes and looked as if he had more he wanted to say but looked down at his breakfast and continued eating instead. Seeing that he was going to stop bothering her with his advances and questions, Ixta breathed a sigh of relief and focused on finishing the little that was on her plate.

At about the same time as Ixta was sitting down for breakfast with her crewmates, Nacón was also eating breakfast, but alone with his father. In an unusual move, he'd made the request that he and his father be left alone to eat. Ordinarily, the warriors who served as bodyguards for Nacón and Chaac all ate together, a relaxed, comfortable crowd of men used to each other's ways. When they were alone,

Nacón started to eat as he would do every day till his father broke into his thoughts.

"Nacón, *hijo* (son) why have you asked for this meeting? Surely there is something on your mind more than that food you're shoveling into your face." Chaac said, somewhat annoyed with the change in routine. He enjoyed the give and take of the warrior crew they spent so much time with. He and his son were able to speak their thoughts around them without having to censor their speech as they did the rest of the day. There was always raucous laughter at the bawdy jokes they often told.

"Well, yes, Father. There is something I need to talk to you about."

"Out with it! Surely, there's no need for a preamble to this speech. Just tell me what's on your mind, son."

"Last night at the celebration, I brought Ixta from the ship to share in the festivities."

"Yes, I remember seeing her at the circle before I retired."

"We spent the night together, Father."

"Yes, that's nice. I'm glad she got to see one of our celebrations." Chaac responded automatically till he looked over at his son's face and saw that there was another meaning behind his words. "Maybe you need to explain more of those details to me, Nacón."

"We spent the entire night together and joined our bodies a number of times and I shared my seed with her more than once." Nacón said quietly and then looked up at his father to see his reaction. For a man of thirty seasons, he felt like a small lad again, being called to defend his actions to his father, his king.

"You did what?!" Chaac thundered, fury clearly written all over his face. He pounded the table with his cup, spilling some of its contents on his plate and sending the rest flying.

Nacón felt defiant suddenly rather than chastened and hesitant as he'd originally felt when approaching his father. Seeing his father's reaction forced him to quickly review and closely examine his feelings about Ixta and what he'd done. Clearly, his father needed to hear his reasoning behind his rash move if he was to move beyond this moment which wasn't quite going as Nacón had hoped.

"As I said, Father, I mated with the Terran woman and shared my seed with her each time we mated."

"Nacón, I heard you the first time. But this isn't some childish wayward act on your part. You are the next in line to the throne, my heir, one who is expected to carry on our family line. There are any number of Uturaxan women who've been chasing after you since you reached your majority. They've made it clear to you, I assume, since it's been clear to the entire tribe that they have been very interested in being chosen as your mate. Here you use the word "mated" with regard to this, this alien woman as if it were nothing. What have you done? Do you realize the chaos this will cause? Have you thought about your responsibilities?'

"Yes, father. I have thought about them and your reaction has made me acknowledge how much I wanted this mating to occur. Yes, I have met with all the women whose families have paraded them in front of me for the past ten years. I have been friendly and even joined with many. But never have I

shared my seed because I didn't want to commit to
any of them. I couldn't imagine spending the rest of
my days with any of these power-hungry women
ruled by their families' interests of political gain. I
want a partner like you had in my mother. Yours
wasn't just a political alliance. You cared about each
other and enjoyed being a mated pair. Tell me that
isn't true. Tell me you didn't care for my mother
beyond her political capital for our family," Nacón
challenged his father.

"I, well, yes, you're right Nacón. I loved your
mother. We were true partners. But did you consider
how the tribe will react to this off-worlder? It's been
expected that you would choose one of the Uturaxan
royal lines for your partner, your spouse to rule with
and provide us heirs with. This will cause much
unhappiness in some circles, son. You have put your
pleasure first above your responsibilities to your
people," Chaac concluded, still angry, but somewhat
calmer as he waited for his son's next words.

"You are right, Father, in that I chose not to care
what unhappiness my actions would cause some of
the power hungry in our tribe because I chose my
own happiness over theirs. I have come to know this
woman over these past months. She is unlike the
other off-worlders we have met. I find my thoughts
occupied with her words and opinions in a way I
have never felt before with the women who have
courted me. She has no ulterior motives for
friendship with me other than gathering information
for her archives and museum on the ship. She does
not befriend me for money or for improving her
standing within the tribe. She doesn't want me to

purchase expensive trinkets to make her happy. Don't you see how she cares about what matters to me, not about what I can give her? She is the first female I have found that kind of relationship with. The Uturaxan women pursuing me with such zeal have provided me with physical pleasure, hoping I would share my seed with them, but nothing in friendship and conversation was never about anything but them and their desires for wealth and position. Those relationships I've had through these past ten years have been so superficial.

These past months Ixta and I have spent together have been a mating dance, a prelude to our joining last night. I just didn't see it at the time till we came to this point last night or I would have discussed it with you. I meant no disrespect, Father. I know you've been waiting for me to find a mate. Well, I have. She may not be what you expected, but I care for this woman and want her to be mine.

"Well, in that we agree. Having shared your seed with her, a pregnancy could likely result, and we can't have off-worlders carrying around the next Uturaxan heir around the galaxies. They are humanoid and more like us than they know so we can assume a high likelihood of conception. We must talk to their captain and arrange for the marriage ceremony as soon as possible."

Relieved that his father had come around to his thinking so quickly and easily, Nacón wondered how Ixta's captain would receive the news that he wanted to marry her. Even more important, how would Ixta receive this news? He didn't know how she would react or what her customs were relating to marriage and courtship. He could only imagine that they were lengthier than an evening together of sharing sexual pleasures.

He knew his father was still angry with him and felt that he hadn't thought this through. He knew his father would have expected to be part of a conversation with him about his thoughts about this woman before he had made the drastic move of sharing his seed. There was no going back after that single act and as he'd told his father, it had happened a number of times through the night. He looked forward to getting it all over with by meeting with the captain. He also wondered what Ixta's reaction would be when confronted with this issue so publicly. They'd never discussed marriage in their talks, especially marriage between an off-worlder and himself.

CHAPTER 4: Captain Wells, Chaac and the Festivities

The day dragged on for Ixta who had a stack of reports to transfer from her info pad that she carried in the field to her computer. She had notes to expand upon and some experiments in the greenhouse lab to monitor. She had a nagging thought that last night's adventure would make for some interesting reading back home if some graduate student had to sift through all the information from this voyage-- if she were ever to write about it. Having gotten up so early, Ixta found herself nodding off as the afternoon wore on. It was almost 1600 hours and nearing the end of her shift when a voice came over the com, snapping her back to focus.

"Ixta Tikal. Report to my conference room."

"Uh, sir. Captain?"

"Now!" was the growled response.

Ixta jumped to her feet, smoothed her hair, and made sure her jumpsuit was zipped all the way up to her neck as per regulations and stepped quickly out of her cubicle immediately en route to the bridge of the spaceship. The captain's conference room served as a general meeting room on and off world. Only on the

planets where colonies had been established did the
captain conduct business off the ship.

Ixta knocked on the door and entered upon hearing
the captain bark, "Come."

Ixta came in, closed the door and turned around.
To her surprise, she saw Nacón and his father Chaac
seated at the big table. She quickly looked at the
captain to gauge his mood. The quick look wasn't
reassuring as he was scowling and the vein in his
forehead was throbbing like it did when he was
furious. Till now, Ixta had avoided bringing the
captain's legendary ire upon herself, but she could
see that today was her day to be the recipient of his
anger. Her gaze turned to Chaac and Nacón and saw
stern solemnity on Chaac's face and Nacón's had a
look of uncertainty mixed with pride and
hopefulness. Pride? What could that be about?

"Tikal, Chaac and Nacón are here to request your
hand in marriage," the captain managed to spit out,
teeth clenched. "It seems they feel you have pledged
yourself to Nacón based on your activities last night."

"What?! Uh, Captain. I don't know what to say.
Surely this is a mistake." Ixta managed to weakly
respond. *'Holy shit! Now where was this going?'*
Remembering the intimacies they had shared, Ixta
felt the blush climb up her neck to her face.

The captain handed the universal translator (UT)
to Chaac who reiterated pretty much of what the
captain had said about Nacón's proposal of marriage.
The captain sat silent, clearly furious, and looked to
Ixta for a response and then, deciding that this was
her problem to work through, handed her the
translator.

"Chaac and Nacón, you do me great honor by offering marriage to me. However, I know that Nacón will one day be king and should therefore be married to an Uturaxan who would be an appropriate spouse of the future king. I am an off-worlder who can no way meet that criteria though I am greatly honored that you might think so."

Nacón smiled encouragingly at Ixta and took the translator from his father's hands and said, "Ixta, I consider you as worthy as any Uturaxan woman to sit by my side to rule this planet one day. You are smart and brave and a fine, strong woman."

Chaac apparently felt like the conversation was taking too long and took back the translator and said to the captain, "At this point, we have gone past the talking part of this situation. I don't think you understand what happened between the two of them last night."

"Well, maybe Ixta can help me to understand. Right now, I would really like to hear from her what happened," the captain said somewhat sarcastically, staring at her intently.

Ixta swallowed and started to tell the captain about last night. Almost before she began, she was stopped by Chaac who said, "Translate this so that Nacón and I may hear your words."

"Yes, sir. I apologize. No disrespect intended." Looking at Nacón while she related her tale, Ixta started with, "Nacón came to the camp and asked me if I would like to attend a party. Since I'd never been to any kind of Uturaxan celebration, I accepted the invitation, and we went a short distance from camp to a bonfire where there were a number of men and women gathered."

Nacón, Chaac and the captain all nodded encouragement for her to continue.

"There were jugs that were being passed around. Nacón's friend told me that it was *pulque*, a celebrational beverage used by the tribe. It was nectar-like in flavor, and I admit I probably drank too much. However, I was very aware of my actions and participated in conversation as well as continuing to observe what was happening. As observation of flora and fauna is my primary job off-world, I felt that I was gathering information that could be useful."

The captain made a dismissive sound and said softly. "Nice try. Not going to fly though."

Chaac determined that Ixta was finished with her accounting of last night's events and said, "The rest of the evening is what we're interested in Ixta. Tell us the rest of it."

Ixta looked uncomfortable and looked at Nacón who nodded encouragingly and then figured there was nothing to be done but come clean with the details since it seemed that Chaac had related additional details to the captain from the look on the captain's face.

"After a while, Nacón and I left the circle and um, we . . ."

Nacón, seeing Ixta's embarrassment and reluctance to proceed, took the translator and said, "We joined our bodies in a sexual way. We joined our bodies more than once and I shared my seed with her more than once."

Ixta gulped as the captain jumped up and thundered at her, "You did what? What the fuck? You had sex with an indigenous? You are in so much trouble, Tikal. You have just ended your career. Was it worth it? Was sex with this alien worth your career?"

Chaac said with a threatening look, "Translate please, Captain Wells. You have us at a disadvantage here."

"Uh, sorry, Chaac. No disrespect intended." Captain Wells took the UT from Ixta and said,

"I just asked her if she had sex with Nacón as that is against her orders as a member of my crew. We take our relationship with the Uturaxan people very seriously and wouldn't want a misunderstanding of any sort. We likewise would not want to offend you, your son, or any of your people."

Chaac said, "I see. There has been to this point no disrespect. Nacón chose Ixta because of their friendship and his admiration of her as a person. The joining of their bodies would have had no consequence beyond that moment, but as Nacón chose to share his seed with her, the situation has dramatically changed for all concerned."

Ixta just listened to the exchange, her head spinning. Since when did a male humanoid ejaculating into a woman have consequences like the ones that seemed to be developing here? She knew that the Uturaxan clan structure had a strict code of morality that was extremely specific in many cases. Evidently, her discussions with Nacón hadn't encompassed enough areas as she was truly puzzled by the chain of events in front of her now. It seemed a point of honor to them that Nacón had 'shared his seed.' It sounded medieval to her. Clearly, she had some gaps in her knowledge base that were about to have disastrous results for her.

Gesturing for the UT from Captain Wells who refused to give it back to her, Ixta just looked at Nacón, wanting to share her thoughts and ask more questions.

"There really isn't more to be said here, Ixta. Chaac told me earlier today, before I called for you, that his tribe and the others on this planet would consider it a grave diplomatic breech should you not accept Nacón's proposal of marriage. He, in good faith, intended to follow this to its expected conclusion when he had sex with you in the jungle last night. I just wasn't aware of all that had happened between you two. I thought he'd just taken a fancy to you and could be talked out of this proposal."

Chaac got an ominous look on his face as Wells spoke to Ixta without the UT. Wells ignored Chaac's obvious displeasure and continued, "Ixta, you will be court-martialed for your escapade last night and returned to earth in the brig. Actually, I think you should take the offer on the table here. If you don't, you will leave this room in handcuffs and taken to the brig to await your court-martial."

"Enough!" Chaac stood, having grabbed the translator and shouted. "No more talk! Do we prepare the celebration for later tonight or do we prepare for war?"

Surprise registered on Captain Wells' face as he truly hadn't realized the severity of the situation in

Uturaxan eyes. Apparently, his anthropologist hadn't either from the look on her face right now. The look on Chaac's face made it clear to Wells that he was serious and prepared to go to war over this issue. He was clearly furious at the lack of expected resolution to the problem.

Everyone in the room looked at Ixta who quickly did some mental calculations about her options at this moment. She felt a pounding in her ears and hoped she didn't pass out. '*Focus! You have to focus!*' She didn't want to lose her career either way, but it seemed she would whether she stayed with the crew or accepted Nacón's proposal of marriage. She was slightly claustrophobic and knew that the brig on the ship was small, smaller than her tiny cabin, and she would be caged in there for many months while here on Uturax and on the trip back home. She couldn't bear the thought of that or the shame of being returned home without her commission and career.

Her life was over as far as she was concerned. Never to return home. . .While she didn't really understand the role of women on this planet, she knew and trusted Nacón not to hurt her or let anyone else do her harm. She only wished that Nacón had explained the details of what was happening between them before they had sex, had told her that if he "shared his seed" that it committed them to marriage! Much as she had wanted to have sex with him, she probably would have chosen not to if she'd understood the consequences. These consequences. However, it seemed as if Nacón was willing to do more for her than her captain who was furious with her now. If Captain Wells were any angrier, steam would be coming out of his ears.

Every crew member who signed on for interplanetary travel was a risk taker with a sense of adventure. This would surely fall under the category of adventure and then some. Making a snap decision since it clearly was her turn to resolve the issue with her response, she decided for adventure rather than disgrace and confinement. Gamely pushing back the sob that threatened to come out of her mouth, her decision was made.

Taking a deep breath, Ixta said, "I accept Nacón's proposal. I am honored to do so."

Chaac and Nacón both looked pleased by her response and using the UT, Chaac said, "Prepare yourself for tonight and gather your belongings as you will move into the village after tonight's ceremony. Captain, you are invited to the ceremony as are your crew. No one is required to attend this event, but all will be welcomed should they choose to come." At that, Chaac and Nacón nodded to both Ixta and Captain Wells, turned and left the room.

Captain Wells faced Ixta as soon as the door closed and sarcastically said, "Well, interplanetary warfare averted at the last moment. That's just great, Ixta. Why did you think you could do whatever the hell you wanted here with impunity? Clearly the enormity of your actions hasn't become clear to you yet. Did you miss Chaac's comment about war? Imminent war on my watch!" Wells finished, shouting.

As Ixta opened her mouth to comment, the captain held up his hand and continued, "I don't know what the hell you were thinking, seaman. You don't ever drink or have indiscriminate sex with anyone anywhere and here you do both in the same night. Chaac wasn't kidding about a war. This is serious business to them. Clearly the thought of a little Uturaxan bastard running around the galaxy is out of the question. It would seem that you haven't learned as much about local customs as you led me to believe. If you had, this whole disaster would have been avoided. You have been irresponsible in the worst way. This indigenous group has been very open and accepting of us, resulting in an alliance that has been and will be very advantageous to us based on the position of Uturax within this star system and the wealth below ground in gems and crystals they all seem to wear conspicuously on themselves. We are just starting to learn a little more about the gems that seem abundant on this planet and the locations of the mines where they're found. Now with you off our crew, it will be harder to find out just how much wealth is here and how to negotiate a beneficial trade contract for us."

"Apparently, Chaac has waited for the last ten years for Nacón to choose a mate, the future queen of Uturax. Ever since he reached his majority, the whole tribe has been watching and waiting for Nacón to take this all-important step in ensuring the continuity of his family's clan. It's a shame that you will never return to Earth, but I've got to say that you're getting off easy here. Many lives would have been lost on both sides of this war that you almost caused. We have more weapons, but they have some mumbo jumbo magic that they combine with their

weapons in warfare that we haven't been able to
dominate yet in our war games. It's almost as if
they're just toying with us when we do mock war
games just to placate us by going through the
motions. If I didn't know that shit like that doesn't
exist, I'd have to say that they have something going
on here beyond my pay grade. On the surface, they
look like a bunch of wild kilt-wearing Scottish
prehistoric men that walk upright, mere savages. But
they have keen minds and are brilliant strategists. It
would have been a shame to lose this alliance
because of your acting like a lush and a slut."

Ixta blushed and hung her head in shame, knowing
that the captain spoke only the truth. Finally, unable
to hold them back any longer, the tears started to roll
down her cheeks. She swallowed the sobs, but the
tears would not stop. She would never return to Earth
again! Her career was in ashes, and she was getting
married to an alien humanoid. *'Peachy,' as grandma
used to say. 'Fucking peachy. What the hell? She had
work to do to get everything she owned together. Pity
party later if she had the time. She surely didn't have
time right now to bemoan her fate.'*

After Wells dismissed her, Ixta bolted out of his
office to run through the corridor to her cabin, barely
containing her tears. She wanted to avoid seeing or
worse talking with any of the crew. Unfortunately,
she saw the first mate step out of the ready room off
the captain's meeting room and knew by the smug
expression on his face that all would soon know her
plight. Justin was not known for his discretion on
matters like this. Her humiliation was complete.
Word travels fast in a close-knit community and

when she arrived back in her cabin area, her shift
mates were all assembled, arms crossed, waiting to
talk to her.

"Tell me it's not true," Preston said. He was angry
that Ixta was leaving the crew and not happy about
the circumstance. "What's the shit they're saying
about you? Impossible! Mother fucking dog had to
have forced you. Did you tell them that?"

"Look, y'all. I don't have anything to say except
it's been a pleasure to serve and work with you.
You're a fine crew. I have to stop by Doc's and then
get my stuff together now. I don't have time to talk
and there's really nothing to say anyway."

"Not so fast, Ixta," said Melanie as she blocked
Ixta's path to the infirmary. "Nothing to say? You
had hot sex with an alien prince and you're not going
to share some details?" Melanie leered at Ixta,
savoring her discomfort. Melanie had been interested
in Preston for some time, and it rankled her that he
seemed obsessed with Ixta to the point that he almost
completely ignored Melanie's advances.

Ixta blushed and said curtly, "No. And that's my
final word on it." Hoping to avoid further comments,
Ixta quickly turned to go to the infirmary, still
hearing them muttering as she walked away as they
continued to discuss her situation. She could still hear
Preston saying, ". . . motherfuckin' slut. . . . . .
wouldn't let me in her pants, but. . ." Since she hadn't
given them details, they would supply their own and
continue their gossip throughout the ship. She was
glad she wasn't going to be here to hear it. She
couldn't decide what was worse: shamed in front of

everyone on the crew or being banned and thrown off the ship to avoid the brig and a prison sentence.

Opening the door to the infirmary, Ixta found Doc on his computer, apparently doing some research.

"Hi, Doc. I'm back as ordered. I'm sure you heard how my day turned out," Ixta said as she gulped a breath, trying to stifle the sobs she felt getting ready to begin now that she was out of sight of the captain and crew. Unable to stop the tears, they started rolling down her cheeks.

As many men are, Joss was appalled to see Ixta crying and felt ill prepared to handle this situation with her but thought to distract her, "Well, Ixta, yes, I did. I don't know whether to congratulate or commiserate in this situation. Anyway, let's draw some blood so I can run some quick tests before you go."

"Joss, the worst of it today was Chaac's and Nacón's going to Wells with the details of last night like they were going over a shipping list or something."

"I imagine that must have been embarrassing," Joss said mildly.

"Try humiliating. In my worst-ever imaginings of awful moments, I couldn't have come up with this shit. Nacón proceeded to tell Wells that we fucked all night long and he pumped his sperm in me again and again. Oh, God, I still can't believe it! It was like someone describing a porn movie or something and then finding out you were the main character. Then to make matters worse, Justin Daniels was listening in the ready room, and he came out to the hall when I did with a shitty look on his face and by the time I got back here, he'd spread the word to the crew who proceeded to add their own little piece of harassment. I feel like a complete asshole."

"Well, it's done. Let's draw that blood now."

Ixta couldn't believe Joss's unruffled demeanor. "You mean you're not going to lecture me on how wrong it was to screw an alien? That's just it? No more comments?"

"Well, since I'm an alien and consider myself fairly liberal, I don't see any purpose in hashing out what's already done and not that radical by my standards. The upsetting thing for me is Well's kicking you off this ship, not your alliance with Nacón. I can't say I know the prince well, but I like him so far."

Sighing, Ixta dutifully held out her arm and then sat on the table to wait for the results. "I wish you were the captain instead of that old bigot Wells. Hey, did you find anything new in your computer today about my situation?"

"Sorry to say that I didn't, Ixta. Just the same stuff I told you about this morning. Here, the report is coming up on the screen, Ixta. Let's look at it."

Doc looked at the screen and then looked over at Ixta and then at the report again.

"Well, Doc. Don't keep me in suspense. You're making me nervous. What is it? Is it different from this morning?" Ixta asked trying to sound casual.

"Yes, it is. You're pregnant!"

"Oh shit! Oh no. Not me! Not pregnant! Will this even work? I thought you said it doesn't work because the alien DNA is too, well, alien to create a fetus. Isn't it too soon for pregnancy to show up anyway? Now what will I do? I can't believe this shit. Am I cursed today or something?" Ixta moaned and babbled on.

"Well, to answer the DNA question, that's been the standard line in med school, but I told you today that there have been so few circumstances of this situation that the research is woefully incomplete. Apparently, you and the Uturaxan physiology are compatible and yes, it is usually impossible to detect pregnancy the day after sexual contact."

"Oh, great. Nothing like making medical history and almost causing interplanetary warfare all in the same day. "At that news, Ixta began to laugh hysterically and then to sob. Concerned, Joss came over to her and touched her arm.

"Joss, I don't know if I can take any more of this today!" She surprised him by jumping off the table and wrapping her arms around his waist, wetting his chest and his shirt with what seemed to him an endless supply of tears. As the sobbing diminished, she unwrapped herself from him and moved back to get on the table again. Joss had been awkwardly patting her back but was relieved when she seemed to have her emotions back under control. While he might have once fantasized about having his arms around Ixta, the reality of a sobbing woman wrapped around him was more than he was ready to deal with and hardly the circumstance in which he'd envisioned her arms wrapped around him.

Ixta continued the conversation as if nothing had occurred saying, "Joss, about lack of research info, you mean that no one has been stupid enough to do this unless they were forced to! There seemed to be some special significance placed on the fact that he came inside me. They called it "sharing his seed" like that was something that didn't happen when they had sex. What do you think that means, Doc, just out of curiosity?"

"You're the expert in fauna and alien cultures, Ixta. You should probably tell me what you think," Doc said mildly.

"Well, let me start with telling you what Wells just told me. In as many words, apparently, I don't know shit about this culture, or I wouldn't have done what I did last night. As far as customs, all I could come up with was that sex is okay among adults, but the male's actually ejaculating inside the female was a life-partner event that apparently happens only after marriage from what I learned this morning. I don't know. I'm just making this up as I go. Maybe it's different for Nacón because he's a prince and can't be having bastards in line for the throne running all over this planet or the galaxy as Wells so bluntly pointed out to me today. You'd think they'd figure out birth control or condoms or something, so this wasn't the issue. It's too late for me now anyway. All I'm remembering after hearing him say we had sex multiple times and that he shared his seed each time is that he came in me multiple times. Each time we had sex, he says we climaxed, and more sperm made its way into my womb. I didn't think pulling out was real birth control anyway though that didn't exactly happen. How could that work? I'm just making assumptions here though about how they have sex."

" Yes, it is too late. As far as not ejaculating, maybe their physiology is different to make that a viable method of birth control. But since he said he ejaculated in you multiple times, there was no attempt at preventing conception. Right? I hope I'll be permitted to monitor your pregnancy. Whether you want to or not, you're making interplanetary history here, Ixta. If you can carry the pregnancy, yours will be the first interplanetary child of record."

"Fantastic. Just what I'd hoped for. In the same breath as they tell that part of it, they'll include the little bit about my being dismissed from my crew in disgrace for violating Rule Number Five about culture and undue influence upon and fraternization with indigenous cultures. Then they'll add that I chose to remain here rather than serve time in prison for grave dereliction of duty. I think my actions would definitely come under the umbrella of 'undue fraternization'," Ixta finished and rubbed her eyes, still not believing the situation that a little *pulque* and a romp in the jungle had gotten her.

Married! And to an alien. Even if the Uturaxans were humanoid in some ways, they were not human. What would that mean for her child if she was able to carry it to term? Mixing of species was not something talked about other than as a taboo. Humans were humans and if the human race were to continue as such, there would be no intermingling of blood with other species of any kind. Humans were quite snooty about purity of race, fearing that the human race would be diluted until it was replaced by alien races. She had certainly not given thought to all these ramifications when she accepted that first drink of *pulque* and when she agreed to leave the circle with Nacón. Even though she was slightly drunk, she was

very aware of what was happening as the evening
unfolded. *I was so naive to think I could be with him
and all those other couples who were obviously there
for sex.* She'd even welcomed the mating after all the
time they spent kissing. It was as if all her training
left her brain for the evening. She should have
thought about the possible outcomes instead of just
going with her feelings and physical urges. Some
professional she was.

Before she was ready to go, Captain Wells called
for Ixta to come to the bridge. She'd put on her dress
uniform, not knowing what would be appropriate for
this set of circumstances and not wanting to appear
too informal and not honoring the Uturaxan
traditions. She had no idea whether this ceremony
would be formal or informal. She guessed the captain
was right. She wasn't the hotshot anthropologist
she'd thought herself to be. She had spent too much
time just talking, even debating, with Nacón about
everyday issues but hadn't gone in depth about the
entire array of cultural customs usually found in
every civilization. Now she was wishing she'd asked
him about courtship and marriage, but as her
grandma would tell her that "If wishes were horses,
beggars would ride." What had she been thinking?
Woulda, coulda, shoulda- that wasn't going to get her
anywhere at this point. In the span of a few hours,
she'd come to terms with the fact that she'd thrown
away her career and life as she knew it because Earth
was now off limits to her as was everything she knew
about the human condition and interactions.

She would need to focus on learning the Uturaxan
culture to avoid any more mix-ups though she

couldn't imagine any having the severity of
consequences that her actions last night had. She
wanted to cry out with pain for the loss of it all, but
her pride wouldn't allow anyone else to see her break
down. She had to pull herself together for her
meeting with the captain. Unless he'd mellowed
since her last visit here several hours ago, she could
only expect more negative comments from him.
Knowing that she deserved all he could possibly
throw her way about her lack of professionalism, she
resigned herself to another round of scathing
comments from Wells.

Knocking on the door to the captain's office, Ixta
entered when she heard "Come." She saw that the
captain was also wearing his dress uniform and when
he looked at her, he said, "Since you're no longer in
the service and a member of this crew, you really
don't have the right to that uniform, seaman." Taking
in Well's statement about her lack of position here,
she also noted that his pupils were again dilated.
*'Shit. This guy's gonna fuck everything up before
he's done if he keeps on like this.'*

Seeing Ixta's crestfallen expression and look of
despair, his look softened somewhat, and he
continued, "I'm sorry, but you'll have to take that off
and put on some coveralls. That's the best I can do as
far as clothing for you. I realize you have no off-duty
clothing with you as interstellar travel has precious
little storage space, and you always have had
coveralls or your uniform to wear to socialize in."

Seeing the look on Ixta's face as she fought to
bring her emotions under control but was unable to
contain the single tear that spilled over and rolled

down her cheek, he said, "You've been a respected
member of my crew till yesterday, but the impact of
your irresponsibility is enormous. I'm losing a crew
member I need, and we almost came to war over your
actions. This is the way it has to be. Use the
storeroom across the hall to get a clean set of
coveralls and quickly change and then I'll meet you
at the door as it's time to go."

"Yes, sir. I'll be right there," Ixta said, feeling like
an outcast, a pariah. Losing the right to wear her
uniform brought home how dire her situation was in
the eyes of the captain and crew. She *was* an outcast.
Why kid herself? No matter how she tried to
rationalize what she'd done last night, the captain
was right to strip her of everything. She'd broken
every important rule and an oath that she'd sworn to
adhere to when she'd joined the service. This error
had no 'do-overs.' Everything she was accustomed to
was about to change in ways she couldn't even
imagine. She felt numb and feared that once the
reality of her disgrace sank in, she would feel even
worse. Following the captain's orders, Ixta found the
least beat up pair of clean coveralls and quickly
donned them and went to the hatch doorway. She was
surprised to see the whole crew there, wearing their
dress uniforms, waiting to accompany her to the
ceremony.

"Geez, y'all. I don't know what to say except
'thank you,'" Ixta said, feeling overcome by their
show of support even though she knew that not
everyone approved of her actions.

As one, the crew nodded at her, some of them
smiling. A few of the female crew members had tear

filled eyes as they looked away, unable to meet Ixta's eyes. They sympathized with her and felt she was a sacrificial lamb today. Others pretended their neutrality, but Ixta could feel their scorn and condemnation as she passed by. Regardless of their censure, the crew was there in its entirety to support and accompany her. *Wells must be going soft if he's requiring their presence. Must be the drugs.* As a group, led by Captain Wells, they stepped out the door and went down the ramp. Before she was ready, Ixta was looking up at Chaac and Nacón and a small delegation of Uturaxans who had approached the bottom of the ramp to wait for her.

Ixta was not a small Terran female by any accounting, measuring a little over 5'9" (175 cm) and weighing 150 lbs. (68 kg) but she had to look up, way up at Chaac, Nacón and the rest of their group. The average male Uturaxan was 6'6" tall and weighed in at 250 lbs and up. They were exceptionally large beings, something that Ixta hadn't really thought much about before. But looking at the lineup of giants waiting for her all in their ceremonial kilts, she likened them to Scottish warriors from many years ago on Earth. They certainly did look imposing was all that she could think as she looked at her new family-to-be.

Ixta looked up and smiled weakly at Nacón who responded by grinning broadly and then putting a serious, solemn look back on his face. Captain Wells and Chaac greeted each other formally and then Chaac turned and led the procession away from the ramp toward the clearing nearby where Ixta could see many Uturaxans assembled, having been hidden by

the foliage surrounding the clearing where the ship
was. Men and women were present, and Ixta was
curious to see so many females assembled, more than
she had ever seen. She noticed that the women
seemed to be older, some even ancient. None of the
younger women she'd seen around the fire the
previous night were present. There were many mated
pairs in the Uturaxan entourage, all dressed for the
occasion. The clan colors were evident in the
women's skirts, head scarves and men's kilts. They
assembled in loose formation, about seventy-five
people in all. Seeing so many assembled from
Nacón's tribe, she had to wonder where the rest of his
people were keeping themselves. There were no
younger tribe members, no children and no marriage
age women. Ixta didn't have to be an anthropologist
to know that this was by design to protect their young
and eligible women by keeping them hidden away
from the Terran's eyes. Why look for trouble when it
can be avoided by just not providing more
information than was needed for the specific
situation? Last night's events and this hurried
marriage ceremony were proof that the Terrans
couldn't be trusted not to take advantage of the
Uturaxan people.

A middle-aged woman approached Ixta with some
beautifully woven folded fabric in her hands, looked
at her for her assent and when Ixta nodded, placed a
beautiful length of soft, intricately woven rust
colored fabric over Ixta's shoulders so that she would
match Nacón's kilt and shoulder fabric like the
tartans worn by the Highlanders on Earth so many
years before. Then, she pinned a brooch on the

shoulder fabric that matched the one Nacón was
wearing. Ixta recognized the woman as the one who
served them lunch many months ago. Since she
lacked a dress uniform now to wear to this occasion,
she was glad that someone in Nacón's clan had
thought ahead to visually mark her as one of their
own. As if anyone would make that mistake! She
looked human, so contrastingly different from the
furry Uturaxan people. As the woman finished and
made to turn away, Ixta put her hand on her arm so
that the woman stopped and looked at her.

"Thanks to you for this. You don't know how
happy you just made me to think of including me in
wearing your clan's colors. I know you don't
understand me, but I hope you understand the feeling
behind my words," Ixta finished with a smile and a
bowing of her head in respect.

The Uturaxan woman smiled back and nodded to
acknowledge Ixta's gesture and moved away to join
the others who had lined up to form a circle around
Ixta and Nacón in anticipation of the wedding
ceremony.

Chaac motioned for Ixta to come up beside Nacón.
Ixta was surprised to see that Captain Wells had
brought the translators to the ceremony. He was so
angry with her that she didn't expect any kindness
from him at this point. The captain offered them to
Nacón and Ixta. Looking at Ixta to see if she had any
feelings on this issue, she shrugged her shoulders as
if to say, 'whatever you want.' Nacón took one of the
translators and spoke into it saying, "It is our custom
to invite friends and family to witness the pledge of a
man to a woman. No one marries us. We choose to

pledge ourselves to each other and the people assembled here with us are the watchers, the ones who witness and speak of this pledge for many years to come. Shall we begin?"

Nacón looked to Ixta for her assent and seeing her nod, joined hands with her, looked deeply into her eyes and said, "Ixta, I pledge to care for you for all of my days. You will be my mate and the one I choose to be at my side as I continue my life's journey. You and no other. Do you accept my pledge?"

Ixta felt like she was swimming without a lifeline, as this ceremony suddenly seemed very serious and solemn. She didn't know what she'd expected, but it wasn't this, a feeling of finality and utter solemnity. From the looks on all the Uturaxan faces, she knew that this was a momentous occasion for them, and she felt like a usurper, someone not prepared for all that this pledge would entail. She'd never been serious about anyone for a long time, having been disappointed several times in relationships. It had been easier to have physically rewarding relationships without having a serious emotional commitment. From Nacón's face and the tone of his voice, Ixta could sense that this marriage wasn't going to be light and uninvolved. She was expected to build a relationship, a life, with this alien male pledging his loyalty and the rest of his days to her. Unsure if she could meet his level of commitment, not knowing if she was capable of that kind of love and caring, Itxa quickly thought about her options. That took only seconds as she knew that she had none.

Lacking confidence, but determined to give it a try, Ixta said, "I accept your pledge, Nacón and offer you mine. I choose to be your mate and pledge to be loyal at your side as I continue my life's journey. You and no other. Do you accept my pledge?"

Gulping a little as the words came out, Ixta figured that she had nothing to lose at this point as all she knew as a crew member was already lost and her friendship with Nacón required that she give this a go, to make a real effort. A real effort on her part to make this work for his sake and the now fragile peace between his people and hers required this of her. Since she'd screwed up everything she'd touched in the last twenty-four hours, at least she could promise to do her very best to do better.

While she still didn't really understand how she'd become a bride and a future queen in the last day, she clearly understood where she was now. She would make this work for everyone's sake. She just wouldn't think about all the ramifications of not making this union succeed. She supposed that could include death as she'd have nowhere else to go if she didn't succeed as a wife here. Well, she guessed she'd brought this all on herself for overstepping the boundaries that were so clearly drawn and dealing with the consequences was just what she deserved. She was a big girl now and couldn't go to anyone to fix her screw-up's.

In that moment, she was mentally transported back in time as an often-repressed memory surfaced. It had been many years since she'd been in that kind of position, and her parents had failed her when she'd gone to them for help during her college years. She

had had an affair with her high school boyfriend and
had gotten pregnant. Her boyfriend dropped her when
she told him of her pregnancy. He'd even asked her if
the baby was his, which really hurt because they'd
been a couple for three years by then. Not wanting to
drop out of college, she'd gone to her parents for
advice and all she'd heard were scathing
recriminations along the likes of: 'You've thrown
away your college scholarship with this
irresponsibility. What do you expect us to do now?
We can't afford to send you to college, so you'll have
to come home. Don't expect us to clean up after you.
You're eighteen now.'

Ixta was horribly disappointed by their quickness
to condemn her. All that she had wanted from them
had been a little comfort and some advice as to how
to sort it all out. Instead, they spent the evening
yelling at her.

She had said to her father finally, "Daddy, I know
I've messed up, but I came to you for advice. It is my
problem; I know this, but I just want to know what
you would advise. I always ask you for advice. "

Her mother, always a little jealous of her close
relationship with her father had broken in, "Well,
darling. You've gone too far this time. Forget some
folksy advice from dear old dad. You didn't get him
alone like you usually do to wrap him around your
little finger. This time, you have to listen to me too.
You've behaved like a little whore who couldn't keep
her legs together. I knew you'd end up like this!"

"Madge, stop it!" her father shouted at his wife,
horrified by her words. I can't believe you'd talk to

your own daughter like that. What's wrong with you?
What kind of mother are you?"

"What's wrong with me? You mean, 'what's
wrong with your daughter?' She went and got herself
knocked up. What about college? What about her
scholarship? You know we can't afford to pay for her
college. She's gone and ruined everything. What will
people say? What will people think? Now what?"

At those words, her father had looked unhappy
and crestfallen as he realized that his wife did have a
point about the cost of college for Ixta and the
importance of not losing her scholarship."

Seeing the look on her father's face and his
complete lack of support froze Ixta's heart. She knew
at that moment that her father's abdication as, in her
mind, her supreme supporter would cause a rift
between them that would take a long time to heal.
She looked at both in disgust and with her heart
broken, turned and left, ignoring her mother's
continuing barrage of scathing comments about her
stupidity and immorality. Everything she said was
hurtful, poisonous, as if she'd saved up all her anger
toward her daughter to spit out all at once.

Ixta had always been close to her father before this
discussion and felt that he'd betrayed their friendship.
She expected her mother to react like this, but her dad
had always been the one she could go to with any
kind of problem for advice. He usually would help
her think through her options, guiding her to make
the best decision. That's all she had wanted with this
new problem. However, that wasn't to be that night
or ever. Her parents had been killed in an accident
shortly after that night, so they had never reconciled

their differences. As it turned out, the situation resolved itself within weeks of her parents' deaths as she miscarried. All that Ixta had been left with though was a distrust of men in personal relationships as the previously most important man in her life had so sorely disappointed her.

"I accept, Ixta. From this moment on, you are my mated partner and my future queen. Let us celebrate!" Nacón said as he clasped arms with her in their formal salute of greeting.

The Terrans shouted their congratulations, joining in the festivities. Since there were no eligible young Uturaxan women to watch the ceremony, there were no hard feelings or signs of animosity on anyone's face. The Terrans were mostly supportive of Ixta and even those who weren't sure this was the best solution, felt that if Ixta was going to try to be positive, then they could too. Even Captain Wells moved forward to congratulate the couple, saying, "I wish you both the very best, Ixta and Nacón. Chaac, I would also like to congratulate you on the marriage of your son. "

Ixta could have sworn she saw an ironic look in Chaac's eyes as he accepted Wells' best wishes but decided she must have fabricated that reaction as she had found the Uturaxans to be guileless in her previous interactions. While they were fierce warriors and outstanding strategists, they seemed to lack the level of reasoning that irony would require. It was starting to worry her how she and her new husband would get along. Hmmm. It made her wonder if this was just another example of how poorly she had done her research here. She was beginning to wonder just what else she had misjudged about this race. Apparently, there was a lot to still be learned here. She felt a tug of regret that she would have no more reports to write and share about all she would learn here living in the village with the Uturaxans.

They all moved a little further into the jungle to another clearing where a long table had been set for the wedding feast. As Chaac took his place at the ceremonial head of the table, Nacón sat on his right and indicated to Ixta that she should take the seat next to him. Chaac motioned to the captain where he should sit, at his left, and then the captain nodded at various officers to take the next seats.

After the officers were seated, the rest of the Uturaxan council approached and took the remaining seats on the half of the table closest to Chaac. The few crew members remaining quickly slipped into seats as did some Uxturaxan elders, men and women, on the other end of the table. Almost immediately, Chaac signaled for their cups to be filled, and the food brought out and served and a long line of serving people brought baskets and dishes of food along with jugs that they used to fill the cups. Smelling the sweet scent of *pulque*, Ixta demurred and asked Nacón if she could have water. Smiling, Nacón said something to the server near his chair who quickly left and immediately returned with a jug of water.

Seeing what had transpired, Captain Wells said to Ixta, "Don't you think it's a little late to avoid overindulging in the native wines, Ixta?" His eyes were cold, and she knew that he was still simmering with fury over the current events even if he was pretending to be civil for Chaac's benefit. The momentary softness she'd seen was gone, replaced by Wells' usual hardass look. He would have to report to his superiors how he had lost a crew member and how close they had come to war. Even if he suppressed the information about an impending war, he couldn't avoid the fact that he would have to account for her absence when he returned home without her. It would not look good on his record, which was already tarnished with his drug use and rehab stint, Ixta knew as she tried to smile to lighten the moment but was able to come up with only a fleeting smile that looked more like a grimace.

Once everyone's cups were filled, Anthony, one of the officers, a friend of Ixta's and a junior anthropologist, tapped his cup and then looking at Chaac for permission, stood and said, "I want to congratulate Nacón and Ixta and wish them both the best in the years to come. Good luck."

Touched by the toast, Ixta raised her cup along with the others and smiled at Anthony in thanks for his toast and effort at trying to make this occasion festive. During the next hour, much *pulque* was consumed along with several native dishes of food that Ixta didn't recognize. She gamely kept on eating and tasting though, not wanting to be disrespectful of the indigenous food. Perhaps, Terrans weren't the only ones who could be affected by too much *pulque* because she heard a disagreement begin at the other end of the table and muttered words she didn't understand."

Even without a common language, it became clear that someone was pointing at Ixta and making derogatory statements and gestures. The Terran crew jumped up as one as did several Uxturaxan men near the upset native man.

Suddenly Chaac roared something in Uturaxan that made several other men appear to escort away the man causing the problem at the other end of the table. He struggled at first but yielded when Chaac gave another very forceful command.

Just then Captain Wells stood and addressed his crew who were by now also standing, "Stand down all of you. Immediately! My apologies, Chaac, but I think we will return to our ship at this time." At his words and nod, the crew got up and began to return to the ship. Chaac nodded his agreement and stood also.

As the Uturaxans made to leave the table as one, the elders, Nacón and then Ixta stood to leave that area, and Ixta found herself flanked by Nacón and the Uturaxan woman who'd brought her the clan colors before the wedding ceremony. Ixta was surprised when this woman wrapped her arm protectively around Ixta but welcomed the warm gesture. They all followed Chaac away from the table into the next clearing where the rest of the tribe was gathered. Ixta could hear some other angry voices in this group along with the voice of the first tribesman who had caused the disturbance at the dinner table. Chaac raised his hand for silence and said, *"Telóm!"* Instantly quiet fell upon the group. A huge, jeweled ceremonial chair was dragged into the clearing and Chaac turned around and took a seat. Nacón took Ixta's hand and led her to a bench that had been placed beside Chaac's chair. Chaac was now holding a tall staff decorated with many colored feathers tied to its end in his hand. Ixta noted that the top was encrusted with beautiful, shining gems.

As he hit the staff against the ground, a group of people approached the throne and knelt on the ground before him. He nodded at the closest person, the man from the dinner table who began to venomously spit out some words, gesturing and glancing at Ixta. A moment passed and Nacón stood up, a thunderous look on his face. Chaac lightly restrained him by touching his wrist and nodded to the man to continue. After looking at Nacón again, he fell silent and said no more as he returned to his seat. One of the younger women began to speak, much in the same vein as the previous speaker from what Ixta could tell. Her Uturaxan was very rudimentary, and she could only pick up a few words here and there, but the expressions on their faces and the tone of their voices left no doubt that they were expressing their extreme displeasure with something. She was beginning to realize that it most likely involved her and Nacón as the gestures didn't stop and Nacón looked furious. He remained seated where he was, obeying his father's request, but his unhappiness and anger were clear.

Ixta didn't need to be a fluent speaker of Uturaxan to figure that out. From the faces of those in the clearing, it seemed that those who had spoken had many others sharing the same thought. The women's comments sounded especially bitter, and Ixta was burning with curiosity and wondered how she would ever know just what was said. Since this was her new home, she felt like knowing what she was up against was essential to her future. She just didn't see a way of knowing more details other than what her knowledge of charades had enabled her to glean from the diatribes just delivered. Apparently emboldened by the speeches of the previous complainers, other women and men asked to speak. By then Ixta was beginning to recognize a few of the words as they were repeated again and again. *'Hell, there seems to be no lack of folks who want to bitch about me!'*

A few more spoke and then no one rose to speak, and all looked to Chaac who had an inscrutable look on his face. Nacón still looked like a thundercloud was hanging over him. He'd remained seated, but his fists were clenched. His lips were drawn back, and his teeth were showing, gritted, clenched together. He looked furious and Ixta knew it had something to do with her and their marriage, but the details eluded her as she had understood really very little of the comments that had been given.

Chaac opened his mouth to speak, and hush fell upon the group as all waited for his comments. Chaac spoke in a level, firm voice, standing so that all in the crowd could hear him.

"*Ixta ubo sposix tupan Nacón. El hed icko scojo e la hid aprobivib. Oide nignuo davo palibris u icko contra sta sumuja. Icko sta icko. Poseis dsara utru rasolum con rospetco a kasar sposix tupan jiho. Solo pnsariu soles mavitona sos comnatius. Codo maviotna soles. Terminemos. No ablaruma nunca maso. Mas, nignuo davo contra sta sumuja cuya vajo protecdada mya y Nacón.*" And to avoid misunderstanding Chaac repeated in the lingua franca of all present:

"Ixta está casada con mi hijo, Nacón. El ha eligido, y yo lo he aprobado. No aceptaré ningún daño en palaba o hecho contra esta mujer. Hecho ya está. Puede que hubiera otro resultado para algunos de Uds., pero está hecho. Sólo puedo pensar en que los celos les da motivo para sus comentarios aquí hoy. La ambición y la avaricia les da motivo para estos celos. Esta discusión se ha concluído. No hablaremos nunca más sobre este tema, pero déjenme aclarar para todos: ningún daño le pasará a esta mujer quien está bajo mi protección y la de mi hijo, Nacón."

('Ixta is married to Nacón, my son. He has made his choice, and I have approved it. I will hear of no harm in word or deed against this woman. What is done is done. You may all wish there were another outcome in my son's marriage choice, but it is done. I can only think that jealously motivates your comments here today. Ambition and greed motivate that jealousy. Let this discussion be concluded. We will never speak of this again but let me clarify for all: no harm will come to this woman who is under my and my son Nacón's protection.')

Chaac's words seemed to have an effect on the crowd as the angry mutterings ceased. While Ixta couldn't really say that the majority of the group looked happy, they at least shut up. Chaac nodded to them and hit the ground with this staff and those assembled got up to leave with only Ixta and Nacón remaining. Ixta felt a squeeze on her shoulder from the Uturaxan woman with the kind face and gestures as if to give her additional support, at least that what Ixta felt it to be. For all she knew, it could have been

a warning, but Ixta had noticed that both Nacón and
this woman had remained at her side once they had
reconvened. With all the angry words, whether she
understood them or not, and looks, Ixta had certainly
felt the animosity of everyone who spoke.

Turning to Nacón once Chaac determined that no
one was left to overhear their conversation, Chaac
said quietly in Uturaxan, *"You have brought this
dissension upon our tribe, Nacón, as you well know.
A night's pleasure has brought this divide to our
tribe. We haven't had open hostility and negative
comments from our tribe in the decade since you
attained your majority when each conversation
started with every elder bringing forward his or her
daughter or granddaughter for you to look at and
talk to as a possible bride prospect. There were
angry words and breaches among families over who
would be your bride and our next queen. You have
upset everyone with choosing this off-worlder,
Nacón. Why couldn't you have just joined with her?
You didn't need to share your seed. It would have just
been a night of pleasure, and no one would have
really cared. I certainly wouldn't have had to
approach their captain with this proposal of
marriage. This young woman is now your wife in the
eyes of her people and ours. You have gone beyond
the point of no return and now must spend your life
with this woman and try to mend the breaches among
our various clans."*

At first Nacón felt defiant; after all he was a
twenty-eight-year-old man, ten years into his
majority and felt himself too old for a dressing down
from his father. It had been many years since his

father had spoken to him in this tone of voice and he
didn't like the feeling. But quickly, he recognized the
wisdom of his father's words. He had caused a
breach by choosing and marrying Ixta instead of one
of their own women. It was certain to piss off a lot of
people for a while. Only respect for his father had
shut down the comments.

*"I'm sorry, Father. You're right, of course, but I
came to love this woman in all the months we spent
talking about Uturaxan culture. She's smart and
honorable and IS the woman I want to spend my life
with."*

*"All right. Enough said. Just let it be known to you
that this is not a simple pairing without consequence.
We almost came to war over this woman. I do not
look to cause dissention between our culture and the
Terrans. I am not happy with the way you have
handled yourself. I will leave it up to you to sort it all
out with her and to instruct her about our ways and
teach her our language as soon as possible. Go to
your hut and try to explain all this to her before you
tire yourself in sharing pleasures,"* Chaac said,
looking at his son with a look of exasperation and
humor and put something in his hand, a translator.

Surprised, Nacón looked at his father quickly and
then said softly, "Thank you."

Nacón took Ixta's hand and pulled her to her feet
and walked away towards his hut, not looking back.
His hut looked just like everyone else's: primitive.
Ixta wasn't sure what she was going to do living in
this world that seemed so backward in so many ways.
Well, she would just have to make the best of it, she
decided again. After all, Terran history told stories of

people living in very primitive conditions and through the years they had evolved and learned technology to the point where they were now exploring the stars. If they could do it, so could she. After all, she had those experiences of summers on her grandmother's farm to help her. While not this primitive, her grandmother had chosen to do many daily tasks using the old ways. Nacón opened the door made of branches bound together and closed it behind them. He motioned for Ixta to sit on the short stool on the far side of the hut and took the translator from the pocket in his kilt and spoke into it, "I have to explain some things to you about what happened tonight, Ixta."

"Good! I got the idea that some things didn't go well, but other than people's expressions and the tone of their voices, I was lost. I mean I didn't know what they were really saying."

"I don't really know how to say this to you, Ixta, but the man who spoke at the dinner was angry because he hoped that I would marry his sister. The women and other men who approached my father in the clearing to speak said the same thing, but with different women and different male relatives. All the same song."

Nacón hesitated, not sure whether he should tell her the rest of what his father said and feared.

Seeing his hesitation, Ixta spoke up, "Nacón. Let's start this marriage by being honest from this point on. However we got here, that's done, and we need to focus on how to make our marriage work. For the friendship we have shared, we need to do this. Tell

me what else was said. Was it something your father
said to the group?"

Looking uncomfortable, Nacón resolutely
continued, "He told them twice that no harm to you
would be permitted."

"Harm? What do you mean? Are they all that
pissed off at me? I heard a few angry people and saw
some angry faces but frankly didn't think that meant I
had to fear for my life. I take it that not everyone is
happy we got married today."

"My father doesn't necessarily think that someone
will try to hurt you but wanted to be truly clear to the
clans that as my wife, you are under his protection
and mine. So just be aware that some people carry
grudges here. My father accused the angry ones of
ambition and greed motivating their jealousy."

"Greed? How?"

"Ixta, I've spent the last ten years being pursued
by every eligible woman on this planet. It was all
about the rank and title of clan chief. Most of the
women pursuing me the hardest didn't even really
know me at all. They knew of my rank and position
within the power structure on this planet and that was
all they really cared about."

"Well, I see I got lucky last night, Nacón," Ixta
said sarcastically, but smiled at him. "I do have a
question for you though."

"Yes?"

"Why did you share your seed with me as you
seem to like to describe what happened last night?
Why are we married? I thought we were friends, and
I can't help feeling like I've been brought into
something I didn't have all the facts about. Do you

realize that my captain was going to put me in prison for what we did? That I lost my career that I'd worked so hard for just because of one night with you? Do you get that yet?" Ixta ground out, getting angrier as she vented her feelings to him.

"And do you know how it felt to be me when you told Wells what we had done down to every intimate details? You were so calm and controlled and showed no emotion when you described us having sex and if you were recalling a breakfast where you ate *atole* or something. Can you imagine how I felt?! To make matters worse the first mate listened to our meeting in the captain's meeting room and then told the entire crew. I had to endure their taunting, hurtful comments till I left the ship. It was horrible."

"Well, Ixta. To be honest, since you asked, I have most of the tribe and my father angry at me. All the political alliances on this planet have just gotten a realignment because of last night. My father is never angry at me about anything that matters. He was furious. With me, with the tribe and with the situation. I guess you can just join that crowd because it seems almost everyone I know here is mad at me for choosing you. Including you."

"Great. So, we're paying the price for a night of you not taking care of your sperm. What a wonderful thing for both of us," Ixta said sarcastically.

"Ixta. We both lost with our actions. But I think we both gained, and you will know this once we calm down and think about it. I shared my seed with you because you are my friend that I care for very much, the first real female friend I've ever had. I can see now that you would have wished that I discuss this

with you before I did so but living my life as a prince
has apparently clouded my judgment. I thought you'd
be honored that I'd chosen you to share my seed
with, to make you my bride. Many women on my
planet would be thrilled to be in your place as you
saw as they expressed their anger with my choice
tonight."

"Honored?! Oh, shit. You're fucking serious,
aren't you? Crap. I really can't believe you just said
that. Let's see. Honored to be threatened with prison.
Honored to be thrown off my ship. Honored to never
be permitted to return to my home planet without fear
of retribution. Maybe I'm missing something here,
because I'm having a hell of a time feeling honored.
I'm just pissed. I wish any one of those women who
were bitching about me tonight were here in my place
married to you."

"Ah, Ixta. I should be pissed, as you say, too, for
your words dishonor my clan and my position in it. I
am a king's son. You forget that. You forget what
this marriage brings you on my planet."

"Well, excuse me, Nacón, for forgetting who you
are. The friend stuff you were just saying was bullshit
then, yes? Friends don't think one of them is better
than the other. You just clearly said you thought you
were better than I am. Now you're prejudiced too.
Did you plan to seduce me at the party to stir things
up on your planet because you were bored? Oh, this
keeps getting better and better."

"Stop! This arguing does us no good. You are
right. We are friends and my words weren't friendly,
but we are now more than friends. You are my wife.

You pledged yourself to me a little while ago. Why did you do that if you feel this way?"

Nacón's words stopped Ixta short, and she bit back her retort when she heard what he said. He had a point. If she was so pissed at him and the situation, why did she pledge herself to him in the ceremony?

"You know I had no choice. It was marry you or go to prison."

"Yes, I know that. You've made that very clear. But I heard truth in your words. I heard the truth in your voice. You meant those words whether you're happy that you did or not."

"You are right, Nacón. I did mean those words when I said them. I saw that you and your tribe were sincere and felt that you deserved better from me than just the fear and bitterness I was feeling. As your friend, I pledged myself to you. As someone who has spent most of her days with you for these past months, I thought I knew you and that you would protect me and try to make this life here with me work. I heard that in your voice. Was I wrong?"

Surprised by her honesty, Nacón nodded and said, "No, you were not wrong. I meant those words. I admit that I let the night get away and my actions were spontaneous. I tell you now that I did not plan to seduce you when I asked you to go to the party. What happened came out of my feelings for you, Ixta. I care for you."

Nacón smiled at a somewhat mollified Ixta and put his arm around her as he showed her more of his hut. The hut wasn't much different than she had expected it to be from its rustic exterior. She didn't

see much furniture or any cooking utensils and turned
to Nacón to ask him about those missing items.

"Uh, Nacón, what about furniture? I don't see how
I can cook us a meal either with no kitchen or even
cooking utensils. I assume one of us has to cook food
here, yes?"

"Furniture?"

"You know. Things to sit on or a bed to lay down
on for the night."

"Yes, well, Ixta. You just sit on the floor and
that's where you sleep too. I have some nice furs we
will use to make our bed this night. And what else
did you ask about? Something about cooking?"

"Of course, we'll sit and sleep on the floor. Why
didn't I think of that? Yes, cooking. I don't see
anything to cook with to make our meals."

"Ixta, you are not expected to cook. As prince, I
have people who work for me to do all those things.
You don't have to worry about picking things up or
cooking as my servants, er employees, will do that."

"Employees?! We live in a tiny hut, Nacón. We
surely don't need any more people in here doing
things when we're able to do them for ourselves."

"Do not worry, Ixta. This will all sort out. Would
you like some more food to eat or something to
drink? I can call someone, and they'll have it here for
you in minutes."

"Nice as that sounds, Nacón, I'm a regular person,
not royalty and having my every whim met as soon
as I can express it sounds a bit extreme to me.
You've grown up like this, so I guess it makes sense
to you, but it just seems like it's too much to me.
First, I can't imagine even one more person in this

house of yours. Let's not be stepping on top of each other. OK? Besides, I ate so much at dinner that I don't think I'll be hungry till tomorrow afternoon. If you're OK, then let's not eat any more tonight. OK?"

Nacón smiled but offered no further explanation. In truth, he felt worn-out and spent from all the excitement, the feast and lack of sleep the previous night. It had been draining and infuriating listening to his clan members complain about Ixta and his marriage to her. They had been insulting and sounded churlish and totally self-centered. In all fairness, he had to admit that his decision last night had been impetuous, and he probably deserved his father's anger and the fact that he hadn't consulted him before deciding to share his seed with Ixta. He knew that for the moment Chaac desired the current alliance with the Terrans and did not want to go to war over a mate for his son. Nacón knew he hadn't discussed this issue with his father or the council because they would have discouraged him, perhaps even forbid him from joining with her.

All that he had known sitting by the fire with her last night was that he wanted to know more about this woman even if she was an off-worlder. He had already shared so much of himself with her with their many hours of conversation. By talking and debating with her, he had learned more about her than any of the many prospective brides he'd spent time with in the years since his majority. It wasn't for his lack of trying that he hadn't been able to locate a mate within his clan. He had met so many women during these ten years, but nothing had clicked. He really enjoyed being with Ixta and he thought that was at least a

positive beginning for their relationship. He was
almost sorry he had his rank because it really
complicated his personal life. He'd chafed at the
constraints placed on him by his father and the
council countless times when he was younger. Now,
as an adult male of his tribe, he was resigned to it and
frankly didn't think much about it anymore. It was
just a fact of life that his family constituted royalty on
this planet. *Pero (but)*, he was just a regular man
when he was allowed to be.

He was looking forward to having Ixta as his
woman and available for sexual pleasures but knew
that Terran ideas about relationships between men
and women were different than Uturaxan ones.
Uturaxans were expected to all contribute to their
clan and play a useful role whatever that turned out to
be. Paired couples were monogamous so as not to
confuse family bloodlines that were especially
important. Spouses formed partnerships often just
based on family bloodlines. Arranged marriages still
happened even though people were permitted love
matches. As a male, Nacón didn't pay much attention
to that as his father had given him permission to seek
his own mate and not be ruled by Uturaxan tradition
or political alliances. He would be eternally grateful
to his father for the sense of freedom he'd enjoyed
these past ten years with that parental edict. From
what he'd seen of Ixta thus far, she was independent
and opinionated and not likely to just do something
because it had always been done. One part of him
celebrated her feisty personality while the other did
worry about her offending the tribe's elders if she
went too quickly trying to change things or flaunt

tradition. By the time he became king, he was sure all this would be figured out and resolved to make them both happy with the outcome. He had never seen her in a bad mood till now and he looked forward to sharing his days with her and raising their children together.

Nacón left their hut for a moment to quickly return carrying two large animal skins with fur on one side. He put one on the floor and motioned for Ixta to sit down. She did so and looked at Nacón for direction as to what he expected next. She took a quick breath when she saw Nacón undo his shoulder throw and then fold it up like a pillow. Next, he removed his kilt and indicated by gesture that Ixta should do the same. Unsure of what was expected, but finding that exhaustion was overtaking her, Ixta began by unzipping her overalls. Feeling his attention on her, she looked over at Nacón who was watching her every move with interest. He seemed very interested, as a matter of fact. She, too, folded her clothing to use as a pillow and then reached behind to unhook her bra. Nacón noted the different type of restraining garment she wore tonight, different from last night's which had unhooked so easily in the front. Looking over at Nacón and finding him focused on her, on her breasts particularly and decided to stop removing her bra and then her undies as she had planned. *'Whoa. What was I thinking? I'm getting ahead of myself here. This big, huge man is looking a little too interested in what I'm doing here. He is my husband now, but being naked with him is something new, too new in our relationship. I still haven't worked through the feeling that I was forced into this marriage. He may think that's all behind us, but I feel betrayed, used.'* Ixta looked over at Nacón to see what would come next, feeling suddenly shy. Seeing his continued interest in her, she felt apprehension that this man she'd erroneously thought she knew well, might have expectations of a physical nature for his wedding night.

But suddenly, he didn't look imposing; he looked tender. Ixta also saw caution, lustful caution on his face. She really did like this man, or whatever he was, and was still definitely attracted to him. Even though she couldn't remember all the details of last night, she did remember having a pleasurable time with him. And from what he'd told the captain; they'd had a good time all night long. Nacón moved closer and then looked at her for permission before he moved to touch her.

After considering a moment, Ixta found that her bruised feelings and emotions were still too raw and stiffened. She had the feeling that physical intimacy with Nacón was inevitable sooner or later between them but couldn't push through the feeling that her life had taken a disastrous turn. It might as well be sooner, and she actually considered trying to work through her reluctance but found she couldn't. But she couldn't articulate her feelings to him and just sat silently. She was tired of talking and explaining and this was all she had now. She might as well suck it up and see if she could make it through this night. Nacón reached around Ixta's back and used both hands to unhook her bra. Ixta froze as he gently slipped the straps from each shoulder and off her arms. Once free, he discarded the bra with a toss across the room and turned back to his new wife and looked down at her now naked breasts and suddenly stopped.

Ixta reacted to his expression, worry on her face and reached for the translator. "What is it, Nacón? Tell me why you're looking at me like that. I don't think I'm ready for all this and especially for you staring at me like that."

Nacón reached over and gently touched her breasts, softly, gently touching the area of her areola, running his finger around it and said, "Your breasts have changed in size and color, Ixta. At least I think they have though the light wasn't the best in the jungle where we were last night. Does that mean something to a Terran woman? It does here."

"What? I don't know what you mean. Nonsense," Ixta said as she quickly looked down at her breasts and saw that their usually pink color was indeed a dusky rose and the nipples looked rounder, fuller and a little larger than this morning. 'What the hell?'

Then Doc Joss's last words and tests came back to her. She was pregnant!"

Seeing no way around the situation at this point and though she might have chosen another time to share her news with Nacón, the situation was at hand right now. Might as well take advantage of it and forge ahead. "Um, Nacón, there's something I need to tell you. . . I'm pregnant." She looked apprehensively at Nacón to see his reaction. It was one thing to be honorable and offer to marry her, but quite another to find that their night of fun had produced an offspring.

"Uh, that is, our ship's doctor says I am, but it's way too soon to be able to detect a pregnancy for

Terrans. The tests don't usually show pregnancy this early, but our doc said that maybe it's because you're not Terran and my body is reacting differently than expected. In the morning when I saw the doc, he thought I had an infection of some sort."

Nacón was beside her in an instant and wrapped his arms around her and began to tell her exactly what he thought. Unfortunately, he wasn't using the translator, but Ixta could only judge by his tone that he wasn't angry and seemed pleased instead. Pushing away to get a better look at his face, Ixta could see his smile and thought maybe she didn't really need the translator to know how he felt.

Unwillingly, tears came into her eyes as she saw his joy; his reception of her news was all she could have hoped for. Before she could stop them, tears filled her eyes and overflowed, making twin tracks down her cheeks.

Touching her left cheek with his finger, he caught a tear and held it up on his finger and then said, "Why do you cry? Are you sad about this news? I don't understand."

"Er, Nacón, I haven't really gotten used to the idea, but it just made me remember about the first time I was pregnant."

"First time? What do you mean? I thought you had no life partner before. You never spoke of a child to me before. Do you have a family back on Earth? If so, how could you choose to leave them to come to my village to marry me?"

"Great! You always jump to the worst conclusions with me, don't you? Yes, I was pregnant. No, I have no children and life partner. I left no family behind

on Earth. I chose you because I used to like you
before you turned on me again. "

"Well, Ixta, it seems like you're just as quick to
judge me, aren't you? Just tell me the facts and then
we'll move forward. Alright?" Nacón said as he
moved back from her and sat on his haunches to
watch her face.

"Wait! How are we even having a conversation?
All these months and even a minute ago, we were
barely communicating with our hybrid language.
What the hell?!"

"I wasn't able to tell you before, but I am learning
your language, Ixta."

"That's it? You've learned that much of my
language that fast?"

"Ixta. We can come back to this. You were going
to tell me about being pregnant before," Nacon said
seriously.

Thinking a moment, controlling her emotions, Ixta
began to tell him her story from many years before.
Her voice almost a monotone, Ixta said, "I was in
college and could only afford to go because of the
scholarships I'd gotten. My high school boyfriend,
my first love, and I were living together in a tiny
apartment near campus. Living together means we
shared the same bed and though we were careful, or
we thought we were careful, I became pregnant. The
day that I found out and told him, he left me. I went
to class and came back later, and all his things were
moved out and he was gone. I never saw him again. I
didn't know what to do, so I went home that weekend
to tell my parents. My mom was horrible and said
terrible things to me, but the worst part was my

dad's, who was my hero, letting me down. He let my mom call me a whore and agreed with her when she said I'd ruined my life."

"What about your child? What did you do with your child?" Nacón asked tensely, hoping not to hear that she'd aborted her baby. He honestly didn't know how he could remain neutral about her decision if she'd chosen to kill her baby.

"There was no child. My parents were killed not long after we had that big fight and I guess the stress of the whole situation got to me because I miscarried. I lost my baby. Whatever was going to happen to me, I would have figured out a way to finish school even if I was a single mother without my parents' support and love. As it turned out, I grieved my baby's death alone and never got to patch things up with my parents. They died without my being able to reconnect with my dad who had always been the parent I looked up to and went to with my problems. He was the best listener and gave me such confidence in my decisions."

"So, this is why you cry now instead of rejoicing about our baby?"

"Ah, Nacón, I'm crying because I can't help contrast how happy you are for me, for us. It makes my pregnancy this time feel right. It's such a different feeling to have happy tears. I thank you for your reaction. I'm glad to share this with you. You have made me very happy."

Mollified and relieved to hear her thoughts, Nacón again reached for Ixta to give her a reassuring hug. He did grab the translator again, however, and asked, "How long is a Terran pregnancy, Ixta?"

"Nine months. How about Uturaxan pregnancies? How long do they last?"

"Two hundred and thirty or forty days is usual for our women. I wonder how long you will carry our child?'

"Crap, Nacón, I don't know. From what Doc told me, there just isn't any research on this topic as there haven't been any births yet between species. Also, Terran births are usually just one baby and from what I hear, your women here have three or four." So concerned about the implications, Ixta didn't notice the look on Nacón's face when she described Uturaxan birth numbers. "I don't think I could carry that many babies, Nacón. I don't think your planet has the technology like a neonatal unit to help babies survive. How do you feel about having a baby this soon? Did you plan on being a father when you shared your seed with me last night?"

"Well, no, Ixta, I didn't think that far. I knew I wanted to make a commitment to you but didn't have the words to ask you how you felt about me. I had hoped that you felt the same as I did but didn't know. I did not know you would be so fertile to conceive on our first night of joining though I did share my seed multiple times and in the back of my mind knew that you could conceive after so many joinings."

Blushing, Itxa said, "From what I hear, we made love all night long, Nacón. That's hardly a onetime event."

"I like what you called joining. I've never heard 'make love,' but I like it. It's a nice way to talk about joining and makes it sound less like just a physical union of two bodies. It implies that it means more than just the momentary pleasure."

"Great. I don't know what to think about that just now since you obviously didn't plan this all out, did you?"

"No, I didn't, but I will not say that I regret last night or your pregnancy. I have 28 winters of age and have been looking for the last ten years to find a mate to make my life with, the future queen of my planet. Somehow, last night, the decision was easy to join with you and share my seed. Whenever a Uturaxan man shares his seed, there is the possibility of conception. Since we joined repeatedly all night long, my body released what I think you would call pheromones of conception that reach out to the female body, telling it to ovulate so that conception can take place."

"OK, Nacón, human reproductive biology wasn't my area, but I don't remember anything about pheromones of conception on my planet and nothing's related to ovulation for me except my monthly cycle. I'm guessing that it doesn't work that way for Uturaxan women, right?"

"Correct. Our women don't cycle monthly or ovulate until they join with a male, and he releases the pheromones of conception. It's an involuntary thing a male does without forethought when he's with his wife, his love. Then her body prepares for pregnancy by ovulating. There are many different things among our people, Ixta. I hope that won't make it difficult for you to carry and deliver our children."

"Too much biology talk, Nacón. I'm tired. I don't
really know what I think. It's all too new to me now.
Let's just go to bed and face all this in the morning."

"Agreed, *mi Cielo (sweetheart)*. Let me show you
our bed," Nacón said as he wrapped his arms around
Ixta and pulled her closer and walked backwards with
her, their bodies pressed together till they reached
and stepped onto the soft furs. Relieved that she'd
gotten over the hurdle of telling Nacón about her
pregnancy, Ixta allowed herself to enjoy their
closeness, his body next to hers. He put one thigh
between her legs and applied some pressure as his
face came down to hers. His lips found hers as he
caught her lower lip gently with his teeth and giving
a little, gentle tug. He quickly released her lip and
moved to cover her mouth completely with his. His
tongue pushed gently inside hers when he felt her lips
part and then slowly sank onto the thick fur with her.
Giggling, she said, "Wow. This tickles, Nacón. This
fur is so soft maybe I could forget about. . ."

Nacón captured her mouth again with his and
began kissing her on her lips since last night's
experience had taught Nacón that Ixta enjoyed this
preparation for the joining of their bodies. All the
while, his hands were roaming over her breasts and
then down her back to cup her ass. When his mouth
moved to her breasts, he noticed that they seemed
fuller and even more sensitive than last night. It had
to be related to her pregnancy, he decided as he
prepared to join their bodies. Another detail he'd
learned was that Ixta apparently preferred looking
him in the eyes as they mated, and he was more than
willing to do whatever she wanted for as long as it

took for her to become accustomed to him and life on his planet. While the experience had been different from the usual Uxturaxan joining, he had enjoyed his time spent with her last night and looked forward to this joining and sharing of his seed again.

The release associated with sharing his seed inside a woman was a new, welcome pleasure now that she was his mate and had already conceived his child or children. His previous experiences had brought pleasure in the joinings without the release inside the female. Sexual release, ejaculation, was a part of Uturaxan premarital joining, but the male's seed was either spilled on the ground or swallowed by the woman. But he found that thus far, married life was very promising in many ways, not the least of which was sharing pleasures with his new wife. He couldn't remember feeling like joining with a woman just by looking at her. Ixta's exotic looks made him want her even more than he had last night and that had been a first for him to desire a woman to the point of distraction.

Nacón decided that this feeling, these thoughts, were something he'd never share with his friends, or they'd never let him forget that he was mesmerized by his wife. It didn't exactly fit the manly Uturaxan tradition of taking pleasure wherever and whenever he felt like it, at least till marriage. But since most marriages were political alliances, couples were pretty matter of fact about their relationships. If love came, it was almost always much later. He didn't want other women now, only Ixta. He wasn't ready to call this feeling, this wanting, love yet, but maybe this was how it started. Love wasn't a topic Nacón's

father had spent much time on. It was probably a
topic a mother shared with her children, but since
Nacón's mother had died fighting beside his father
when he was very young, no one had ever talked
about it to him. His friends were still as young as he
was, and fighting, training, having a good time
together and with the willing women on his planet
took up much of their time. Deep conversations about
anything beyond strategies for war just didn't
happen.

Sitting with Ixta on the bed of fur, Nacón repeated
his actions of the previous night as it seemed that Ixta
had enjoyed his actions in preparing for joining to the
extent that she desired joining as much as he. Aware
of the changes in her breasts, Nacón very carefully
licked one of her swollen nipples before taking it into
his mouth. Ixta gasped and reached for his head to
clasp it to her breast, thus telling him that she wanted
him to continue. Clearly, she'd gotten over her earlier
feelings of anger toward him or she wouldn't be so
accepting of his sexual play right now. However,
now that they were a married couple, he wanted to
share other pleasures with her that he hadn't done last
night as a courting couple. He licked and sucked his
way down her body, swirling his tongue around her
navel. While he did this, his fingers found her private
folds and finding them already moist, gently inserted
his fingers inside her. She responded with another
moan and opened her legs for him to gain easier
access.

Ixta held her breath as his mouth moved lower, not
sure how alien culture approached what she was
hoping would happen next. Her mental analysis soon

gave way to the waves of feelings of pleasure that swept over her as Nacón's tongue found her clit and as he swirled his tongue around and around on her. Then, finding the response he hoped for from her, Nacón began to gently suck on her before he resumed licking with increasing speed. Alternating between both, he was gratified that his second venture into interplanetary lovemaking was proceeding so well. Ixta moaned loudly and then went stiff and then limp as she climaxed. Nacón knelt beside her, watching his new wife as she lay satisfied. He would definitely have to say that their species were very similar.

As he sat on his heels, musing about his new state of affairs in his life and planning the next step in their mating, he noticed that Ixta rolled over till she rested her head on his thighs. Soon, he no longer cared to analyze what was happening because he felt Ixta's lips and tongue move around the head of his penis. Then she began to mimic the actions he had done to her as she sucked and then licked up and down the length of him while sliding her hand up and down the shaft. Unable to focus on more than the feelings she was causing as she continued, Nacón gently pushed her off him before he came, positioned himself as he knelt between her legs and clasping Ixta's hips, thrust inside her and began to pull himself slowly out to thrust inside her again. He leaned over and swirled his tongue around her right breast and then the left before abandoning her breasts for a moment to concentrate on the goal at hand. He found that as his rhythm increased, he thrust as far inside her as he was able to touch her womb before withdrawing slowly enjoying every part of each thrust and he again began to suck on her breasts with more force. The mating rhythm increased for both. Ixta responded by pulling his face up to hers when her newly tender breasts could take no more as she kissed him, her tongue mating with his. The tempo increased till both could stand it no longer and climaxed, finding the completion to the act they both needed and wanted.

Sated and relaxed, Nacón reluctantly withdrew from Ixta and moved to settle his body behind hers on the furs. Ixta and Nacón quickly fell asleep almost as soon as they finished joining their bodies. Ixta was ready to sleep and her newly pregnant body was tired. Also, her mind was exhausted by all the changes today in her career, her life, and her future. So much had happened in the last twenty-four hours that she needed time to put it all into perspective. Marriage had not been high on Ixta's list of things to do in the foreseeable future, so she was surprised to find herself not only married but expecting a child as well and enjoying the physical benefits of regular sex that came with this marriage. Her final thoughts that night were that there would be more time to think about all of that in the morning.

CHAPTER 5: Next Day

Morning found them asleep on the big fur, legs entwined and still covered by the lighter fur on top of them. Ixta deduced it was morning because someone tapped lightly on the hut's door and then entered with a tray of food. Hearing and then seeing someone beside her bed, she yelped and then sat upright, covering her naked body with a corner of the fur.

Two women approached the rug and the older of
the two said something to Nacón that Ixta understood
to be related to food. Ixta recognized her as the
woman who had brought her a Uturaxan clan fabric
to be married in and who had stood by her side after
the marriage dinner when things got tense. The
younger women, who Ixta recognized as one of the
women who spoke last night against her marriage to
Nacón, gave something to Ixta first and then Nacón,
her expression changing wildly from hostility to
desire as she offered a dish to Ixta and then Nacón .
Both women motioned for them to eat. In no hurry,
Nacón lazily rolled over and smiled at Ixta and then
got up and walked across the room to retrieve clean
clothes. He was unselfconsciously nude and Ixta
noticed the younger woman greedily eyeing him
before she turned back to Ixta with malice in her
eyes. Ixta gasped at the malevolence in her eyes.
Apparently walking around nude in your own home
in front of two women was not worth mention or
note. Ixta, however, was still trying to process what
was happening with the younger woman. Finally, the
older of the two noticed how the younger was
looking at Ixta and Nacón and barked something at
her that was unintelligible. At that, Nacón and Ixta
looked up in time to see the younger women hang her
head as she was sent from the hut. The older woman
looked at Nacón and then at Ixta and nodded in a
friendly fashion.

Nacón supplied the information that Ixta lacked
about his nana, "This is my Nana who raised me after
my mother perished in the winter of '09 where many
in my tribe died. We were at war, and the weather

conditions were very harsh, thus complicating the battle. She was the only living relative, though distant, of my father and had been widowed years before. She had no children of her own and seemed happy, at least I think she was, to take over my care. I was still many years from my majority, and my father was not inclined to take another wife though many women in our tribe would have been glad to share his bed and his title."

Turning to his nana, Nacón then said, "Nana, this is Ixta, my wife."

Ixta reached out to clasp the arm that Nacón's Nana offered in friendship and the edge of the fur cover fell and revealed her upper body. At once, Nana exclaimed something in Uturaxan to Nacón.

Looking at Nacón for explanation, Ixta said, "Is something wrong?"

"She has noticed how your breasts look, Ixta. Their color and shape are like those of our women in the early stages of pregnancy. Remember how different human women look than Uturaxan women also, but maybe this is a similarity. Look down at yourself."

"I don't think I'm ready to discuss my breasts with you and a stranger just yet, Nacón."

But Ixta did look down at her breasts and gasped when she saw yet another change in them. The color of the areolas had darkened and deepened from last night and they had grown larger and felt more tender. She didn't know what to think or say, so just looked up at both Nana and Nacón helplessly.

"It is a good thing, Ixta. It means that your body is embracing our child or children rather than rejecting the pregnancy. Nana has a sharp eye, and she's been waiting like my father for me to marry and produce an heir to ensure the continuity of our line. This is proof to her that we're on the right track. If you'd thought of keeping this a secret for a while, however, I think we can forget that now. She will be knocking at my father's hut as soon as she leaves ours. We had better plan on visiting my father as soon as we break our fast to tell him the happy news that he's going to be a grandfather though Nana will already have preceded us with the news. Your physical state will be viewed and commented on by my whole tribe from now on. Prepare yourself."

Not sure if she wanted the affirmation that this pregnancy seemed to be taking root inside her womb, Ixta was still in the "thinking about it" stage of pregnancy and trying to figure out just how her life was going to work here on Uturax. Seeing the hostility on the younger woman's face, Ixta was quickly brought back to last night when so many spoke against her and Nacón's union, even his father. Hopefully, his father would at least welcome the news that she was expecting the Uturaxan heir already. At this point, she wasn't going to guess about anyone else's feelings since her own were so conflicted. Clearly not everyone on this planet was magically going to change their opinion of an off-worlder being allied to their prince. She wondered how long that would last or if it would ever go away. The chief's words about not harming her weren't exactly reassuring as he must have felt the need to say such a thing.

Nana quickly left once she saw them reach for the food to break their fast and Ixta tentatively tasted the unfamiliar fruit placed on the tray in front of her. Nacón must have been starving as he quickly ate the first fruit and then the second while Ixta was still dealing with the first. As soon as she swallowed her second bite, everything started to come back up. She jumped up and rushed over to a pot in the corner of the hut and promptly threw up. In an instant, Nacón was at her side, his hand on her forehead. "What do you need, Ixta? Is the pregnancy making you sick to your stomach?"

Ixta nodded miserably and said, "I think I need something like dry bread or toast. I don't even know if you have that or crackers which are unleavened pieces of baked dough. I think fruit seems a bit too adventurous at the moment. No rush though. I think I probably need to eat, but it can wait a while."

"Nay," Nacón said as he opened the door and shouted for someone. In an instant, he was telling still another woman what he wanted for Ixta and the person hurried off.

As if this wasn't enough ruckus to start the day with, there was a hard knock on the door a moment later.

"Enter."

Chaac stuck his head in the doorway first and then seeing Ixta sitting on the ground holding her head between her hands, said, "Nana just came to see me. Is your wife all right? She doesn't look good."

Ixta looked up as she did understand some of what Chaac had said, quickly covered her nudity with the fur and responded, "I'm fine. Just a little nauseous."

"Son, this is not as it should be. Something must be wrong with your wife."

"Father, give us a moment to figure this out. She just woke up and tried to eat a little fruit which obviously didn't agree with her system."

"Ixta, is this stomach problem normal for Terran women?"

"Well, sir, since I've never been pregnant with an alien baby, I can't really say much about it, but I have heard that some Terran women become nauseated when pregnant. It was just that bitter taste of the fruit that didn't sit well with me."

"What are you talking about, Ixta? Say that again, please, Nacón said."

"The fruit looked tasty, and you were devouring several pieces, so I was surprised when I ate it, and it was bitter. It tasted awful with a bitter, metallic aftertaste. Frankly, I couldn't imagine how you were eating it with such enthusiasm. It came up almost as soon as I swallowed the second bite. Both pieces ended up in the pot over there in the corner."

At her words, both Chaac and Nacon went to look at the pot and then returned to the tray with the fruit that Ixta had eaten from. She watched them each smell the fruit and then each lick a finger, touch it to the fruit both on the skin and then the fruit inside and then back to their mouths. Each made a face as they tasted it, spat it out and both said, "*Veonum!*"

"What? What are you saying?'

Grabbing the UT, Nacón muttered, "Poison. Someone tried to poison you, Ixta." No sooner had he finished saying the words, they both looked at the door after hearing it slam shut as Chaac quickly exited. "Get dressed, Ixta. We need to go speak with my father and work with him to figure this out. This is serious business. I'll be right back for you."

Shaken by Nacón's words and the thought that her first day in Uturax had gotten off to such a poor start with an assassination attempt. Wonderful. It was going to be harder than she'd imagined integrating herself into Uturaxan society when the native population, at least some of them, wanted her dead. Then there was this pregnancy issue to deal with. Even though it was an unexpected speed bump in her life, she was starting to get used to the idea even though there was no certainty that it would end with a successful pregnancy. In doc's words, she was making medical and interstellar history here and it was anyone's best guess how this would all end.

Having someone try to kill her this morning so obviously and without much subterfuge was a harsh reminder that some people would go to any length to influence the line of succession on this planet.

For a seemingly peaceful group of people, their feelings about the political structure seemed to be extreme. This was probably another misconception she had about these people along with everything else. The captain was so right about her: she was a shitty anthropologist who was a rank amateur when it came to figuring out the important things about this alien culture. All those months of observations and conversations with Nacón had produced truly little real information now that she was mentally cataloging all that she knew about Uturaxan culture. However, she'd not seen that before and now it was potentially too late to figure out the things she might need to know to survive living here as an unwanted alien intruder. Feeling drowsy, Ixta succumbed to the residual poison still in her stomach and slid bonelessly along the wall where she was sitting to lay in a crumpled, ungraceful heap.

Nacón came back in a few moments later to find Ixta on the floor and became concerned when he couldn't rouse her. He sent one of the women to get his father back inside and then confronted him saying,

"What now, Father? Do we let her know all about us to save her? This may still seem like a crazy move on my part, but I care about this woman. She interests me like none of ours I've met through the years since attaining my majority. I've come to care for her and am excited that she is carrying my child. I don't want to lose her or my potential heirs. Do you?"

Chaac was taken aback by the intensity of Nacón's words. He really hadn't given much thought to the bond that had been formed with his son and the Terran woman but was starting to realize that his son was serious about this relationship and did understand the implications of this alliance with the Terran woman.

Neither of them had realized the extent of the Uturaxan enmity against this woman. Nacón had raised an important issue: to expose everything about their people to this woman, notwithstanding Nacón's wife, or possibly lose her to an assassin's attempt on her life this morning. So brazen. However, until they knew more about Ixta on a more intimate level, Chaac wasn't comfortable with taking her into their confidence just yet. He saw that his son was and would do anything for his woman. The potential heirs she carried made this more problematic for them both. However, maybe there was another alternative. The Terran ship had a doctor who had sophisticated equipment and who might be able to help them through this crisis. He would also know more about this woman's physiology and that could ensure a quicker cure if there was one to be had.

"Nacón, let us notify the ship's doctor and petition Captain Wells for his assistance in this matter. It could solve our problem in a more expeditious way as their doctor knows Terran physiology, particularly of this woman, and we don't. If you're in agreement, I will go to the ship immediately. I want you to stay with your woman to protect her from further harm at the hands of our people."

"Yes, Father. Their doctor is also a friend of Ixta's, and I feel he'd be happy to help her out. Please, send someone now."

"I will go, *mi'jo (my son)*. Wells is more likely to take our petition seriously if it comes from me. He's still trying to win me over, remember?"

Chaac wasted no time on arriving at the ship's ramp and waited to be acknowledged. Captain Wells himself came down the ramp and extended a translator to Chaac.

Not really wanting to reveal what had happened, Chaac, however, decided that honesty was needed to impress the gravity of the situation on Wells. "Captain. We would like to request your assistance by sending your ship's doctor to our village immediately. Ixta is quite ill."

Surprised, Wells took a moment to think about the request and the precedent that would be set. "Well, Chaac, I have to admit to you that I am surprised."

"Captain, Ixta was poisoned a little while ago and I fear for her life. We would be very grateful and appreciative if your doctor could aid us in trying to save her life. It is a very grave situation."

"Poisoned?! Fear for her life. . . Hell," hesitation and precedence thrown aside in that instant, the captain spoke into the comlink, "Dr. Tvitmpr, report to the ship's ramp with your medical equipment. Call me on the captain's channel for more detail." The captain figured that so many rules had been broken on this voyage that he was willing to intervene to try to save Ixta's life and would explain himself later if the need arose. He still felt a little guilty for throwing her off her ship by forcing this marriage on her by offering no alternatives. She had been a hard-working valued crew member before this incident. Early retirement was probably already in his future for losing a crew member in the manner that Ixta had exited the ship's crew. He had to admit to himself, albeit reluctantly, that his drug use might be affecting his better judgment.

Joss heard the strange summons from Wells and hastened to call the captain on his secure, private channel. "What is it, sir?"

"Ixta has been poisoned, so bring what you need to diagnose and cure her if it's possible. She's not doing well, so hurry it up, Tvitmpr. Chaac is waiting here to take you to her."

Joss quickly assembled what he would need to help Ixta, he hoped, and cleared his mind of all else as he focused on the drugs he might need to help her and save her life. He figured there would be time later for questions about how this had come to happen. How quickly things could change in twenty-four hours.

Joss went with Chaac back to the village, hurrying along behind him. He was taken to Nacón's hut and went inside when the door was quickly opened for him. He saw Ixta propped up on a lush bed of furs and went to sit beside her. He inserted the tip of his portable medic-eval unit into her arm, pressed a few buttons and then waited for the readout. Chaac and Nacon and an older native woman all waited looking anxious. His findings told him that she still retained some of the poison in her system but from what Nacón told him, she was lucky to have vomited up the tainted fruit almost immediately after consuming it. He turned to his bag, found a suitable antidote that shouldn't harm her fetus and prepared the injection. Quickly administered, Ixta started to feel its effects right away. Her eyes opened and she looked up at three people plus her friend Joss and said, "Am I going to be OK, Joss?"

Joss smiled at Ixta and said for her benefit and that of Chaac and Nacón, "You already are. You were lucky, Ixta."

"Er, Joss. Is my baby OK?' she asked tentatively as she put her hand over her stomach and tears welled up in her eyes. She hadn't wanted to be pregnant, but now that she was, she found that she didn't want it to end this way, by an assassin's hand.

"Let me check you for a heartbeat first."

Joss dug around a moment in his bag, pulled out some equipment and then put the monitor over her lower abdomen and turned on the volume. All could hear a strong heartbeat and Joss looked up to see all three other people smiling along with Ixta. He didn't even bother to tell them that this was much too early on the human scale to detect the heartbeat so strongly but figured that at the rate the pregnancy seemed to be progressing for her that it was worth a try. Apparently, the Uturaxan half of the fetus was speeding things along.

"Things sound good, Ixta. I think we caught this in plenty of time. The poison is strong but slower acting. That and the quick thinking of Chaac and Nacón to come for me right away saved you and your baby."

Hearing Joss's words lifted a weight off Ixta that she hadn't realized she was carrying. It was a relief to know that her baby was alright, and that the danger had passed. No longer needing to maintain her calm during the crisis, she burst into tears and began quietly sobbing.

Ixta reached for Joss's hand and clasped it tightly. "Thank you, my friend."

Seeing Ixta's sudden emotional moment, Nacón moved over to kneel beside her and wrap his arms around her, giving her a reassuring squeeze though he honestly was out of his element and didn't know how to handle an emotional woman. He felt his lack of information on daily living with a woman as he'd been raised much as fosterlings were in olden days where warriors raised the young men. Girl children were raised by women and boys were raised by men to inculcate all the values needed and expected in them to be successful in the art of war.

"My pleasure," Joss said as he packed his bag and stood. "It's important that there be no repeat attempts on her life. At some point, her baby will be affected if this continues and Ixta could lose her life as well. You have to take care of her!"

Nacón met his eye and swore that would be so. "Perhaps you would like to continue to visit our camp to monitor Ixta's pregnancy as long as your ship is here. Yes?"

"I would be very happy to continue to care for Ixta."

Chaac used the translator to thank the doctor and praised his quick, calm approach to finding a solution to Ixta's health crisis. He ended by saying, "If you should ever need a home here with us, you will be welcomed."

Surprised, Joss nodded and then turned to leave. He had never been invited to join anyone on the planets he'd visited and was often barely tolerated. This was a nice change in his situation here on Uturax. When he stepped out of the hut, Chaac followed and barked some orders to several warriors nearby. They stepped to Joss's side, evidently planning on seeing him safely back to the ship. All this made him wonder about what they really knew about this planet. Clearly it wasn't the peaceful, idyllic place they'd first assumed. From last night's dinner drama, Joss understood that Ixta's marriage to the prince wasn't universally popular but hadn't realized how deeply the negative feelings ran till he was called to save Ixta's life. From the reaction of

Chaac and Nacón, he felt that they would do all they could to protect her. They had been very worried about her survival and transparently happy to hear the new heir's heartbeat.

Back in the hut, Nacón knelt beside Ixta and offered something to drink and some dry cakes to nibble on after he first tasted them both. Chaac entered and shouted at Nacón, "What are you doing?! You cannot put yourself in such danger. We will find tasters from several of the clans for all the food both of you consume. Neither one of you is safe. I want you to be part of the tribunal later today to question Camila about what happened along with your Nana. We must resolve this quickly and mete out the appropriate punishment today."

Nacón nodded in agreement and turned to Ixta when his father left the hut to assemble the elders who would take part in the tribunal. She still looked shaken though some color had returned to her cheeks. *"Mi Cielo (sweetheart)*. You scared me. I thought I would lose you," Nacón said as he cupped Ixta's face in his hand and then gently stroked her cheek with his finger. Surprised that he cared so much so soon, he remained by her side, anxious to assure himself that she was really feeling much better.

"I really didn't have time to think much, but I must admit that Joss's words about someone poisoning me makes me rethink how people must feel in your tribe about me, rather against me, wouldn't you say? I just didn't realize how mad people are."

"Do not worry, *mi amor (my love)*. Not everyone spoke out yesterday to voice their displeasure. Not all the royal houses are unhappy. Some are even pleased that they didn't lose to one another in this race for the queen's position. Now that an outsider has taken the prize, they no longer must compete, and the balance of power has not been disturbed or altered in any way. When they have time to think of it in these terms, they will be quite happy with my choice. "

Nacón's words were meant to soothe her, but he couldn't help silently questioning his line of reasoning that he'd just put forth for Ixta.

Ixta responded, apparently having doubts of her own. "Well, that's an interesting way of looking at it. Are you sure you're not just looking at it this way because it's easier than thinking that your people would be so bold in trying to take your own life? Also, have you considered that while the younger woman handed my plate to me, that you could have taken some food from it too? You could have died today also!"

Horror dawned on both their faces as Ixta's words sank in for both. Nacón truly hadn't thought of it that way. Since Chaac had made such a public declaration of not harming Ixta because she was under his and Nacón's protection, this was a challenge that was treason. Someone was trying to depose Chaac's house from power either way.

"Again, you show me your worth as my wife, Ixta. You have a quick mind and a way of looking at things with a warrior's eye. Both are especially useful as part of the ruling party on this planet. Rest a bit as we will be summoned to give testimony later this today once my father assembles the tribunal."

"Tribunal? Is that a justice court here?"

"Yes. Did you not think that we would follow up and see justice done?" Nacón asked puzzled at the thought that Ixta might think that nothing should be done.

"I haven't had time to think, Nacón. But I do see that something must be done. Let me know what I have to do."

"*Mi amor*, you just have to be there and tell them what happened this morning."

Ixta fell asleep curled up in Nacón's arms as he gently stroked her hair. Somewhat surprised by the easy, relaxed way he treated her today, Ixta felt good to feel safe in his arms. After this morning, her new life here seemed filled with peril. Wanting a pregnancy and marriage or not, that's the situation she found herself in, regardless.

Ixta had given Nacón a lot to contemplate. He wondered if his father had come to the same conclusion that she had but dismissed the idea of going to discuss it with him as he didn't want to leave Ixta alone. Recalling Chaac's anger at seeing his son taste the food newly brought to Ixta after the attempted poisoning, he figured that he had come to the same conclusion. After her ordeal, Ixta needed to rest and gather her strength before the tribunal began in a few hours' time. Nacón knew his father had left to summon tribal elders and all members of the tribunal.

Each of the royal houses had a representative on the council and all would want to participate in this gathering as the implications of what had been done were a direct challenge considering Chaac's warnings last night. Even if he hadn't made a point of making

sure Ixta came to no harm, just the idea of someone
trying to kill the prince's spouse was treasonous. He
could only hope that all the information could be
gathered that would allow them to deal with the
perpetrator or perpetrators quickly and completely. A
crime like this could not go unpunished. There would
be no pardon today.

It felt like she had just closed her eyes, but when
the door opened to summon them to the tribunal, Ixta
could see that the suns had risen quite a bit and that it
was past midday. Quickly trying to gain her bearings
and find her coveralls to put back on, Ixta was
stopped by Nacón with a hand on her arm.

"No, you are my woman now in all ways, by our
custom and law and by the body bond we now share.
You will wear my clan colors today unless you object
and I would hope that you do not."

"Oh, of course not. I just didn't think. Where are
these new clothes? It all sounds rather cave man
Nacón, but if this is important to you, I'll wear
whatever you like. Your home is now my new home.
Your people will be my people if they decide to let
me live long enough."

"Cave man?"

"Never mind. Oh, that's nice!" Ixta said as he put
several lengths of soft cloth in her hands. She
recognized leather undergarments like his and put
them on and then donned the kilt. However, when she
wrapped the shawl around her upper body, she
looked down in dismay as she saw one breast bare for
the world to see.

Nacón laughed when he saw her face and reached
for another shawl-like length of fabric to exchange

for the first. It was longer and wrapped around her in a way that her breasts were completely covered. "Here let me help you with this," he chuckled as his fingers lightly tweaked the slightly swollen nipples when he adjusted the fabric. "If there were more time. . ." he said as he leaned down and breathed softly on the breast he exposed again for a moment.

"Nacón, we have no time and certainly not for that right now though I wish I could eat a little something."

"I have brought you some grain cakes that I think you call oat. You can at least eat a little of that until this is over and we have dinner."

Ixta took the flat brownie-like oatcakes from Nacón and quickly ate both and then it was time to go to the door. She blinked in surprise at the contingent of soldiers that was waiting for them. Ixta recognized all of them from the group that had accompanied her and Ethan on their explorations of the planet.

Nacón nodded at his men who formed a phalanx around him and Ixta to escort them to the tribunal. He was glad that his father had contacted his squad to have them waiting to protect him should the need arise. He hoped that it wouldn't be necessary to always have his guard around him, but he'd rather be prepared for the worst at this point. He looked at several of his men and met their eyes, seeing excitement and commitment in their eyes. He knew they were more than ready for this challenge and probably hoped they'd be called to action, though Nacón knew that would mean another threat on either him or Ixta. He nodded to each as they reformed

around him and his bride to accompany them to the
tribunal.

Several minutes later, they arrived at an area of the
camp that Ixta had never seen. Instead of the rustic
benches she expected, there was an amphitheater
with seating fanning out and up in a semicircle. The
seats looked almost natural but were too uniform to
have just occurred in natural stone in that fashion.
Clearly someone had been at work here to construct
this area that must serve governmental functions. Ixta
saw many people sitting on the first two rows of
stone benches and then an open area and then the
upper area was tightly packed. They must be the
observers, and the members of the council were on
the lower benches. They seemed more controlled and
regal somehow. Their clothing was more heavily
ornamented, and they had an air of privilege about
them. At least that's what Ixta decided about them as
she quickly took in the scene before her.

Looking to Nacón for guidance, she followed his
armed guards, walking at his side. They were
escorted over to the left side of the amphitheater and
sat on a bench up front. Chaac was seated on an
elevated platform in an elaborately carved chair, a
mate to the one he had sat in last night when he had
told the tribe not to harm her. This chair was a little
larger and more formal looking somehow. She saw
what couldn't have been real gems, though she didn't
know what to call them, outlining the top and sides of
the back of the chair. She could have sworn they
looked like diamonds, rubies and emeralds, but that
couldn't be on this primitive outpost. Or maybe this
was just another example of how little she really

knew about Uturax. Given her current situation and married state, she was betting it was just another example of her ignorance of this planet and its resources as well as customs.

Ixta saw the staff with feathers and other decorations on it that Chaac had held last night and waited for him to pound it against the ground for everyone's attention as he had done last night. This was more and more like some sci fi horror movie unfolding in front of her. Unfortunately, she was IN this morality play rather than just observing it. She looked at Nacón beside her and saw him sitting composed, if a little serious, just waiting patiently.

"Este tribunal está convocado. De parte de todas las casas reales, ¿tienen representante aquí?"

(This tribunal is called to order. Do all the royal houses have representatives here?) There was a universal grunt of response that Ixta assumed was agreement.

"As leader of the house of Palenque, I will call people to witness and give testimony unless there is opposition to this proposal."

Chaac looked around to see if any of the other royal houses would dare to contradict him. If they did, then that was another indication that this attempt on Ixta's life comported something bigger and darker. He had come to the same conclusion as Ixta that while the tainted fruit had been handed directly to Ixta, there was no assurance that Nacón wouldn't also partake of it and thus die alongside his bride.

There was no negative response to his proposal to conduct the trial and act as prosecutor and Chaac began by calling Nana to the chair placed to the side and below where he was sitting. Nana got up and walked carefully to the front of the amphitheater and took her seat.

"Nana, whose name as you all know is Hattie Castañon Lara, I have only one question: Who prepared the food to break my son's fast this morning? Be very specific."

"I prepared the beverage, and the oat cakes and Camila came in to help me by bringing fruit with her that she had already peeled and cut. They were nicely arranged on the platter, so all we did after she arrived was go directly to Nacón's hut to feed him and his bride."

"Thank you, Hattie. Did you see Camila Obregón Castillo put anything on the fruit while she was with you?"

"No, sire. I did not."

"Did you request Camila's assistance in preparing the meal?"

"No, sire. I did not, but when she appeared with the fruit, it appeared to be a tasty addition to the light fare that I was preparing. Also, it's widely known that *durazno* (peach) is Nacón's favorite fruit, so I knew he would like it. I accepted her help without thought and I can see I bear the blame for her having access to Nacón and his bride. For that, I am sorry," Hattie finished and looked at her nephew and his wife with sorrow.

"Tis of no import. Your integrity is not being questioned here. It appears that Camila took advantage of the situation and your trust. That will be all for now, Nana, except how do you feel about Nacón's bride?'

"I am very happy that he has finally chosen a mate, and even happier that his woman is so fertile that she is already carrying his child, the new heir. I saw the changes in her body myself this morning."

A gasp rose from the seats higher up in the amphitheater as apparently news of Ixta's pregnancy hadn't reached the rest of the tribe yet. Convening the tribunal and the speculation about the assassination attempt had occupied everyone in the hours since morning, so the news of the pregnancy had yet to circulate.

Nana preened in her chair, her ample bosom swelling as she sat up straighter, proud to have been the one to share this information about her much-loved nephew, her almost son.

Chaac looked up to silence the crowd who was eager to hear more news as this day was becoming more interesting as it progressed. Who knew what would come next? "Thank you, Hattie. You may take your seat. I think there are no more questions we need to ask you."

"Nacón, please step forward to testify."

Nacón rose and walked slowly to the witness seat. He stood tall and proud, handsome with an angry look on his face as he took his seat.

"Tell us what happened this morning when the door to your hut opened."

"We greeted Hattie, my nana, and Camila who had brought us food to break our fast." Nana gave me my morning beverage cup first, then another to Ixta. While she was pouring our drinks, Camila served the fruit, putting Ixta's on an eating platter which she handed to Ixta and then she did the same for me. I didn't notice anything unusual about her actions with the food, but she was looking at Ixta in a most unfriendly manner. It was so noticeable that Nana said something to her and then sent her out of the hut. The breakfast fruit was *durazno (peach)*, my favorite fruit, and I quickly started to eat it. I noticed that after only one or two bites, Ixta got up quickly and ran to the pot in the corner of my hut where she vomited the fruit. Shortly after that, she fell ill and passed out."

"Did you become sick also?"

"No. I did not and did not notice anything odd about the fruit."

"What made you think there was a problem with the fruit?"

"You mean other than my wife throwing up and losing consciousness?" Nacón asked sarcastically.

"Yes. Be specific," Chaac instructed with a stern look at Nacón to focus without the sarcasm.

"Before she passed out, Ixta said that she didn't like the bitter taste of the fruit and was surprised that I had eaten mine so quickly and with such relish. That was it. The fruit I ate was very sweet as *durazno* should be. You and I both tasted a small bit of residue of the fruit she ate from, and it did have the bitter taste of poison. Knowing that, we immediately spit it out unlike my wife who did not have that opportunity."

Chaac nodded and said, "I confirm what Nacón has said about tasting the fruit. Nana had come to find me to tell me of Ixta's pregnancy and when I returned with her, I found Ixta ill and heard her say that the fruit had a bitter taste and then my son and I both touched the remaining fruit on her plate and tasted its residue on our fingers. It was bitter, not sweet as it should have been. Is there anything else you have to tell us?"

"Yes, I want to say that while this seems to be an attempt on my wife's life, to kill my bride, it could have also killed me. There was no way to know if I would eat some of her fruit also. It is well known that *durazno* is my favorite fruit and it could be assumed that the assassin planned to kill me also."

An uproar arose at Nacón's word as all present realized that while an assassination attempt on the wife of a royal family member was extremely serious, an attempt on the life of the prince was grave, of the highest importance. It was a treasonous offense in either case.

After letting the crowd buzz for a few minutes, Chaac brought down his staff on the stone floor and it make a resounding smack as he nodded to Nacón. "You may resume your seat. I call Ixta Tikal de Palenque to witness.

Nacón grasped Ixta's arm to help her to her feet and then held her elbow as he escorted her to the witness seat. He wanted to show his support and commitment to his bride and was also concerned about her steadiness as she had eaten almost nothing today and he knew the demands on her body were increasing with every hour of her pregnancy, even if she wasn't aware of it yet.

It was noted by the crowd that Nacón was marking her as his woman by his solicitous care of Ixta as he helped her to her seat. The upper seating area was buzzing with comments.

"Ixta, can you tell me what happened in your hut this morning beginning when the door opened?" Chaac inquired.

"Well, yes. I saw Nana come in with a jug and cups and she gave us each a cup and then poured Nacón a beverage and then did the same for me. While she was doing this, the woman Camila was just looking at me like I'd stepped on her favorite cat's tail. I mean, she was looking at me like she was very angry with me, but I didn't know why. She served me fruit and handed me the platter and did the same for Nacón. By then, Nana noticed her negative attitude, said something to her I didn't understand and apparently told her to leave because Camila looked embarrassed and then immediately left. I saw how Nacón was really chowing down, I mean devouring the fruit, so I figured it must be pretty good to be eating it like that. I took one bite that wasn't very good because it was bitter. But I figured maybe I'd gotten a piece that wasn't that ripe, so I ate another and then that's when I felt like I had to vomit. I got up and ran across the room and threw up the fruit I'd just eaten. By then Chaac came into the hut with Nana, and I made a comment about the fruit's bitter taste. I felt worse and worse and passed out next, I guess. I woke up later when the ship's doctor was checking me out to figure out what was wrong."

"When did you find out you were pregnant, Ixta?"

"Yesterday afternoon right before our wedding ceremony, Dr. Tvitmpr did a blood test on me and the results said I was pregnant."

"Do you understand the importance of this pregnancy, Ixta Tikal de Palenque?" Chaac asked, using her new last name, a name she hadn't even known before a minute ago. This was even more bizarre than yesterday, finding herself married to a man whose last name she didn't even know. Won't that make a great entry in the family Bible or in her diary? She thought she'd probably omit the fact that she hadn't even known her last name.

"Yes, it is a sign of the ties that bind me and your son. We are linked in more than words, but by a new life that will one day rule this planet, I hope many, many distant years from now as I think you're doing a good job. At least I did till somebody tried to kill me and my baby and your son this morning," Ixta finished wondering if her big mouth had gotten her in trouble again.

Ixta saw Chaac's stern expression change at her words just for a moment before he spoke again. "You are correct, my daughter. You carry the future king or queen of Uturax and Camila was the executor of the plan that could have killed you, my son and your child all in one action. That is why I consider this action high treason. I warned you all last night about being sure no harm came to you. To have an assassination attempt come on the heels of my declaration makes my blood boil. We are warriors first on Uturax and this is an act of war. I will have retribution!" Chaac shouted as his anger rose.

There was an answering roar from the amphitheater as others joined in his shout and began chanting, "Blood must be spilled. Blood must be spilled."

Ixta looked around and then up the crowd and then at Chaac wondering what the hell was going on and cursing again her rudimentary command of the Uturaxan languages. She thought she understood the word blood but couldn't see how that related to the incident they'd been discussing.

Suddenly it grew very quiet when Camila, the woman from the hut earlier in the day who had given her the poisoned fruit, was brought to the edge of the amphitheater, her hands and feet bound by something metallic. They weren't chains, but whatever bound her glistened in the sunlight like metal would. Ixta looked over at Chaac and raised her eyebrows and gestured to her previous seat beside Nacón and when he nodded, Nacón rose and quickly helped Ixta from her seat. A change in his demeanor was clearly visible, his jaw was clenched, and he walked stiffly, drawing himself up to his full height. He looked imposing and very angry. As soon as Nacón and Ixta were seated again, Chaac motioned to the guards to bring Camila all the way into the amphitheater to the witness seat.

The guards saw that she was seated and then attached the metallic restraints to the chair and stepped back.

"Woman, state your name."

"Camila Obregón Castillo, of the house of Castillo," she said sullenly.

"Camila Obregón, do you deny anything that has been said about you thus far?" Chaac inquired.

"No, I do not."

"Tell the tribunal how the fruit came to be poisoned."

"I put the poison on the fruit in my hut and brought it to Hattie Castañón's hut because I knew that she would take the food to Nacón to break his fast and that of his bride. I knew she would think I was just being helpful. I took care to find *duraznos* to bring because all of us know that they are Nacón's favorite fruit."

"Where did you get the poison for this fruit?"

"I found it in the forest."

"How did you know it was poison? Who helped you do this?"

"Nobody helped me. I just knew," Camila said quickly and defiantly.

"You just knew," Chaac said, disbelief evident in his voice. "I find that very hard to accept as truth, Camila. Now why don't you tell me what the truth is? Did you intend to murder my son as well as his wife?"

"You have to take it as truth because I'm not saying anything more about the poison. Oh, yes, I saw that Nacón's wife was pregnant this morning and was glad that I would be killing her, her baby and hopefully your son," Camila said coldly, turning to look at Nacón as he stood and roared at her.

"Do you refuse to tell us who is behind this plot? It is impossible that you planned this yourself. You never leave the pleasure house, spend your days intoxicated and are months behind in your training program with the new weapons. You don't have the initiative to go outside, let alone plan an assassination this big," Chaac said with contempt and asked the council to weigh in, "Think you that the House of Castillo planned this coup attempt?"

"No! This woman does not act nor speak for us and hasn't for many months. She is a disgrace and has not been in contact with our house for as many months. Do not think we would seek to depose the House of Palenque who has provided a just rule for so many years. Palenque won the right to govern in the last Gem Wars and we seek no change in that rule. Believe us! We speak the truth. We are disgraced by this woman using our name."

When the other royal houses indicated their agreement about the innocence of the rest of Camila's family, Chaac accepted it on face value for the moment. However, the problem remained that he didn't believe Camila. She wasn't smart enough to have found a natural poison just out in the jungle though he knew many grew there. With her current lack of ambition, he didn't think she could have found the money to buy it from someone, so it was logical that she had accomplices. It was probably the *Sin Raíces* faction. They had to be behind this though Chaac hadn't thought they'd ever have the balls to try to kill his family. Nacón was well liked and respected on Uturax and a warrior in his own right. No one would have dared face him in combat and it made sense that this underhanded way of killing without honor would be the method *Sin Raíces* would choose.

"One last question, Camila. Why? Why did you do this foul act? You have brought disgrace on yourself and on the house of Castillo."

"I wanted him for myself! Is that so hard to understand? Several months ago, we joined our bodies after one of the fertility celebrations and I knew then that Nacón was destined to become my mate," Camila said and looked smugly at Ixta as if challenging her right to Nacón.

"Did my son share his seed with you in that joining?" Chaac asked carefully.

"No. Unfortunately he did not. If he had, I would be the one carrying the royal heir, not that alien bitch sitting over there!" Camila said with venom in her voice.

"Well then, is there anything more you would like to add at this time?" Chaac asked, clearly relieved by her response. Camila shook her head negatively and looked defiantly at the crowd and the tribunal members. The buzzing of comments and various conversations in the upper levels of the tribunal seating area in the amphitheater could clearly be heard by all.

"For the House of Palenque, I accept the profession of innocence of the House of Castillo and would like the members of the tribunal to make a guilty or innocent ruling on Camila Castillo Obregón's testimony here today. What say you?"

Each member of the council that comprised the tribunal gave a thumbs down sign, an age-old method of passing judgment. After all had voted, Chaac said, "I too vote 'guilty' and impose a sentence of death by beheading. I appoint the warrior of Nacón's choice to execute the sentence, which is to say, to execute the woman Camila Castillo Obregón."

Nacón ignored Camila's gasp and looked at his men near him and around the prisoner. He nodded to Ulises, his first swordsman whenever the need arose.

Before another word was said, Ulises moved quickly over by the witness seat, drew back the huge

battle axe the guards all now carried and separated
Camila's head from her neck. The cry she started to
make never made it past her lips as her head fell and
rolled several feet from the chair. Ixta's eyes were
drawn back to the weaponry that all the guards now
carried from a primitive skull cracker war club to the
fierce battle axes to other things hanging from their
belts that Ixta couldn't identify. When had this
happened? The phalanx of guards that had before
looked imposing for their height and physical
strength now looked lethal.

Nacón heard Ixta's quick intake of breath and
hoped she would maintain her usual calm demeanor
without reacting. Proper Uturaxan behavior at
beheadings was not a topic they'd touched on in their
many hours of conversation he thought wryly. He
squeezed her hand, and she seemed to understand as
she made no further sound. He knew she had
probably understood only a little of what had
transpired but the result was evident and must have
been surprising to her. He doubted that her people
dispensed justice so swiftly and in this manner.
Nacón felt admiration for her ability to control her
feelings and reactions during an event that must seem
extreme and violent to her.

Ulises stood at attention with his sword held aloft
and then he reached down and grasped Camila's head
with her hair and held it up for all to see. There was
unease in the crowd but also a sense of rightness
because whether Camila had had an accomplice or
not, her actions were without pardon. If anyone here
sympathized with her, they were silent, not having a
death wish to ally themselves with a convicted

assassin. There was no excuse for attempted murder on the royal family, angry or not about Nacón's bride choice.

The ruling of death by beheading was appropriate and any less of a punishment would have seemed weak and ineffectual on Chaac's part. The tribe was reassured that their king had displayed no hesitation in carrying out this severe punishment. Clearly last decade's peace had ended if some faction was willing to try this direct of an assassination attempt. A challenge had been issued and met by Chaac's swift justice. Time would tell what would happen next and if the balance of power would shift in the tribe.

Ixta was glad that Nacón had clasped her hand as it reminded her of her place and to hang tight. It was as if the past few moments had happened in slow motion in her mind. She knew that something awful was going to happen after she'd seen the tribunal members each give a thumbs down sign, but she hadn't realized just how awful the sentence would be to watch. The anthropologist in her noted that all the bodyguards now carried a huge axe with a metallic blade that looked much more sophisticated than the wooden weapons she was used to seeing them with. Nacón's touch brought her back to reality and forced her to leave all her thoughts that were swirling around in her mind for later. Without words, Nacón had communicated to her that what she did and how she reacted was important here.

As a crew member that had made two previous interstellar trips, Ixta had seen battle, if from the fringes. She usually ended up working with the ship's doctor Joss or a medic in the triage area rather than being actively involved in any fighting. She had seen her share of deadly wounds and watched her crewmates die at times. It was never easy, but she accepted it as part of her training, as part of life in service for her planet. It wasn't all exciting exploration and discovery every moment. Clearly the captain had been right about this planet being inhabited by warriors even though none of the aliens had displayed this kind of capability in front of any of the crew members before.

She could see that this was one more example of information that her questioning of Nacón as an anthropologist should have revealed. '*Great. Just another reinforcer that I am shitty at my job, as if I needed another.*' If she seemed dispassionate, she hoped Nacón would understand that this alien woman who had just been executed had tried to kill her and thus her baby. No one could do that to Ixta without a fight from her. Feeling slightly bloodthirsty by her current line of thinking on the issue, she agreed with Chaac's ruling and was glad that this woman wasn't alive to try again. She had to wonder if it was so simple. Was this woman acting alone? She hoped that Chaac had covered that in his questioning of Camila and cursed again her lack of fluency in Uturaxan. The pidgin language she and Nacón had concocted didn't include as much pure Uturaxan vocabulary as she needed now.

Ixta hoped that Nacón would fill her in on more details later as she had many questions and hoped to be able to quiet her worries about the continued life of her unborn child. She hoped the tribe took this as proof that she, along with her baby, were important to

the House of Palenque. Funny thing, not knowing her
new last name. She figured there'd be no next time of
casual sex with anyone as Nacón seemed pretty
committed in his vows, but she would never, if the
situation ever came up, have sex again with someone
whose culture she didn't understand and whose name
she didn't fully know. She vowed that to herself, and
she composed her features and turned to Nacón to see
what was next.

Just then, Chaac pounded his staff on the rock slab
floor again and said something to his people. It must
have been a dismissal as all stood and began filing
down the stairs from all the seating levels to the
ground to head back to their huts. Chaac turned to
Nacón and said something that must have involved
going along with him as Nacón took her by the elbow
and they followed Chaac out of the amphitheater and
back toward his hut in the village.

The amphitheater certainly was grand by any
standards, Ixta thought, especially when she
compared it to the hut she was sharing with Nacón.
The tribunal's setting was simple, but there was
something about its construction that bespoke a level
of technology that she thought wasn't present on this
planet. At least until confronted with the fierce, well-
designed and honed battle axes, she had thought
technology wasn't present here. Perhaps that meant
other off-worlders had built it long ago and the
Uturaxans just took it over later as they could have
done with weapons they found. That would be a good
question for Nacón later if she ever got enough of the
language mastered to have a conversation on that
level though she guessed that he might soon outpace

her in language skills from what she'd observed very recently.

The party of three, accompanied by a full squad of Chaac's guards as well as Nacón's men who surrounded just them, arrived shortly at Chaac's hut. Ixta was curious to see what the king's hut would look like, wondering if it would afford more creature comforts than Nacón's which had the bare minimum.

Upon entering, they were greeted by Nana who brought a seat for Ixta to sit on and placed it beside the other chair in the room, clearly Chaac's. She hesitated and looked to Nacón. "You sit. You are the prince here. I'm just the bride."

Nacón shook his head 'no' and sat cross-legged beside the offered chair. Waiting for Chaac to sit first, Ixta sank into the chair, glad to be sitting as she realized she felt weak from hunger. Her mealtime today had been less than fortifying to say the least. "Oh, hell. If someone doesn't manage to kill me, I'm going to die of starvation. I could eat or at least chew on Nacón's arm like a chicken leg right about now."

Not even noticing that Nacón understood her words, Ixta heard Nacón say something quickly.

Nana looked at Chaac who nodded in assent before she brought them platters of food.

"Who has tasted this food, Hattie? All our meals must go past tasters now."

"Each of the royal houses sent a child in the line of succession of power and all of the food has been tasted by them before I bought it out to you. Will that suffice?"

"Yes, Hattie. Thank you for seeing to that detail so quickly." Chaac indicated to Ixta that the food was safe by putting some into his mouth and smiling.

"Eat, Ixta. This food is safe. You must eat to take care of yourself and our child," Nacón said as he handed her a platter, taking a handful of what looked like green beans and putting them in his mouth as he reached by his own platter and began wolfing down the food there.

'Whoa, cowboy. Eager to eat. A zest for all life's pleasures, I see. From what I've experienced with you these past two nights, your appetites are all strong.'

"Thank you. I eat, "Ixta said in Uturaxan that brought a smile to both Chaac and Nacón's faces and a surprised look to Nana's. And she dug into the platter of vegetables and what seemed like fish, though she couldn't really be sure what it was. The texture was like fish, but the taste was well, out of this world. Or at any rate, her world. Ixta ate with gusto. It had been since the previous evening that she had eaten well and with all that had happened this morning and then the tribunal, she was running on empty and was truly hungry. Hungry like she hadn't been in years. It brought back memories of her life after her parents died when she was so upset that she forgot to eat and had little interest in anything.

As the day progressed, Chaac, Nacón, and other members of the ruling family met to discuss what Ixta assumed was the failed assassination attempt on their lives. They all paraded through Chaac's hut and glanced curiously at her each time. Hearing about her pregnancy, no doubt, Ixta saw that they all looked at her belly area with thoroughness. Some were pleased, but others had a false smile pasted on their faces as they were introduced individually to her. It was obvious to her that her safety and that of her child could be in further jeopardy on this planet. In the space of several days, she'd gone from carefree, dedicated anthropologist, a respected member of the ship's crew, to a banished outcast in her crews' eyes and an unwelcome addition to this village and tribe. At least Nacón still seemed happy with her and his Nana was another friendly face. When she heard who the food tasters were, she felt bad about children's lives being at risk for her and Nacón, but knew it was a necessity and that Chaac would accept no less. Hopefully because the royal houses' children's lives were at stake, she and Nacón would be left alone. It wasn't a comfortable feeling though knowing that someone wanted to kill you. Nacón had explained more of the trial's proceedings to her and added that he didn't believe that Camila had acted alone for the reasons that Chaac had mentioned in the trial. Camila was not clever or ambitious and would have needed help to even think of the assassination attempt, let alone the method.

Finally, another meal was brought as the day grew late. Who knew it could cause hunger just sitting around in a tense atmosphere trying hard to concentrate on what was being said as the parade of nobles trooped through Chaac's hut? The last one left and Nana quickly appeared with trays of food which she set on a table she pulled over so Chaac, Nacón and Ixta could eat. Ixta appreciated her solicitousness and real concern for her and her appetite. Strange

food or not, Ixta kept up with Nacón as he wolfed
down the food. Her hunger satisfied, Ixta leaned back
in her chair and watched her new husband.

Nacón was still eating with gusto, and she enjoyed
watching him. He was, she decided, handsome. She
could have done worse! Odd how all this had worked
out. She had come to value his friendship in all the
months they'd spent talking and had a real fondness
for him. Now that he had turned into her sexual
partner, that dramatically changed their casual
friendship. It was different in so many ways being his
wife. There were the incredible sex and his real
concern for her well-being. She knew that was
motivated by his interest in the baby she carried, but
the result felt the same to her. She felt something
with him she'd hadn't felt in many years--cherished.
*'Crap, my hormones are making me sappy. I don't
know when I've ever said anything like that. I've got
to control my emotions, or I'm going to be sitting
around and crying like a baby just because I'm
happy. I'm sure Nacón wouldn't understand that.
Before anything, this is a warrior culture. He's got
enough to worry about now just keeping me safe from
his people without having a weepy wife on his hands.
Must be the pregnancy as I've never been the
emotional type. I've had to be strong and working on
a ship required that I be as tough as the next man. No
time for sissies.'*

The next few days were tense as Chaac met with
Nacón to do what she could only guess was a threat
assessment, waiting to see if there would be a
backlash to Camila's execution. Nacón never let Ixta
out of his sight, so she sat in on the war councils.

After the initial looks of distrust that the members of the royal houses gave her, they dismissed her from their minds and talks began in earnest to try to discover who was really behind the assassination attempt. Ixta found that after three days of sitting in the council room all day, more of the Uturaxan words were becoming understandable. She had a facility for language and was able to use her very personal knowledge of the details of the assassination attempt to help provide a context for the new words swirling around her. She didn't say anything to anyone about her improving language skills as she felt it was a tool she could use to her advantage and safety if few knew she could understand far more than they expected. She would talk to Nacón about it once these non-stop meetings concluded, but as yet, there had been little time alone.

She looked forward to some alone time with him, not just for the physical side of their relationship that she found enjoyed so much and looked forward to, but for the friendship they had been building prior to their wedding. She did count him as her friend, a better friend than she had made in quite a while. Her one real friend on the ship was Joss, but his being Argentian had precluded their hanging out with the rest of the less liberal crew. So, Ixta had many acquaintances on the ship, had been well-liked and many would have counted her as a friend. But she knew the limitations of those friendships and had seen their distaste for her choice to ally herself with the alien race in this place. Some were puzzled, others horrified at the implications of her union.

Since the crew refused to let Joss participate in most social events, Ixta had learned to compartmentalize her activities and friendships. As a crew member, Joss had access to all social areas and functions, but the reality of it was that if he ever ventured into any of those areas, conversation either stopped or became stilted. She knew that no female on the crew would date him or allow her name to be connected with his in any capacity. She felt that he had considered asking her out but had probably decided it would cause them both too much trouble if the censure they'd experienced by eating lunches together was any indication. Fraternization with aliens was tricky because the official policy line was that all races were equal. However, there were many unwritten rules about how far this fraternization could go. It was just easier to avoid making friendships across races because friendships could deepen and then both individuals were in jeopardy of retaliation from their crew mates, of loss of rank, or even dismissal as had happened to her.

Her friendship with Nacón had seemed so uncomplicated after all the political nuances of relationships among the crew and on the outposts they stopped at. Hell, even off duty, you had to watch your back when hanging out in alien bars. With Nacón, neither of them had an agenda other than spending time together while she did her former job. Since it had all blown up about their marriage, she came to understand why he was pleased to have a friendship that didn't seem to hinge on getting his wealth and position for a political alliance. She had fallen into a nice place, she decided, though having someone try to kill her and her baby wasn't exactly a plus. However, it was nice to have someone care for her and pledge themselves to her since it was someone she admired and liked. It had been so many years since she had had someone care for her and worry about her other than in a professional way. If they could survive the enmity of some of Uturax's tribal members, she hoped they could build on the friendship they already had. Looking back, Ixta guessed it wasn't as uncomplicated as she had thought. *'How could I have missed all the signs? If I had been sharper, I might still be working on the ship, a member of the crew. Whoa, girl. If that were true, then you wouldn't be expecting a baby. Admit it. You're happy about that even if it is inconvenient and unknown. You want this baby.'*

Ixta's musings ended abruptly as she looked up and saw someone she didn't recognize slip in through the back of the hut. Strikingly different in appearance, he was different from the rest with no body hair, looking almost completely human. His movements were furtive as he quietly replaced the piece of wall he'd moved to enter. She looked around quickly, but no one noticed this intruder because there was a heated argument going on among the council members. Without knowing why, Ixta felt an impending sense of doom. She felt the hairs on the back of her neck stand up. The intruder gave off what she would call "bad vibes." She didn't like the look on his face and if pressed for a word to describe that look, would say "evil." *'Didn't regular visitors enter through the front door? Who slips in the back of a house except someone up to no good?'* Ixta quickly glanced around and noticed that Chaac's and Nacón's guards had been sent to stand outside the door of the hut. Apparently, no one thought anyone would try to enter the hut through the back as there was no door but the one in front and they had already caught the attempted assassin.

From her vantage point, Ixta could see that this man carried one of those strange rods she'd seen hanging from the warriors' belts at the tribunal. That and his very human hairless body look made this man stand out as someone out of the ordinary. She hoped that she wasn't misjudging this situation as her recent expulsion from the crew had bruised her confidence in her judgment. *'Crap, what are the odds of this? Another assassination attempt? Here? If this was karma, I must have really screwed someone over in my last life. Shit, I can't make a mistake here. What if I'm wrong?'*

However, Ixta decided she wasn't going to take chances with her new husband's life. There was nothing reassuring about this man's presence here nor the look on his face. Ixta saw that he hadn't even looked her way, or she would have shouted out about his presence. The lighting was poor in the back areas of the hut, and she was hidden in the shadows that he was also trying to take advantage of as he made his stealthy progress through the hut. While she wasn't a warrior like Nacón and his men, she had the training and skills to sneak up on someone from behind certainly when there was so much background noise. What person hadn't played hide and seek as a kid? That very clamor of angry voices that the intruder was using to cover his stealthy entrance could also cover her pursuit of him.

Ixta clasped the skull cracker club that she'd taken from the stack of weapons in Nacón's hut earlier today. She didn't know why she had grabbed it, but she had held it and found she liked its weight and feel in her hand. Serendipitous decision. As the alien man made his way undetected toward Nacón and his father, Ixta readied herself to spring into action. She really didn't have time to analyze whether this was the best or the worst idea she'd come up with lately. She knew that she was afraid that he would slip out the back of the hut where he came in if she raised the alarm and then still be a threat to them if he resurfaced later, if he was a threat. He was closer to the back of the hut where he'd sneaked in, and she didn't doubt he would quickly disappear. After Camila's attempt to poison them, Ixta didn't trust anyone here any longer, if she ever had, other than Nacón and Chaac.

Without a sound, Ixta crept behind him and suddenly hit him over the head with the war club. Then she did shout as she brought the club down on his head again as he started to sink to the floor, "Down, you son of a bitch!"

Suddenly the room changed in that instant, the argument ending abruptly. Chaac and Nacón saw the alien on the floor and Ixta standing over him brandishing the war club. Her shout had gotten all their attention certainly. Nacón shouted for the guards to enter and Chaac walked over to the man on the ground to see who it was and what had happened. The hut became a hive of activity in that instant. The guards rushed in and over to the unconscious man on the floor. They bound his hands and took his weapon to secure the area and their prisoner.

As one, all the people in the room looked at Ixta. *'Oh shit, I hope I haven't just bashed in the head of some important royal family member here.'* She lowered the club and looked at Nacón expectantly, hoping he would take over for her now in the aftermath of her actions. Seeing him looking back at her with that same expectant look as the others, she then said, "I saw him sneak in the back of the hut. The look on his face was evil, and he acted like he wasn't meant to be here. I was afraid he would escape if I said something, and I didn't want him to hurt you. After Camila, I'm not sure who is a friend here."

By now, the guards had disarmed and restrained the man; they then gave the weapon the prisoner had held to Chaac. After looking at the weapon which he found was set to kill, Chaac uncharacteristically started shouting, "What have you to say for yourself, *hijo de la chingada (motherfucker)*? Kennan, to come into my hut armed and uninvited through a hole you made in the back can only be interpreted as an act of aggression. Did you plan to murder me or my son or the council of elders on this day? A man does not kill someone by striking them in the back. Only a coward approaches a fight like you did!"

"Camila was afraid to say it, old man, but I'm not. *Sin Raíces* is done with waiting patiently for your recognition of our group. We wanted to unite with the old houses of Uturax, but you have avoided meeting with us and giving us our rightful place in this government. Since you won't recognize us, you must be eliminated. Your days are over!" the man shouted.

"Silence! Your group is a bunch of lawbreakers who have no good to offer to Uturax. All that you live for is to cause pain and suffering in the name of some vague ideological platform. What say you, members of the council? Do we convene a tribunal for this man? He has admitted his guilt. I see no questions that remain to be answered."

"Nay, no tribunal is needed. Death to the traitor!" the cry rose among the council members.

"Now, could someone tell me how this traitor got into our midst with a stun rod?" Chaac looked at the rod in his hand and added, "A stun rod set to kill. Did no one cover the perimeter? You are a band of warriors, but it fell to this pregnant alien woman to save our lives. How is that? Explain yourselves, warriors."

Nacón's men looked ashamed because they had failed their king as well as their immediate leader. Chaac's guard had similar looks on their faces, knowing that they deserved the criticism. They were warriors but had acted like raw recruits in the past hour. They had been complacent thinking that the threat had been removed with Camila's execution and never considered that someone could enter the rear of the hut to make mischief because there was only one door at the front. Their leaders could have been killed by this *Sin Raíces* rebel. The kill setting on the stun rod he carried confirmed that assassination was his motive. Kennan's words also confirmed that the rebel group was behind the assassination attempt on Nacón and his bride earlier. So many years of peace among the clans had robbed them of their fighting edge, it seemed.

The lead man in each group of guards said, almost in unison, "We have nothing to say in our defense, my king. We have failed you. We accept demotion and punishment."

"Much as I would like to do both, we need you right now as you are or should be. Figuring out how to change your training protocols will be your first task tomorrow, my son. Right now, we owe thanks to your woman. She seems to have a side to her we had not realized. Congratulations on choosing so well. She will be a warrior queen one day at your side."

Ixta missed a little of what Chaac said but did get the message that he was pleased with her, and she smiled in return. *'What a day! She was ready to go home to their hut and forget all that had happened today. Too much to process.'*

"Guards, bind this man and keep him in custody till tomorrow. I think that his execution for his deeds should take place in front of an audience. Do not fail me again. He must not escape. Call in more of your guard to post a perimeter around the village that is impenetrable. We are officially on battle alert. Bring out your weapons. Follow all protocols for that level of defense. Do I need to be more explicit?" Chaac asked tersely.

"No, my lord. It will be done immediately." The team leaders responded again in unison.

Chaac turned to the woman who had separated herself from the council and appeared at his side, waiting to be recognized.

"Esmeralda, do you wish to speak for your kinsman before tomorrow?" Chaac said, frowning as he turned to her.

"No, my chief. I want to clarify that his elders knew nothing of this shameful plot of aggression. We do not support him or *Sin Raíces* in any way. He has brought shame to our name."

"Esmeralda. Thank you for your words, but you have been a council member for many years, and your loyalty is not in question. I do have to ask if you would speak against his execution though. That is what I am going to recommend. This is too grave an act to not be punished severely."

"While it will bring my niece pain, she will have to realize that it is just. Our family supports your judgment here. It will be a while before we can live down this shame."

"Do not worry, my old friend. Your position within the council will not change and I will welcome your opinions as always," Chaac reassured her. Her mate had died soon after Chaac's wife in another battle in the long war. They had been good friends for many years, and he had considered accepting her invitation to make their relationship closer when Nacón was younger but eventually decided against it. He didn't want another mate, and it made their official political relationship all that much easier without the undercurrent of a romantic attachment. However, he did appreciate her efforts to clarify her clan's feelings on the situation as well as her support for his decision.

Nacón went to Ixta, took her arm and indicated that they were leaving. Several of his guards fell into step behind him. The village was quiet as it had grown late during all those discussions during the day. There was no activity, but at this point, no one wanted to take a chance on anyone else out there looking to harm him and his wife.

Arriving at his hut, he gave an order for three of his men to stay outside the hut and he went inside with Ixta. He said, "I must thank you, my wife, for saving my life and that of my father today. Only your quick thinking prevented Kennan from firing his weapon or detonating the explosives he had brought with him when he came in by the back hole in the hut he had made. He could have killed any or all of us but given what he said about belonging to the rebel group *Sin Raíces* , they are desperate to make a big statement. Killing me or my father is the kind of publicity they are looking for."

"You know, Nacón, this planet is suddenly seeming a lot more complicated than it did just a few days ago. I am glad that I could help. I must confess that I had a moment of worry that I was going to bash someone over the head who was an important person. I didn't know how I would deal with the aftereffects of that."

"Intuition is sometimes the most important weapon any of us can use. That feeling you get that something isn't right is usually correct. You are a good woman to raise a warrior's son. I am proud to have you as my wife."

"Uh, Nacón, what if this baby is a girl? Have you considered that?" Ixta asked smiling at Nacón, relieved that he approved of her making such a rash decision.

"Ixta this is probably more than I should say, but at the time of conception, the male determines the sex of the child or children. Is it not like that on your planet?'

"Well, yes, but while the male determines the sex, he has no choice. It's a 50/50 chance either way unless they are having the conception done in a lab because they can't conceive on their own or lack the time to spend together to do so. Hell, it's complicated where I come from, and people often live far apart even though they have chosen to be married."

"Here, the choice is made by the male at the time of conception. It's part of sharing seed in our culture. Ordinarily the mated pair discusses which sex children they desire prior to each conception and a joint decision is made. I made that choice for us, Ixta, as we didn't talk about much of anything that night. The fact that I shared my seed with you multiple times that night, each time choosing ensured that our child or children would be male. I'm sorry if that is not to your liking, but our custom is that the first-born children of the ruling king and his heir will be males to ensure the bloodline and succession to the throne. While women do share in ruling our planet, ours is a patriarchal society in that our highest rulers are kings and thus are male."

"This is more than I think I can absorb right now. The biology of your tribe is different from mine clearly, but a boy is fine. You have thought more about this than I have, that's for sure. I look forward to raising your warrior child or children for you, Nacón, if we can just avoid getting killed by this rebel group. What's that all about?"

"That is a discussion for another day, wife."
Nacón said with finality.

"Wait a minute, cowboy. Don't do that little
woman act on me now. I deserve an answer," Ixta
said with annoyance.

"Ah, Ixta. Don't be angry with me. I will talk to
you about all of this tomorrow. But first, I must ask
my father for guidance as your place on our planet
and in our family has changed dramatically. You
must understand that until today, we didn't know if
you were with us or with your ship in your
allegiance. Our planet has not had much luck with
off-worlders before you and we cannot risk our safety
too soon in any alliance. Do you at least understand
that? Do not be angry. Let's talk about this tomorrow.
Tonight, we must rest so that we are ready to face the
new day. It has got to be a better one than this has
been. I can still see the look on the guards' faces as
my father chastised them for not being on top of all
security in the hut. They were majorly embarrassed
that you, my wife, saved the day instead of one of
them."

Ixta smiled at Nacón's words and agreed that it
had been amusing to see their faces. Being upstaged
by a mere woman, an untrained off-worlder, was a
blow to the egos of a group of warriors. There was
more to all of this than was on the surface. She had
more questions than ever before: the stun rod weapon
that was very advanced for this civilization, the rebel
faction, two assassination attempts, Nacón's mention
of lack of luck with other off-worlders when he had
never mentioned any planetary visitors before. As she
continued thinking about these questions, she noticed

Nacón walking the perimeter of the hut and he had some strange device in his hand. She watched fascinated as he seemed to be sweeping the exterior wall with the instrument. This instrument looked far more advanced than anything she had ever seen on this planet. Something was off here. It just didn't fit together with the crude village, these weapons, the tribunal's physical appearance that had the look of the modern world.

Nacón noted that Ixta was watching him with interest even though she said nothing. Tomorrow he would have to see his father right after breaking his fast to clarify Ixta's position within the tribe. She had seen things today that he knew she wouldn't ignore. Her questions were growing, and he felt she had a right to know the details and to be a real member of the tribe. However, he knew how carefully his father guarded the tribe's secrets and his policies had kept them safe all these years. It might even have to go to council.

Finishing with his sweep and setting the shield around his hut's perimeter, Nacón turned to Ixta and asked, "Do you want anything to eat or drink, Ixta, before we sleep for the night?"

"No, Nacón. I'm just tired, really tired. Too much happened today. I'm exhausted and I don't think it's all related to the pregnancy. Let's go to bed. And sleep."

Nacón laughed, getting her meaning. She looked spent and badly in need of rest and sleep. He would forgo sharing pleasure with her tonight though the last few days had awakened a thirst in him for his wife that he hadn't known he would feel. He liked joining with her on so many levels: the physical pleasure and the feeling of sharing on a level he'd never felt with another woman. Maybe he would grow to love this woman like his father had loved his mother. That was unexpected, but something he decided would be another benefit to his alliance with Ixta. Resolved to go to bed to sleep, he unrolled the furs and arranged their bed on the floor. He wondered how much longer he'd have to sleep on the floor. He hoped his father agreed tomorrow to take Ixta into their confidence and then they could enjoy the regular creature comforts instead of this rustic existence. He took off his kilt and leather thong and then motioned for Ixta to join him on the furs.

She laughed and said, "Having you naked beside me isn't a good guarantee of rest, Nacón. When we get naked near each other, we end up making love. "

"I can do what's best for you and our child, Ixta. Come over here; lay your head on my shoulder and go to sleep. No more talk." Nacón said smiling as he laid his head on the furs. Ixta complied and almost as soon as her head touched his shoulder, she relaxed and was soon lightly snoring.

Nacón chuckled to himself. I'm sure she's going to say to me that I snore, but now I've got the proof that she does too. He felt like he could sleep without one eye open because he had swept the room for any weapons or explosives one of the rebels might have installed and he'd also set a shield around the perimeter of their hut. Also, there was a full contingent of his guard surrounding his hut and patrolling the perimeter. He decided that protecting himself and his wife was a necessity even if his father hadn't cleared his letting Ixta see anything more about their technology. He couldn't really see how his father could keep all of these secrets anymore since she had seen the tribunal gathering area and the stun rods on two occasions. She was smart and wouldn't be fooled by some vague explanation. Maybe one without the other, but he knew she would be full of questions tomorrow when she regained her strength.

He lay on his side and watched her sleep in the dim light resulting from the glow from the shield. While he hadn't really thought about her being beautiful before, now he did. She had always looked attractive to him, but he saw her in a different light now. She was so much more than any other off-worlder he had met as well as the women he'd spent time with on Uturax and now she was his woman. Her strength of character was there in her face as she encountered every new situation. She had never judged his people nor thought them less because they appeared to be different and primitive in so many ways. In such a short time, his feelings for her had grown and multiplied. If he had thought about their marrying at one time when they first met, he would have laughed, calling the thought ridiculous. But now that they were wed, he was glad that he'd made that spontaneous, poorly thought out, independent decision to share his seed to make her his mate. Even his father had quickly come around from his initial fury at what he considered Nacón's irresponsible actions. He could see it on his face and hear it in his voice when he had chastised the guards. He was proud of her actions and her quick "what the hell" thinking. Her boldness had saved his life and his father's, and he didn't know how many others in that hut and its vicinity.

Kennan was unstable and probably would have tried to eliminate as many of the ruling council as he could. They had also found an explosive with a timer hidden in his belt. It appeared that he was ready to commit suicide and destroy everyone and everything in the hut and nearby. The stun rod was the least of the problems they had been facing with his intrusion. The *Sin Raíces* faction must be getting desperate, and their actions had escalated to what he considered a desperate stage. Nacón wondered how many others were part of this group. Without the DNA marker implants, they were easy to spot. As far as they knew, they were all natural born Uturaxans so would have had implants when they joined this group. Someone within the group must have medical training to surgically remove them and cause them to revert to their normal humanoid appearance. The holographic disguising amulets wouldn't work without the implants, so they had no real defense against discovery. That meant to him that they had gone underground somewhere or established a base camp deep within the rain forest part of the jungle as their refuge for their dystopian society. That was something he would have to discuss with his father tomorrow. He hoped that Chaac would allow Ixta to be part of those discussions about the *Sin Raíces* as he felt that she had the type of analytical mind that could benefit the discussion and help them search for answers.

Nacón woke suddenly and looked up to find Ixta's face staring intently at his. Her breasts touched the side of his chest, and she was putting one leg over him. She saw him awaken and continued climbing over him and then sat astride him, first leaning down on her arms, and then resting her forearms on his chest. She looked down into his eyes and smiled as she rubbed against him and felt him rapidly growing under her pussy. She moved her hands to run her fingers through his hair that fell back from his face. She was fascinated by it perhaps because he'd never allowed her to touch him before, only those few times when she had broken protocol and grabbed his arm or hand. His hair was soft and silky as she pulled it away from his face to expose his neck better. She nuzzled his ear, sucking lightly as she moved her way back around to his face. Her mouth found his, and then she kissed him all around his face after several long, deep kisses. She shifted slightly and moved back a little to lean forward putting her breasts almost in his mouth and then sat down slowly on his penis as he took a deep breath, wanting to prolong this moment. He felt her warmth and wetness as she took him inside her, inching her way down all the while watching his face and expression.

What a way to wake up! Congratulating himself again on his decision to make this woman his wife, Nacón reached up to take hold of one of her breasts to guide it to his mouth. Keeping in mind that she was tender from her pregnancy, he gently suckled first one breast and then moved to the other before moving to take the nipples of both breasts into his mouth. Without that confining undergarment she

wore, her breasts were larger than he had first
imagined and very malleable in his hands. He laved
both with his tongue, ending with taking the tip of
each breast into his mouth to suck it, drawing the
nipple out, lightly gripping it with his teeth. He
reached to grab her hips, to better control the rhythm
she had established, but she pushed his hands back up
to her breasts. Perhaps in response to his attempt to
control her movements, he vaguely noted that Ixta
did respond by moving up and down on him more
quickly. They could both hear her wet pussy slapping
down on his balls and thighs. Then quiet would ensue
as Ixta would languorously pull herself up again,
arching her back, never losing hold of Nacón on the
upswing of the delicious rhythm she had found. She
would build up the intensity and then almost stop as
she felt both of them moving along too fast. They
were both breathing heavily and sweat covered their
bodies where their torsos met. Instead of detracting
from the intimate moment, their mingled sweat just
added to the extremely sensual experience. Nacón's
mouth was wet and hot as he suckled her tender
breasts with just the right intensity to almost drive her
through the roof while not rough enough to hurt.
Though her breasts were tender, the sensations were
too much for her to ask him to stop. She couldn't
have stopped; though when she slowed for a moment
to give herself and Nacón time to slow down their
bodies' determination to find release, she managed to
speak.

"I want to savor this moment, Nacón. I've never
woken up to sex with a man before. I think I like this.
I want to ride you till we both come. I want to fall

onto your chest when I'm done, too tired to move," she managed to gasp out between her up and down motions that she found she could not stop herself from resuming. Deciding to forego the conversation and focus on the pleasure she knew was close at hand for her to experience an orgasm and she hoped that he was ready also as she wanted to share that feeling again with Nacón.

Ixta picked up the tempo until she felt Nacón stiffen beneath her and then she shifted slightly and felt herself start her climax. Her pregnant body seemed to be perpetually turned on these past two days and she was glad to have this man beside her, rather under her, to take care of those urges. She didn't know when she'd had so much sex and was enjoying all the sensations. She had left her "toy" on the ship but couldn't imagine needing it any more with her new husband. She lay limply on top of him, breathing heavily. For a newly mated pair, they felt very in tune with each other's wants and needs.

"Don't tell me you do this often. Wake up with other men," Nacón said grumpily.

"No. Actually, not ever. I've never slept with a man, Nacón," Ixta said shyly, feeling foolish. She didn't know much about Uturaxan sexual customs but knew from Nacón's casual comments that unmarried couples often had sex and prior to marriage, were not often monogamous and it was considered normal on his planet, not promiscuous. She had been circumspect in her relationships not wanting to get the crew's tongues wagging as gossip was a favorite pastime with little else to do on long voyages and hops between outposts. Thus, her love life had many periods of celibacy marked by a few periods of intimacy with a regular partner.

Nonplussed but pleased by her confession that she'd never slept with another man meant to him that her relationships hadn't been close or deep enough, "Well, Ixta, I am glad to hear that, but if you had had many partners, that would have been alright with me too. We have discussed how my tribe is very casual about sex, haven't we?"

"Yes, but I just feel funny telling you that I'm not especially knowledgeable about other men's habits. I have had lovers but have never been this close with them."

"We have never talked about this before, but our custom is for sharing of seed to only happen in a mated, married pair. Once a pair is mated, they no longer join with other people by our custom. They are true to their mates. We do not share seed in casual relationships because it could result in conception and that is something carefully managed because of political alliances and our harsh winter weather cycle on Uturax. I imagine that sounds strange to you, but it is our custom. I have never shared seed with a woman before and spending the night with a woman is not part of our dating customs and expectations. Our joinings before marriage don't have much emotional attachment and are just superficial alliances for physical pleasure. I like waking up with you beside me, I mean on me," Nacón laughed as he slipped out of her and rolled her over to his side.

"Can we bathe before we eat breakfast? I, er, haven't noticed any baths or showers around here.

Where do we bathe? What happened to that tub they brought in before?"

Nacón laughed, wishing he could show Ixta a real bathing room, but until his father gave his approval, he would have to continue with the elaborate charade they played for every off-world group that visited Uturax. In moments like this, it seems ridiculous, but he would follow orders at least for a little while more.

"Let me call Nana to bring us a tub and water to bathe and I'll tell her that we will be eating right after bathing."

Before opening the door to the hut, Nacón brought out the small device he'd used last night to go all around the hut before they had gone to sleep. He repeated his actions of the night before and then opened the door and called out for Nana and the bath. In short order, the tub was brought into the hut first and then water by the bucket. When it was ready, Ixta got into the tub and washed her hair and body with Nacón helping her by pouring water over her hair to rinse out the sweet-smelling soap that Nana had brought. Then, Nacón helped her out of the crude tub and wrapped her in a length of soft, fluffy hand-woven cloth and then used the remaining buckets of fresh water to give himself a 'bucket bath.'

There was a knock on the door and Nana stuck her head in, "*Se puede entrar?* (May I come in?)"

"*Sí*, Nana. Pasa; pásale. (come in; come on in)" Nacón said and made a place on one of the tables for their food. He looked at Nana, nodded his head at the food and looked questioningly at Nana who smiled and said, "*Sí.*"

"Let's eat, Ixta; it's safe. Let's hope this breakfast goes better for you than the last one we ate here together."

"Don't even go there, Nacón. I don't want to relive those moments. I'm so glad that Chaac called Joss from the ship, and he was able to come with an antidote to the poison I'd been given. It scared me, Nacón. I don't want to lose our child, and I've decided that I'm sure as hell not ready to die. Let's eat."

This time, the fruit Ixta ate was sweet with no bitter aftertaste and it went down well and stayed down. Nacón and Ixta had an uneventful breakfast with Nana smiling indulgently at them. She seemed as happy for Nacón as he was about this marriage. Nana had almost given up hope that he would choose a woman as his mate. She felt he was past the time for the sexual alliances that never led anywhere. She wanted him to find a mate and secure the succession of Chaac's clan by fathering an heir or heirs. She had none of the reservations that Chaac had about upsetting the political balance on the planet with Nacón's marriage to an off-worlder. She liked Ixta and frankly didn't care about the politics among the royal families. She just wanted to see Nacón happy, and she had seen the happiness on his face when he was around Ixta and knew he was pleased that they were expecting a child together. He was so deliberate about his choices that she had initially been very surprised to hear that he and Chaac were going to the off-world ship to ask that Ixta marry him. She had seen Ixta around the planet talking with Nacón for months and they had seemed extremely comfortable together, enjoying each other's company. Nacón's friends had been talking about how he spent all his free time with that alien woman instead of hanging out with his friends as he always had before. Nana supposed she should have put more importance on those comments. She didn't like feeling like she was behind in all the information relating to Nacón whom she thought of as her adopted son. This campaign against Chaac and Nacón and now Ixta had her worried. It was no small event to attempt to assassinate members of the ruling royal family, worse even since Chaac had made that public announcement the night of the wedding about no harm coming to Ixta. Nana worried that worse times would come before this was all resolved. She would herself have to be more vigilant to protect them in any way she could.

Chapter 6: Revelations

After breaking their fast, Nacón sent one of his men to ask his father if he could speak with him privately this morning before he met with council. When the news came back that he could, Nacón turned to Ixta and said, "My wife, I must speak with my father alone. You will be safe here with Nana. Ulises leads the guard outside the door. He will be sure that nothing happens to you."

Puzzled, but figuring that it was just a regular happening for Nacón to have a private morning audience with his father, Ixta said, "Don't worry, Nacón. I'm sure we'll be fine here. Nana will teach me something useful about being an Uturaxan wife."

Nana was more than happy to stay to entertain Ixta and asked what she would like to learn.

"Nana. I want to start making some clothing for my child. Do you have sticks made for knitting or weaving fabric by hand and some soft yarn, the product from spinning wheels?"

After some questioning back and forth and Ixta drawing a picture on the ground to illustrate, Nana understood and called to Ulises to come inside. In rapid-fire Uturaxan, she told Ulises to send one of his men for the materials Ixta would need to knit: knitting sticks and soft yarn. Soon, Ixta was sitting with Nana on the floor, and both were casting on stitches for knitting projects. Nana was using very small knitting sticks and told Ixta she was making little foot casings.

"Oh, Nana, I call those 'booties. I'm going to make a little hooded sack for the baby to snuggle in. Later we can both make a blanket. This will be fun, and I hope I can remember. Did I tell you about the day that Nacón took me to the spinning hut, and I was able to spin some yarn? The fleece we were using was so soft, perfect for clothing next to the skin. I told him that day about my grandma who used to work with fleece and spin yarn. She taught me all the old skills to prepare and spin the yarn and how to knit. I never knew I would need all those things she taught me, or I might have paid more attention," Ixta said with a laugh.

"*Mi niña (my child)*, I think Nacón has made a good choice in his mate. You will be a good wife to my great-nephew and yes, we were all very surprised by your skills that day," Nana said, pleased with her latest discovery about Ixta, her skills and her willingness to learn and improve on those she already had.

Several hours later, Nacón returned to find Ixta and Nana sitting side by side and using some sticks to create small garments for the baby he supposed. They were chattering pleasantly, and he mused how it seemed Ixta had a knack for fitting in everywhere. He wondered what she would say when he took her to see his father, and he told her more about his planet and his people. Putting himself in her place, he would probably be furious for having been deceived and lied to by everyone she'd met on his planet. He only hoped he could make her see that his planet's safety was the reason for all the subterfuge.

"I'm glad to see both of you passing the time in such a productive manner. I hate to break this up. However, Chaac has granted us time to speak with him together."

Looking up in surprise at his entrance, Ixta said, "I didn't realize you were back. Look how much we've both gotten done this morning, Nacón. We are making things for the baby when he's born. What do you think?" Ixta held up her baby cocoon and Nana joined her with a pair of booties.

"Impressive. Just another thing I didn't know you could do. You never cease to amaze me, Ixta. Come. We need to go to Chaac's hut now. He has another meeting after ours."

Exiting their hut, Ixta was again struck by the level of security around them and the absence of people in the village. They were soon at Chaac's door and were ushered in. He was sitting on what Ixta called his throne chair and awaiting them.

"Good morning, Ixta. I want to thank you again for your vigilance last night. You saved our lives, and we are indebted to you."

Seeing Ixta's quiet smile of pleasure, he continued, "Now I have a question I must ask of you and want you to understand that you are the first and only off-worlder we have ever taken into our tribe as one of us. Contrary to what your captain has told you, there have been many ships that have come to Uturax over the years. We have tried to make alliances in the past but found betrayal at every turn. We are peaceful people who have become warriors to protect our own. Do you understand that?"

Stunned by Chaac's revelation, Ixta managed to say, "Er, yes, I guess so. I thought Nacón told me that we were the first off-worlders. I'm not sure what to think. My question for you is if anything I've been told about Uturax and its people is true?"

"Fair question, Ixta," Chaac responded. "My answer is that very little of what you think you know and have learned about Uturax in these past six months is true. You were allowed to see what we tell off-worlders who come to our planet." Seeing her poorly disguised look of anger quickly move across her face before it became neutral again, he added, "Let me assure you that this has been necessary. Our safety has depended on not revealing our secrets. I think on your world, you call it national security. What my son has told you is what I have instructed him to do to protect our planet and our people. Do you understand that?"

"Do you mean that everybody here has lied to me?"

"Simply put. Yes," Chaac responded, awaiting the inevitable next question.

"Is this whole thing about my marriage to Nacón a sham also? Is my pregnancy not real? I know I have a life growing in me!"

Nacón stepped up beside her and reached to take her arm, but Ixta stepped away, shrugging off his arm, wanting to put distance between them. "You! Were all those sweet words you said to me about caring for me and our unborn child lies too? Is that part of this elaborate charade to con a crew member from the ship here to get more information from them, from me? I've been honest and shared information with you without the need for deception. I can't believe this is happening?' Ixta said between clenched teeth, angry and exasperated. She briefly considered slapping Nacón but felt that wouldn't solve anything and maybe piss off both him and Chaac. Clearly what she needed was a cool head and more information. Trying to bring her emotions under control, she still felt stupid, a fool.

Chaac looked at his son and said in rapid Uturaxan, *"Mi'jo. Qué esperabas? Claro que se siente usada, traicionada y confundida. Tienes que convencerla de tus sentimientos verdaderos."*(My son. What did you expect? Of course, she feels used, betrayed, and confused. You have to convince her of your real feelings.)

Nodding briefly at his father, Nacón said earnestly, "Ixta, you must believe this. The feelings we share are real and I have never said anything to you about my feelings that is untrue. I am proud and happy that we are expecting a child together. Never doubt that."

Somewhat mollified, Ixta said, "Well, what has changed that you've decided to tell me this now? I'm still the off-worlder I was a few days ago." She directed her look at Chaac, challenging him to answer, but concerned about what she might hear next.

Chaac answered her dryly saying, "That's not quite true, Ixta. Since then, you have become pregnant with the next heir to the royal family that leads this planet, and you saved our lives last night."

"Shit!. You mean that a baby and some quick thinking and head bashing suddenly made me worthy of your secrets? Please. I'm no fool. At least I didn't think I was."

"Yes, that's exactly what I mean. But I have a question for you. Do you plan on making your life here with Nacón or would you leave here if you had the chance?"

Nacón and Chaac both looked at Ixta closely, wondering what her answer would be. Nacón hoped that she would choose Uturax and him, but realistically her new life had been forced upon her by her captain and Chaac and he couldn't blame her if she chose to leave. He hoped she would choose him because he didn't know what he would do if she didn't. He cared about her and there was also the concern of her pregnancy with the Uturaxan heir.

"Maybe the captain didn't make it perfectly clear to y'all, but I have no choice but to stay here. If I don't, I will be put in prison and taken back to Earth for trial and a dishonorable discharge from the armed services."

Persisting, Chaac said, "Yes, we understand all of that, but IF you could, would you choose to leave us and return to your home?"

"Well, I can imagine anything, can't I? What is there here for me?"

Both Chaac and Nacón looked disappointed in her answer and Chaac started to speak, "If that is the case, . . ."

"Wait a minute, sir. You didn't let me finish. That wasn't a real question, but a prelude to what I want to tell you. Let me tell you what is here for me assuming that Nacón's words about caring for me are true and I hope they are: a husband who seems to like me a lot and wants to protect and take care of me and a baby that we would share as parents is what I have here. Back on Earth, I have no one. My parents died years ago, my grandma whom I dearly loved is gone too. I have some friends, but no one there is special to me. My whole life was the crew and the ship. Now my transgressions in their eyes have taken that life from me. There is nothing of my old life that I want or need. Here, I have hope to be happy.

Since I've been here, it's been scary; I almost lost my life in an assassination attempt, and I've had the feeling that y'all have been holding out on me. I know there are secrets about Uturax that no one has told me yet, but I've been happy with Nacón and Nana has been so nice to me. These are things I haven't had in a long time, or ever really. It means a lot to feel like I could have a family again here on Uturax. Do you need me to say more about why I

choose Uturax? I can go on if you need me to," Ixta
finished in a rush as she realized that the reason's
she'd just listed off the top of her head were real. She
had been without family for so long that she wistfully
hoped that the life she hoped for here with Nacón
would come true.

Chaac felt relieved at her answer though his face
indicated no emotion and said, "No. That will be
sufficient. I am glad that you choose Uturax. Now, I
ask you to forswear this oath to me: "I, Ixta Tikal de
Palenque, do swear to never reveal the secrets of
Uturax and its people to anyone. I would add that
there could be occasions where I or Nacón would
give you permission to break your oath but not until
then."

Looking at both strangely, Ixta nevertheless
complied and repeated the oath, wondering what
she'd gotten herself into now. She hoped this didn't
end badly for her like her life-changing romp in the
jungle had done for her a few nights ago. *'Shit. What
have I got to lose? I have no people, no country, no
family other than Nacón and his world.'*

"Excellent. You may both go now back to your
hut and Nacón will tell you some information that
may help you understand more about Uturax and its
people. Go now. I have council members coming to
go over last-minute details. In two hours, we will
execute Kennan and we want to prepare in case any
of the other *Sin Raíces traitors* want to cause any
more trouble.

*'Crap, another execution. There sure is a lot of
bloodshed here.'* She wasn't used to seeing heads roll
daily. Clearly, she'd been sheltered. She had thought

herself a seasoned traveler who had faced everything, but her preparation didn't include the level of violence on a daily basis that she was now experiencing. Just another example of her life having been lived in such a limited fashion as far as she was concerned. Interplanetary travel was no longer as perilous as it had been in the early days when territories and alliances were claimed and formed. Thus, Ixta had seen almost no battle time and what she had seen had been on the fringes helping Joss care for the wounded soldiers so they could return to fight while she and Joss waited for the next wave of injured to arrive at the M.A.S.H. (mobile army surgical hospital) tent. Come to think of it, why had it always been MASH meaning "army" since they were navy? I guess MSSH was too unpronounceable.

Arriving back at their hut, Ixta looked at a strangely silent Nacón. She looked up at his face expectantly wanting to once and for all clarify facts and details since her preconceived conclusions had all proved wrong. It seemed that every day brought new examples of her lack of competence as an anthropologist. She decided she would just have to try to put her ego aside, get over her feelings of foolishness and betrayal, make the best of it and move forward.

"Ixta, I just don't know where to start. I would first ask that you not be angry with me, please. I have not told you all about my people for the safety of our tribe and our village. Too often in the past, off-worlders have come as you did saying one thing and meaning something entirely different."

"Wait a minute! Other off-worlders? That's what

Chaac was referring to by "others." You told me we
were the first. That was a lie. You told me lies!"

"Stop, a minute, Ixta. Yes, I lied to you, but it was
for my planet's safety. I already told you that. Can't
you understand that?"

"I feel like a complete asshole! Just what of all
that you told me was true? Was any of it? You have
to understand now why all of what you have told me
is in question. I need to hear that part again where
you assure me you weren't lying to me about our
future and our child. Was the part where you pledged
yourself to me for all our days real? Am I really your
wife or is that another lie? Where am I to go? What
about my baby?" Ixta said in a rush, angry and
concerned about her baby's future, her resolve to
suck it up and move forward quickly forgotten.

Nacón thought he'd already answered this doubt
of Ixta's in his father's hut, but clearly it had all been
too much to take in at once. Sighing softly, he said,
"Ixta, all of that was true. I have pledged myself to
you and now to our child for all my days. I do care
about you. The lies were only about my culture, my
people, not about my feelings for you and our future
together," Nacón said as he reached for her.

Ixta sidestepped him and looked up in his face
again. "You do pledge to care for me and my child. Is
that much true?"

"Yes, but the pledge is for you and **our** child. We
made this baby together. When I shared my seed with
you, I was wrong not to consult you, but I had chosen
you for my mate. That was all I could think about
that night. To use a word you seem to like, 'shit' is
how I feel about deceiving you."

In spite of herself, Ixta smiled at his odd use of one of her most frequent swear words and looked up at his face again to gauge his reaction, "Just so you understand that I don't like being lied to. We said we were going to be honest and try to build a relationship. Was that true?"

"Yes. Completely. I hope to form a marriage with you like my father had with my mother. She also was brave and strong of conviction. Theirs was a love match and I would want the same for us. Do you think you can work at my side in this manner?'

Ixta felt reassured by Nacón's words and what he'd said was quite romantic. What woman wouldn't want a love, even lust, match with this man? Alien or not, he was like the man of her dreams even though she'd given up dreaming about finding him years back. She'd resigned herself to always being a space bum wedded to her work. Her future had looked bleak in terms of her chances for a husband and children. Now, he was holding this promise out to her about the kind of marriage every little girl on Earth still dreamed about. *'Whoa, let's not get ahead of ourselves. Let's clarify a few more details about what he hasn't told you. What I told them before is still true. I have nothing left back on Earth and lost the right to be part of the crew here. I hope he's being honest with me now.'*

"Nacón, what else were you going to tell me about your planet that you couldn't before?" she said sweetly.

Nacón wasn't fooled by her tone and knew her ego was bruised, and she felt foolish. However, he felt he had to at least make a start to rectify the situation with her. "Ixta, we are not as simple as we may seem to your crew. It is a defensive disguise to protect ourselves. While your crew is still here, however, we must continue the charade."

"What do you mean? Could you give me an example?"

Instead of talking, Nacón decided a demonstration was in order. He touched the large gem on the amulet armband he and the others always wore, giving it a twist, and immediately, he was standing before Ixta unmasked, no longer the fur-covered alien she was accustomed to seeing.

"Shit! Well, I'll be damned," Ixta said as she reached out to touch him more astonished than angry at discovering his disguise and finally seeing him as he really was.

Instead of avoiding her touch as he usually did, Nacón let her run her hands up and down his arms and over his chest. She then reached up to touch his face. Her fingers ran over his body, enjoying the feel of it. He was no longer covered in fur as he'd always appeared to be before. Except for his massive size he looked like most Earth men except his body was in excellent condition. She enjoyed feeling his muscles beneath the smooth skin. *'Well, this IS a surprise. A nice surprise. Who woulda' thought?'*

"Well, that sure is a surprise. I think I like this new look for you though I was ready to go for the old one if you'll remember."

"That is something that I admired about you, Ixta. You accepting me even though I looked like a furry beast told me about you and your values. It never stopped you from becoming my friend and sharing your ideas with me. I respect that in you. You were not allowed to touch me before because the disguise is visual only. I think you call them holographs. Actually, I was surprised that you hadn't figured that one out when we joined our bodies."

"I have to admit that I was too involved in the moment to worry about the details except the ones directly related to my sexual pleasures and yours. At some point, all I wanted to do was come and I think you did too. Obviously, you weren't too worried about discovery, or you would have never let me on your body, under your body and put my mouth around your body."

Nacón listened to Ixta's describing recent sexual encounters between them and his mind, he had to admit, was starting to wander from the task at hand. As her hands wandered over his belly, he felt his penis start to swell. Forcing himself to focus on the talk he was trying to have, he said, "Ixta, you have seen some of our regular weapons which are much more advanced and complicated than the ones we showed to your crew. Our goal was to have them think of us as primitives. We also understand and speak your language and that of many of the other trading nations but take care not to reveal this as a defensive tactic. Your crew and others are often unguarded in their comments when they believe we're beneath them in intelligence and civilization. By listening in on these conversations, we are able to protect ourselves. Does this make sense?'

"I hate to but have to agree with you. It's an ingenious ploy for your planet and culture's safety and very clever. O.K. Let me get this straight: you're not hairy though you are tall; you have advanced weaponry; you're multilingual. Anything else?"

"There are many more details, but I won't go into them today. As they arise, I will disclose them to you if that meets your approval?"

"Fair enough. You speak English as well as I do now that you're talking to me normally. I can't believe you let me muddle through trying to communicate with you when you could speak my language. I don't see how that was playing fair. I thought we were friends."

"We were and are, but our planet's and my people's safety had to come first. Our culture and its safety have always come before individual wants and desires. I hope you can understand that."

"For now, I guess I must, but it still makes me feel like a fool and nobody likes that. How much time do we have before the next execution? I'm asking to see if we have any free time left," Ixta asked playfully, her eyes focusing on the bulge in Nacón's kilt that was swelling as she watched, tenting the fabric in front over his erection. She figured that arguing any longer had no purpose and she enjoyed sharing their bodies as much as Nacón and if losing herself in another activity was ever needed, this was certainly the time for a distraction.

"About two hours."

"Can you lock up this hut, so no one disturbs us?" Ixta asked as she looked up at Nacón. Already turned on by her fingers as they had explored his body, Nacón quickly swept the perimeter of his hut and then turned to find Ixta already disrobed. He wondered if they were making new biological rules for their species in their intense sexual interest in each other. He stopped to look at her and was surprised to watch her cup her breasts and then look him over at him, meeting his eyes after removing her undergarments. Nacón hurried over to her side to see if he could help her in the process. He came up before her and sank on his knees, grabbing her by the waist. She was a visual feast to him after discovering how much he enjoyed making love with her.

Before he had time to decide where he wanted to start his strategic assault on her body, she put her hand down between her folds in the triangle of red, curly hair. He felt like she was highlighting areas for him to focus on in the next moments. She drew her fingers out and then placed her hands on her waist, one on each side, as she squared off to stand facing him as if challenging him to make the next move. Nacón grabbed her hand and brought it near his face. She watched him softly sniff her scent in an act that seemed very primal to her. Then he put first one and then the other two fingers that smelled of her scent in his mouth and sucked on them till he moved to kiss his way up her arm to then nuzzle her neck.

He gently laid her down on the furs and then quickly removed his kilt and loincloth which was straining with his erection. Taking a moment to put his mouth where her hand had been, he first gently and then with more enthusiasm sucked on her clit. Ixta squirmed under him, reaching down to clasp his head closer to her pussy, opening her legs even more to him. Nacón built her sexual tension in that moment, licking and sucking on her and then leaving her unfulfilled, just beginning to get hot, moved up her body to grab her nipples in his mouth, first one, then the other. She may have been sensitive, but he couldn't tell from her response as she thrust her breasts up higher into his mouth while writhing under him. His thigh was pushed high between her legs, and he could feel her moist readiness for him.

Nacón let go of her breasts and moved up to press a kiss to her lips. Ixta thrust her tongue in his mouth and began sucking on his as he joined his mouth with hers, tasting her sex in his mouth. While engaged in the mating of their mouths, Nacón reached down and caressed Ixta's red triangle of hair a moment, feeling her push it into his hand, rocking a little to increase the pressure of the contact. Then he inserted first one and then another finger inside of her, enjoying the wet warmth.

Saying, "Stay with me, wife," Nacón rolled her over on her belly, pulling several furs beneath her to raise up her posterior. He mounted her from behind, reaching around to find her clitoris, her center of pleasure, to ensure that he kept her actively involved in the moment. From their few encounters, he knew she preferred to look at him but wanted to share a more common Uturaxan form of mating with her today.

He leaned over her, massaging her while he thrust in and out of her vagina in a steady rhythm. His other hand reached around to her left breast, and he found the nipple extending beneath his fingers as he explored it as it had done for her moments before when she had caressed her breasts. He had never seen a woman touch herself quite in that way with such a challenging look and found it had driven him crazy

with desire for her. Later he would wonder why that
simple act had been so erotic to him. He nuzzled her
neck and back, kissing her shoulders in his tour of her
body. All the while, he kept up his massage and the
penetration and then retreat from her pussy. Finally,
both were gasping, and Ixta was as ready to come as
was Nacón. He shuddered his release as he ejaculated
into her, and she came in a rush. She felt him touch
the edge of her womb and the sensations were
enough to cause her to climax again. Nacón gently
withdrew and laid her over on her side so he could lie
down beside her and mold his body to hers. He
congratulated himself on having gotten through the
first hurdle of undoing all the lies he'd told her
through the months. This day's talk had ended very
well, and he thought he would enjoy each talk even
more if they all ended like today's had.
Remembering to set the timer for an hour's nap,
Nacón soon joined Ixta in sleep to awaken to the
alarm all too soon.

"What's that noise?' Ixta groaned, rolling over to
lean on her elbows so she could look at Nacón.

"That's the alarm. I know you have those on your
ship. You've mentioned them before. I'm afraid we
have just enough time to wash up, get dressed and
then head over to the tribunal area for the execution.
This is what I have heard you call a power nap.
Come, let me show you something."

"Forget what I said, this doesn't feel like it gave
me much power."

Nacón led her to the corner of the hut, pressed
something on the handheld control he had in his hand
and a very modern looking, even futuristic bathroom

with shower appeared, materializing out of the wall where it had been camouflaged. He stepped into the enclosure and pulled Ixta in beside him.

"You mean I've been struggling with medieval toilet facilities when all this was hiding right under my nose? I don't know whether to be pissed off at you again or just grateful to finally have a real shower. I'd better not have to go on a chamber pot again. With all this hardware, I should be able to take a shit and shower in peace without the primitive approach again."

Nacón laughed, glad that Ixta seemed willing to accept that she had a modern bathroom right under her nose without further discussion or a renewal of their previous argument. They quickly showered mindful of their limited time before having to leave the hut. When Nacón wanted to get too enthusiastic in his scrubbing of her back and then chest, Ixta laughed and grabbed the soap from him. She scrubbed his back and then pushed on his shoulder to turn him around and after scrubbing down his chest said, "You'd better do the rest, or we will never get out of here."

Nacón laughed again, agreeing that they had a schedule to keep and mentally planned on resuming this activity later. He didn't know when he'd laughed as much as he had since marrying Ixta. The introduction of soap and water into their sex play would prove to be fun for both. After showering, Nacón hit another button, punched in a code and the sprays of water were replaced with a blast of air, not too hot, not too cold.

"Nacón, you'd better not hold out on me on more of

these modern conveniences. I know. I have to keep this a secret from my crew should I see them or have the chance to talk to any of them."

Pleased that she understood that she was now part of the secret and honor bound to keep it, Nacón put aside his worries about her reaction when she really understood the extent of their subterfuge. He only hoped she would be as accepting as she had been today. Once she'd gotten over feeling foolish, she had seemed to understand the reasoning behind their tribe's decision.

Stepping out of their hut, Ixta was reminded that things were not all idyllic and simple here when she saw Nacón's guard assemble around them.

Now that he was "uncloaked," his guards looked at him in surprise. "She knows. Chaac approves," Nacón said in way of explanation and watched as they grabbed their amulets and looked at him questioningly. When Nacón nodded his agreement, his guard also shut off their holograms and Ixta was surprised by the change in the features of each man. She, however, said nothing and looked up at Nacón to see what was next. He grabbed her elbow to guide her along, always the gentleman with her, protective and solicitous. They arrived at the tribunal amphitheater within moments and saw that many of the same faces that had been at the last tribunal gathering had returned. Ixta's gaze went up to the upper rows and saw many sullen faces there interspersed among others who looked eager for the proceedings to begin.

Chaac walked up with his heavily armed escort and took his seat in the ornate ceremonial chair as he had before. He reached for his amulet to dial the gem to appear before the assembled people who were in costume as they were all here as their furry counterparts. However, since Ixta knew their secret about their physical appearance, he saw no reason not to appear as his natural self. Chaac turned the amulet and then he hit the ground with his staff. The sunlight streaming through the foliage lit up the area and Ixta noticed the gems twinkling as the suns' rays hit the heavily gem encrusted staff. She was surprised to see that Chaac was younger than she had imagined. Seeing him in this light, he looked different than on previous occasions to her for some reason. Apparently, he'd married in his twenties because she judged him to be fifty or perhaps in his mid-fifties. She wondered if she would recognize all the people she'd previously met while they were disguised by their holograms. She noted that when Chaac had deactivated his hologram, so had the crowd. Chaac hit the ground again with his staff as there were still a few murmurings from the seats above. Instantly, silence fell. The crowd and the elders all looked at Chaac expectantly.

"For any of you who do not know what happened, last night, a *Sin Raíces* rebel Kennan Eisenberg Ramírez entered my hut during a council meeting without invitation with a stun rod drawn and set on "kill." Additionally, he carried an explosive belt to cause more harm and destruction." It was only through the quick thinking of my daughter-by-marriage that my son and I are here to tell this story. Any of our royal family or council members who were meeting at that time could have been killed or injured. Kennan confessed that his intent was murder, and we determined that there was no further information to be gathered through a tribunal. Uturaxans, what say you? Is there any among you who wants to see a full tribunal conducted? Speak up now or forever lose that right."

Chaac paused and looked up at the crowd assembled. Silence reigned. Nacón stood beside his seat and scanned the crowd. The silence continued and became almost painful as if people were holding their breath to see what would happen next. Finally, one of the elder women raised her voice and said, "Off with his head! Off with his head!" Her words were quickly taken up as the crowd chanted along with her. Chaac allowed the chanting to continue a while and then raised his staff and quickly brought it down on the rock floor with a crack.

"It is so decided. My son, your woman has shown great courage and a remarkable quickness in her thinking. If she would prefer, she can carry out the sentence of death. What think you?"

Without having to look at Ixta for her answer, Nacón said, "As your son and daughter, we thank you for that respect you show us. However, this is a sentence I would ask that you allow me to carry out, Father."

Ixta thought she understood that Chaac was offering her the option of personally chopping off the head of the man bound beside them and hoped that she was wrong. She was horrified at the thought of it. Shooting rounds into a target dummy were very far removed from killing a person right in front of her by cutting off his head no less. *I'll never be able to pull*

this off. Shit! She was relieved when Nacón said he
wanted that honor.

Chaac considered or pretended to consider for a
moment and then said, "Nay, son. After more
thought, I say that it is something that as leader, I
must do. This has gone too far. Much too far. Let the
rebels understand that our way of living is not going
to end or change to meet their demands. If they
choose to continue, they will all suffer this same fate
when caught. Give me your sword."

Nacón stepped over beside his father and handed
him his personal sword which was more of a
broadsword with an axe on one end. Chaac grasped
the heavy weapon from his son and stepped over to
Kennan and said, "You have brought dishonor to
your family. Before last night, your family was
known for good works in our tribe with a long history
of service. You have shamed them."

Unable to respond because his mouth was covered
with a band, Kennan could only look at Chaac with
anger smoldering in his eyes. He sat there, resigned,
his eyes opening wide suddenly as Chaac swung the
sword and cut through his neck swiftly. When his
head remained atop his neck, Chaac used the tip of
the sword to give it a nudge and then it rolled off and
onto the ground.

Ixta relaxed once it was over, relaxing her fingers
that she'd tightly gripped into fists at her sides.
*'Christ almighty! Two in less than a week. For what I
thought was a peaceful, idyllic place, a hell of a lot of
violence happens here. Good God! This is the place
where I'm going to bring up my child. My father-in-
law just lopped off someone's head. Granted this*

asshole came in that hut intent on killing at least some of us. I guess if you live by violence you die by violence. Shit!' She didn't know if she was getting used to this level of violence but found it didn't seem as horrific as Camila's execution a few days ago. *'This is as bad as any campaign I've been on off-world. Too up close and personal. Christ, if I understood him right, Chaac was asking if I wanted to do the honors. For once, I'm glad my man took charge of that situation. I hope I won't be expected to participate in one of those executions any time soon.'*

Lost in her thoughts, Ixta was startled when Nacón grabbed her by the elbow to escort her out of the tribunal area. She noticed that Chaac had already left, heavily guarded. She and Nacón were quickly surrounded by their own heavily armed troop as they followed Chaac's contingent back to his hut.

As they were just arriving, they heard a commotion before they even got into the clearing. Out of the corner of her eye, she noticed that everyone activated their holograms in that instant. When they moved from the thickly growing plants on the path into the clearing near Chaac's hut, they saw that some of the men from the perimeter guard were holding someone prisoner. The prisoner was yelling and struggling violently. Ixta saw his face and then exclaimed, "That's Ethan, from the ship!"

Nacón looked at her and then at Ethan in surprise and then moved up to the group of soldiers. By then Chaac and the council had stepped out of his hut to see what all the noise was about.

In the space of a few days, all chaos had broken out on their usually peaceful planet, and this promised to be another situation to deal with that looked to have negative consequences. The council members had almost resigned expressions on their faces.

"Diego, tell me why you have a Terran in your custody who has a knife stuck in his leg."

"We found him near the older mines already wounded. He was muttering something about, "By God, I'll have those diamonds. Those diamonds will be mine.""

"The rest of our perimeter patrol found Yesenia Tenoch Tatanka-Iyotake on the paths on her way back to our village and they should be arriving any moment. She can better tell you the details of why she put her knife in this man's leg."

Just then Yesenia burst into the clearing, running with a soldier on each side of her. Their long legs easily covered the distance to the area where Chaac was. She stopped suddenly when she saw Ethan and then purposefully walked over to him, spat on him and slapped his face."

Ethan lunged, struggling against being held but stopped when he was given a touch from the stun rod in Diego's hand.

"Permission to speak, my lord. Please let me tell you what this man did!" Yesenia begged, clearly upset.

Chaac nodded at her, and all listened to Yesenia recount her tale. "I was looking for samples for my biology report in the jungle near the old mines. This man surprised me and then grabbed me. He said, 'Tell me where the diamonds are. I have to find the diamonds before the captain comes looking. I want some for me, just me. I know there are plenty for all of us. Tell me now!' and he had kind of a wild look in his eyes."

When I just looked at him and shook my head, he grabbed me and said, "Well, if I can't have the gems and you won't help me, I'll have you," and then he kissed me hard on the side of my face. He would have kissed me on my mouth, but I turned my head in time. He was gross! I'm going to be fourteen this winter, but I haven't started kissing yet or even thought much about it. Let alone with this ugly Terran monster. As soon as he did that, I pulled my knife and stuck him as hard as I could on his leg. He started to squeal and let me go and I ran. Then part of the guard ran in and grabbed him, and some came running after me. I could hear them as I started running back to the village."

Faces grew grave as the import of what Ethan might have planned to do to the adolescent girl became clear. Anger was reflected on all their faces. Chaac looked at Ixta and asked gravely, "Is this customary Terran behavior? Do you routinely assault children?"

"No! Ethan must have lost his mind. Terrans do not accost and assault young girls, at least most do not. When that does happen, the punishment is severe. Every Terran male knows better than to accost a young girl. I'm so sorry. I know Ethan to be impulsive, but never before vicious and cruel and capable of attempting such a vile crime."

"Very well. Diego, take this man to the holding hut and prevent him from saying any more. I tire of his whining cries over there. Bind him tightly and place a guard. I do not want retaliation against him at this point. Yesenia, girl, are you alright? Did he do more than what you have described? Do not be afraid to tell us all. There is no shame in the telling."

"No, sir. When I stabbed him and he relaxed his arms, I ran before he could do me more harm."

Looking to Chaac for permission to speak which he received with a nod, Nacón said, "You make us proud today, Yesenia. You acquitted yourself as befits a warrior in training. Well done. A warrior travels prepared and your preparedness and bravery in a difficult situation saved your life today."

Yesenia blushed and then looked again at Ethan and spat again, but on the ground this time. "May I go home now, sirs?"

Chaac nodded and said, "Dismissed, soldier. Good job."

Chaac motioned for the council, Nacón and Ixta to join him inside his hut and then said, "I fear this is going to get much bigger before it's over. I think the ship's doctor should be brought here to check this man to be sure that he's all right. I don't want to have to explain to Wells that our men hurt him today in the scuffle. The issues should remain separate and clear. Also, I would like to try to verify what he said about the captain looking for diamonds. That is concerning to me. This man Ethan was armed and up to no good. It was expected that at some point, the off-worlders would notice the gems we wear and are on our ceremonial things like my staff. Their greed always surfaces."

Ixta said to Nacón, "I wonder what this is about. I've only been gone a little while and I never heard anything about searching for gems while I was still on the crew. I think the captain would have said something to me or Ethan about it because we were always here exploring. Oh, maybe he didn't in front of me because Nacón and I spent so much time together he was afraid you and I were friends, and he couldn't trust me with that kind of information."

"Yes, I think you're right. Ulises go bring the ship's doctor. Say we want him to check a problem with Ixta's pregnancy. I am afraid that I will have to go talk to Wells tonight, but I will not board his ship as I fear they would try to kill me right then. They will probably have noticed by then that Ethan is missing. Very quickly this has gotten out of control."

Ulises took several of his men and turned to head to the ship to see if he could fetch the doctor. However, as he was midway on the jungle path, he met up with the ship's doctor who was heavily loaded with equipment. Returning much sooner than anyone expected, Chaac and his group were told that their guest had arrived.

"Well, Doctor. That was sooner than expected," Chaac greeted him, surprised that he had almost miraculously appeared as Ulises had left just moments ago.

"I met your men on my way toward your village from the ship and they helped me carry some of my gear. I was in a hurry to get here to talk to you before anything happened. I sent word to Wells that I needed to check some things about Ixta's pregnancy for my research. I was able to leave without incident."

"What is your reason for coming to our village? In a moment I will tell you why we were going to request your presence here."

"Last night, I was in the mess hall eating a late dinner when I overhead first mate Justin Daniels talking with some of his mates about the captain's plan to loot the mines. The mess hall, our eating area, is not that large and sound carries very well. Apparently, he'd had too much to drink and too little food because he's usually not one to talk over much, especially about things the captain has told him to keep quiet about. He had an interested audience as he went over the captain's plans to locate the gem mines and loot them. Any conversation that had been going on soon stopped as virtually everyone there stopped to listen to what he was talking about. The captain figured that if your people wore gems as a routine part of their dress, there must be plenty of them here that would sell for quite a lot of money in any market, legitimate or the black market. Daniels spoke at great length about the surprise attack that is planned with a 'take no prisoners policy' in effect. He said that Ethan, the biologist, was going out this morning to do some scouting to try to locate some of the mines."

"Why are you telling us this information, Doctor? You are betraying your captain with your words," Chaac inquired frostily, unsure of the doctor's motives and not feeling inclined to trust any of the ship's crew at this point.

"That I am, sir. But I did not sign on as doctor to this ship to loot other planets and kill alien races which is what my captain clearly has planned. What he is planning is in violation of all the rules of this voyage and the Interstellar Planetary Exploration Consortium. I am not Terran, however, and apparently my race has a different view of honor and what is right. If I must betray my ship to try to save lives in a greedy, dishonorable takeover, so be it."

Nacón first looked over at his father and the doctor and said, "We told you when you saved my wife's life that you had a home here should you ever need or want it. Are you asking for sanctuary here with us?"

Joss looked serious but was glad that Nacón had brought up the only remaining concern he had which was where he could go now. "Yes, I would ask for sanctuary here on Uturax. I hope that my skills as a physician could be of some service to you."

Chaac was surprised by Joss's request and the exchange between his son and the doctor. When he'd made the offer after Joss had saved Ixta's life, he hadn't expected to see the doctor here asking for sanctuary so soon nor having to deal with an impending coup by the ship's captain. Shaking his head at the strange twists and turns of this off-worlder ship's visit, he sent the doctor outside so he could confer with his advisors and to ask Ixta what she knew of the doctor.

Feeling that the walls of the hut were closing in on her, Ixta stepped forward. She had no idea that Wells would be that despicable and dishonorable. Everything was taking a violent turn everywhere she looked. People she thought she knew well were clearly operating out of the boundaries of the personal guidelines she thought defined them. At least Joss seemed to be still on the same page that she expected him to be. "The doctor is a friend of mine, a very fair man who is skilled as a doctor. He is always calm and brings much experience from previous voyages as well as his preparation on Argentia. I admire and respect him. He does not lie and values the truth above all. Evidently it is a core Argentian value."

Nacón added, "We cannot forget that he saved Ixta's life and my unborn son's life as well. That he comes from the ship is not something to be held against him. He is not Terran, and he came of his own free will and offered us information that is very useful to us, especially after apprehending Ethan a little while ago. His information fills in the gaps in what Yesenia told us that Ethan said."

"I agree, son, but we must be cautious."

"Yes, Chaac. Off-worlders cannot be trusted. That is evident. Yet another ship has come to try to rape our planet and kill our people," one of the council interjected, concern on her face.

Nacón said earnestly, "Do not say that all off-worlders cannot be trusted. That is too broad a statement. Recall that my wife saved all our lives when Kennan tried to kill us all right here in this hut. Has that been forgotten so soon?" Nacon growled, angry that Ixta could be considered as unworthy of their trust.

"Apologies, my prince. Of course, your wife has proven her loyalty to us. She has proven worthy to be your bonded mate. However, we must be cautious, and we do not know this doctor. But it speaks well of him that he has come to offer us insight into the plot against us. I do not see that as a betrayal of his people, but an effort to be rational and righteous."

"Let us put this to a vote. All indicate their approval of granting sanctuary to the Argentian doctor by raising your right hand," Chaac said as he raised his hand.

With a few grumblings, the rest of the council joined with approval of granting asylum to Joss. When brought back to the council hut, his expression was clearly one of relief when he was told he could stay as he did not want to return to the ship after what he had learned they were plotting. If the Uturaxans had not chosen to grant him sanctuary, he would have had few options this far away from civilization and trading routes. There would be no ship tomorrow or the next week or month for him to buy passage on to return to Argentia. He looked around the hut at the people present. Other than Ixta's and Nacón's smiles and looks of acceptance he saw only wariness and suspicion on Chaac's and the other council members' faces. He saw that he would have to prove his loyalty and usefulness to Uturax and its people before he could win acceptance from its people. *'Not an unfair expectation on their part,'* he figured. *'It seems I'm always in a situation of having to prove myself ever since I left Argentia. Ahhh.'*

Ixta wasn't sure what protocol was, but she squeezed Nacón's arm and smiled up at him, pleased that Joss had been accepted. Nacón looked down at her and they shared a look of agreement as he, too, was pleased that the Council had backed up Chaac's original offer to the doctor of a home here on Uturax should he ever want it. Honestly, he didn't think the doctor had expected to take them up on it and he certainly hadn't thought a crisis would arise so soon that would provoke the doctor into asking for asylum. He had been surprised when his father made the offer as his own mind was still taken up with Ixta's brush with death. When he heard Chaac's words, he felt the rightness of them in that moment and was glad his father had thought to make that offer.

Nacón was also pleased that he had judged the man, rather the Argentian, correctly based on very little information. He knew him only superficially but had spent a little time with him on the information gathering excursions prior to the medical rescue mission of his wife. Joss would sometimes come with Ixta and Ethan or instead of Ethan to gather samples. He had also met other biologists who came in Ethan's stead if he was occupied on the ship. While Joss wasn't a warrior, he was fit and Nacón found him funny. He enjoyed his sense of humor and way of finding amusing things to comment on while watching Ixta and Ethan pick through the ruins of Uturax. Once he'd investigated the local plants in the area and taken samples he felt he could use, he would usually wander over near Nacón and his men and begin his running commentary of how odd it was to be picking through what was probably the garbage of early Uturax. He also found Ethan to be less than a man and had little to say that was positive about this Terran, an assessment that Nacón shared.

Nacón had looked forward to the days spent with Joss and felt they would have been friends in other circumstances. Nacón felt that his intuition about Joss had served him well because this alliance had already provided the Uturaxans with a tactical advantage to what was about to unfold. Nacón surveyed the room and saw much of what Joss had seen but knowing the members well, he could read beneath their expressions. At this point, the council was solidly behind Chaac and his decisions. The reluctance that some had shown about accepting the doctor's request for sanctuary was only superficial. No one had expressed real concern or dismay about Chaac's support for acceptance of the doctor's request. That was good for his family, and he felt also for the safety of his people. If the *Sin Raíces* group was stepping up its treasonous activities and the Terrans were planning an attack, then a united ruling coalition was beneficial to Chaac's ultimate success. It was strategically possible to fight on several fronts at once, but hopefully not more than one. Having political bickering behind the scenes would only slow down the fight. Nacón would lead the army in whatever was required, but he felt reassured knowing that his father wouldn't have to divide his concentration on internal power struggles within his council simultaneously.

Nacón asked Joss to follow him out of his father's hut and said, "You will stay in temporary quarters with my men till we find you a more permanent setup. Will that meet your needs?"

"Ha! Any kind of roof over my head will meet my needs. I appreciate that you and your people granted me asylum as I really don't know what I would have done knowing what I know about Wells' plan to attack and loot your planet. I'm not that good an actor to pretend that I agree with something that morally wrong." He looked at his watch and noted with surprise that the suns had risen high in the sky and afternoon was almost over.

"Ixta, would it be possible to get something to eat or maybe you could tell me when the next meal is?' Joss looked at Ixta hopefully.

Smiling, "You always have been a chow hound, doc. Dinner will be served in an hour. I don't know yet if there will be something ceremonial."

"If not, the doctor may eat with us, Ixta. We will tell him once we hear plans from my father."

"Perfect. I suppose there's still time for a little rest?" Ixta asked questioningly. She felt tired after all the excitement of the day. Each day was more filled with events and disasters than the last and she couldn't ever seem to get caught up on her sleep. She supposed it was the pregnancy, her hormonal body requiring more rest.

"If it wouldn't look undignified, I'd race you to our hut," Nacón said laughing.

Joss watched the interchange and was happy to see that Ixta and Nacón had an easy, friendly relationship. He had wondered if the shotgun wedding would produce rancor and distance between the two, but apparently the opposite was true. They seemed extremely comfortable with each other, teasing each other gently.

To the surprise of both, Ixta turned and took off running, Joss supposed toward her hut. Nacón nodded at one of his men and quickly told him to take Joss with him to the barracks and then turned and ran in pursuit of his wife who had just disappeared. He was pleased to note that two of his men had followed

Ixta immediately when she left without waiting for orders from him. He trailed the three of them as he sprinted toward his hut with two of his men right on his heels.

Nacón caught up with Ixta just as she entered the clearing right in front of their hut, came close behind her and lifted her off the ground, laughing at her surprise.

"I didn't even hear you! How do you do that?"

Nacón replied laughing, "A warrior must be able to sneak up on his prey even if she is his wife. You yourself know this trick as you demonstrated this technique last night when Kennan entered my father's hut to kill us."

They entered their hut leaving their guards outside and Nacón swept it, using his small device to sweep the perimeter along all the walls. Once finished, he said, "All's well. If you're going to take a nap before dinner, you'd better get at it."

Ixta was already kneeling on the furs, moving her clothing into a more comfortable pillow. She yawned and said, "Wake me. OK?" and then closed her eyes. Within moments, Nacón could hear her gentle snores. He set the alarm and lay down beside her, his arm laid loosely over her hip. He decided that if he wasn't going to get much sleep at night as a newlywed, he probably needed a little sleep as much as she did but for different reasons. He needed to be refreshed to be battle ready now that things were taking another lethal turn with the threat from the ship's captain and crew.

The alarm sounded and after sending one of his men to ask Chaac about dinner plans, Ixta and Nacón freshened up, Ixta luxuriating in the running water in the bathroom she used to splash on her face. "I should stay pissed at you for keeping this bathroom a secret from me. I can't believe you had me using icy water from the well to wash with and that awful chamber pot to go to the bathroom. Argh!"

Nacón laughed and said, "Let's go, wife. My men will bring Joss along with them. Ulises just told me that Chaac is having a small dinner with family for Joss and we're going to be late if we don't hurry up."

Ixta smiled and grabbed Nacón's hand as they walked to the doorway. Met with the armed guard, she was reminded that all was not well here, and things were simmering in an ominous way on several fronts. However, that could be faced later, and she looked forward to chatting with Joss and helping him run interference with Chaac if needed. They paused at the doorway and activated their amulets and Ixta saw she was again surrounded by a furry group of guards as well as her husband in disguise again.

Entering Chaac's hut, Ixta saw that Joss was already seated as was Chaac and surprisingly Nana, who usually served them, was seated on the ruling family's end of the table. She was family but didn't usually sit down with them for meals. All the Uturaxans were cloaked with their holographic disguises which made sense as Joss was just newly arrived and had not earned his full acceptance into the clan yet. Ixta noted with pleasure that Joss had been accorded a position of honor by being seated with Chaac and Nacón. Nacón and Ixta took their seats near Chaac and looked at Chaac to see if he would speak to them all.

Never ignoring an opportunity to say a few words, Chaac said, "We, the Palenque family, are gathered here tonight to welcome Joss Tvitmpr, formerly the ship's doctor, who has asked for and received sanctuary here with us on Uturax."

Several of the elder family members who had not been present at the meeting earlier looked over at Joss in surprise. He wondered if his being Argentian had anything to do with that. As a group, the Uturaxans all looked so similar. He supposed it was fur, but he imagined they felt the same about his purple scales that obscured his features. He saw a few nods and surprises on others' faces but no outright hostility. He had been told this was a family dinner but saw that the table had been extended and others added since this afternoon to accommodate the large group. He counted almost thirty people in the room including Chaac, Ixta and Nacón.

After the murmurs of surprise, Chaac nodded and the serving folk started to bring in the various food dishes, some to serve the dinner guests from, others to set on the table for self-serving. As they all settled into their meal, Joss heard the woman next to him say, "Doctor. Are you mated on your planet?"

Gulping in surprise as a question about his marital status was the last thing he expected, Joss said, "No, ma'am. I am not now, but I was when I was younger."

"Well, young man, don't stop there. What happened? Did you not stay with your bonded mate?"

"Uh, well, she died in childbirth along with our first child. It was a rare blood disorder."

"Sorry to hear that, young man. Now that you are staying on our planet, how do you plan on being useful to us?"

Joss was somewhat taken aback by the persistence and probing of his dinner companion but gamely forged ahead to answer her. "I am a doctor and hope that my skills and training can help the people of Uturax. I also hope to help Ixta with any problems that might arise during her pregnancy."

"Good answer. Good enough. I like you, doctor. Will you seek a mate among us? Are you averse to mating with one of the older women or are you looking to procreate since you created no heirs earlier in your life on your planet?"

Joss choked on what he was trying to swallow and looked over at Ixta whom he saw convulsed with laughter but trying to hide it behind her hands that were covering her face. He looked to Nacón for guidance but other than an amused smile on his face got no clues. "Well, ma'am, I haven't really thought about any of that."

"Well, you're not getting any younger and while you're probably younger than I am, you're no longer a young man. If you want an heir, you'd best get after it. If, however, you want a companion, there are many of us who are no longer in our childbearing years that you should consider."

To Joss the conversation kept getting weirder with everything the woman told him. "Er, what did you say your name was, ma'am?"

"I am Nacón's nana and his great aunt, but my name is Hattie Castañón Lara. You may call me Hattie."

"Hattie, do you have a spouse and children?" Joss asked politely. Seemingly, there were no out of bounds questions about family issues and family seemed to be of great interest to Hattie and he felt he needed to be sure of some boundaries where she was concerned given the drift of her conversation.

"No, Dr. Tvitmpr. May I call you Joss, doctor?"

"Yes, of course."

"Joss, I have no spouse nor children. When I was young, I had a mate, but my husband Halldorr was killed in battle when we were both young. Unfortunately, we had no children yet when he died. But when Nacón's mother died in battle, Chaac chose me to care for his son and Nacón became like a son to me. He is my child in all but the formal sense. I will care for his and Ixta's child as my own grandchild and look forward to that day."

Joss looked at her and saw a warmth and tenderness in her eyes that reached out and touched him in a way that hadn't happened to him in many years. She certainly had a sense of humor too as he'd seen a twinkle in her eye as she had as much as propositioned him a few minutes ago. He laughed out loud as he reached over and grasped her hand.

Allowing his touch, Hattie smiled, and Joss was surprised at himself by his bold touch even though her words sounded suggestive and inviting to him.

"Hattie, I think you and I will be friends."

"I think you are right, Joss. I look forward to it."

Nacón and Ixta watched this last exchange and looked at each other first with surprise and then amusement as it seemed that Joss was settling into Uturaxan culture easily and quickly, more quickly than either of them had anticipated. They looked over at Chaac to see if he had observed what had happened and saw that he had but were unable to discern how he felt as his face showed no emotion.

Nacón thought about what he had just witnessed, still surprised at how the encounter between Nana and Joss had unfolded: *'I wonder if my father will accept Joss and Nana's budding friendship? He has taken her for granted as a woman all these years. I had hoped for years that they would fall in love and marry even though Nana is a little older than Chaac and is his distant aunt. There is no stigma here if pairs are not of the same age though circumstance usually unites couples closer in age for childbearing. But after those years have passed, it is of no importance. This should be interesting to watch.'*

'Wow! That didn't take long. Who would have thought Nana would see Joss and be interested in him? That sure sounded like a romantic encounter to me. After so many years alone, maybe Joss will form an alliance with a female here on Uturax. There hopefully won't be the same kind of prejudice he's experienced on the ship. Being Argentian hasn't seemed to matter to Nana at this point. For looking like a dull, jungle planet, there's a lot of romance going on here. Who woulda' thought?' Ixta mused.

Chapter 7: Sin Raíces

Dinner concluded without incident and Ixta and Nacón decided to go for a walk in the calm before the storm tomorrow. They had guards posted all around

so none of the crew would be able to approach
without raising the alarm. Nacón wanted to go to the
spot where Ethan had been apprehended to see if
there was anything of note they hadn't yet discovered
about the incident. Taking another route, they came
into a small clearing not far from the old mine and
saw four naked hairless people all tangled up together
on the ground. Ixta flushed with embarrassment when
she saw that they were having sex together and that
was why it was hard to figure out where things
started and stopped as far as the bodies went.
Nacón's guards shined a light on them, and they all
looked up in shock, their faces slack with their lust.
They snarled their displeasure at being interrupted in
their group orgy and Nacón shouted, "Are you *Sin
Raíces*?"

"No. No. We're just out having a little fun," one
of the males said with a defiant look on his face, his
words slightly slurred.

"Cover yourselves and leave this place. Go back
to your village and do not return to this side of the
planet. Is that understood? Be gone!" Nacón again
shouted at the group that seemed reluctant to
disengage and do his bidding and took a step in their
direction.

Deciding that he was serious, they scrambled to
their feet, grabbed their clothes and hastily left the
area, running out of the clearing.

"Is that wise, my lord?" asked Ulises quietly of
Nacón, looking around to be sure no one was nearby
to hear him.

"Ordinarily, no. I would have brought them in for
questioning as they know better than coming over

here. But did you notice their eyes and their smell? They're on peyote from the looks of it and we have too much to do tomorrow with Ethan and the impending attack from the ship's captain to waste on this scum. They just didn't look to be part of some resurrection forefront as part of *Sin Raíces* or not. Do you not agree?"

"Agreed," Ulises concurred, relieved that Nacón had truly considered all the angles of the situation. Ordinarily he wouldn't have even voiced a concern but since Ixta had joined with Nacón, his leader seemed preoccupied with this woman. It appears he thinks of little else than his new wife. He had to admit that she was beautiful though Nacón would kill him if he knew he had these thoughts about her. That he was sure of.

They continued along the path to the mines but found no new clues there but could see the signs of a struggle from earlier in the day. Ixta asked Nacón about the people they had seen, "Er, Nacón, those people did not have hair on their bodies. They looked human. What are they? Also, is it a custom here for groups of people to have sex together and so openly?"

"No, Uturaxans do not have group sex or have sex out in the open like they were. Also, they have no hair because they have no amulets. They have removed the DNA markers in their necks they were given at birth, and the amulets will not work without the DNA markers. The fact that they engage in indiscriminate group sex marks them as outcasts. I've told you how important joinings are to us between mated pairs to safeguard familial lineages. The markerless don't care about family lines or who the father of a child is. This goes against all we believe and have worked for as a culture.

The first ones of their group were outcast and sent to the far side of the planet so as not to be seen by off-worlders to create problems for us. Their children do not have DNA markers implanted any more as originally done with them; they flaunted that custom and today it's their lack the technology. For the most part, they have not caused problems until the *Sin Raíces* revolutionary group was formed several years ago. I don't know if all the markerless folk are in this radical political group seeking to overthrow my father and our way of life, but since they all look so similar it is hard to tell at a distance. The obvious first determination is they are not one of us because they wear no amulets whether they've been activated to project the hologram or not. They removed their markers, and their amulets were taken away as a visual reminder of their shame and defiance. I don't even know if any amulets are still hidden in their possession.

I never understood their motivation or reasoning on this basic belief. Uturaxans are allowed a lot of freedom to experiment and form alliances prior to marriage. No, we don't have group sex, but promiscuity is not a word we use to judge others as do humans. Having multiple partners is not judged as a negative behavior among us though we do not believe in more than one partner at a time in a joining. The first were cast out because of their propensity for orgies and indiscriminate sowing of male seed without thought of repercussions or who would claim the children that were conceived. Not providing for children and their future is an egregious offense here as our children are cherished and their futures assured through strong family alliances. These people fought over who had to take responsibility for children born of these joinings. Their children were not cherished or planned for."

"Well, isn't that ironic? I'm pregnant with a pregnancy that we surely didn't plan for. Are you putting yourself in that category with them?" Ixta asked.

"*Christo*, no! While it's true that you and I didn't plan this pregnancy together, our child or children will be cherished and well taken care of. Do you not agree?" Nacón said earnestly, looking at Ixta for her affirmation.

"Agreed. I was just checking. The ones we saw looked like they were high. Is drug use common here?"

"Yes, you're right. They were. As there are no real industry and little technology on their part of the planet, the markerless young often turn to natural drugs, maybe to self-medicate their misery away. Peyote grows wild in parts of the planet and is not hard to obtain. As a result, these young people spend their days under the influence of that drug and others they can find growing in the jungle. That's why I can't understand how *Sin Raíces* continues to recruit and grow. Who would want to promote that way of life over ours? Why would anyone choose that? Our youth serve as warriors and if they prefer after their time in the army, can go into any number of technological jobs that give them purpose or remain

in the military as their career path. We have so much
to offer and other than a backward life, the revolution
offers nothing. Drug use is not tolerated on our side
of the planet. Some of the rich youth of parents with
positions in our community have had their parents
buy them exemptions from military service and they
sometimes fall into bad habits like drug use. They
don't want to serve or work unless they are forced to.
That is something my father is working to try to
change as he sees it detrimental to our collective
future."

Well, apparently it offers something to some
because they do have their followers even after
Camila's execution; Kennan was not deterred and
tried to kill us all in Chaac's hut," Ixta commented
dryly.

"Maybe you can help me get another perspective
on it to try to understand them better. Understanding
the enemy is important in any war and we are at war
on all fronts now."

"We can talk later. It's dark now. Shouldn't we be
getting back to the village? Is it safe for us out here?"

"With my men here, we are safe, but you're right.
. ."

In that moment, they all heard a hissing sound and
the sky was briefly lit up with a flash and then with
what Ixta could only identify as a weapon headed
their way. Nacón and his men heard and then saw the
danger even before she did, and they turned and ran
as one to the old mine with Nacón grabbing her hand
and pulling her along beside him. Not questioning
what was happening or the urgency, Ixta blindly fled
with Nacón. When Ixta struggled to get her balance

and gather speed, Nacón grabbed her to his side and lifted her off the ground as he ran with his men to cover. Hurrying inside the entrance to the mine, they turned away toward the interior waiting for the RPG to hit. Nacón wrapped his arms protectively around Ixta, shielding her with his body. Almost as soon as they thought it, the hit came with a thunderous sound, missing them and burying itself into the earth not fifty feet from the mine entrance where it exploded. A few small rocks dislodged from the mine's ceiling and fell, hitting them on the head and shoulders. A big cloud of dust surrounded them in the mine's entrance, and they coughed as it filled the space. Though their ears were ringing, they could hear pieces of earth and rock raining down after the explosion.

"Shit! That was close. So much for being safe. Do your people have weapons like that or was it one from the ship?"

"Yes, we have those weapons and that sounded like one of our old ones which would make sense as being of the vintage and quality of the weaponry of the rebels. Using them on us is highly unusual, however."

"I'd say the quality of that weapon was good, good enough as it could have killed us," Ulises interjected.

"Agreed. Send out Gael and Kachay to scout the area but be careful. If it's clear, we will leave for the village. Do you both have your infrared eyepieces with night vision?"

"Yes, my lord. We will report back shortly. Do you want us to engage and kill if we encounter any of these predatory traitors?"

"Yes, shoot to kill. I expect they left running by now like the cowards they are, but if they're still there, do not risk injury by capturing them. Kill them if you have the chance. Try to determine if the four we found fornicating were involved in this. If so, I made a grave error in letting them go. They were using drugs though and high and I doubt they could have pulled off such a close shot with that old RPG in their altered state. The old weapons must be aimed with great skill and accuracy to hit even near their targets. But I want to know."

Ixta sighed, trembling after the adrenaline rush that had propelled them to safety in the mine. She was glad she could still run swiftly enough to keep up with Nacón at least for a while. She knew that in a few months that would not be the case. Turning to Ixta and noticing that she was trembling, Nacón put his arm around her shoulders and pulled her to him. "Are you alright, *corazón (sweetheart)*? You were not hurt by the running?"

"No. I am O.K. Just a little shook up by what almost happened. It's been quite a day, a week, a month."

Smiling at her tenderly, Nacón kissed her briefly on the top of her head and turned to his men to give additional orders. Within five minutes, Ulises came back with Gael and Kachay who had no news to report. They'd found where the rebels had been, but their tracks indicated they had left quickly and were no longer in the immediate area.

"They were not the same we came upon earlier fornicating, my lord. There were only two of them from where the RPG was launched. Their tracks came from another direction, and they wore boots on their feet. Those we came across on the path wore no shoes."

"Thank you for that news. It seems the markerless are overrunning our territory though. Report to Chaac when we return to the village to give him an updated report. I'll meet you at his hut as soon as I get Ixta settled in our hut. Let's go back to the village before anything else happens tonight. I think we're all ready to relax without having to look over our shoulders."

With Nacón's men scouting ahead and the rest keeping a protective shield around them, Nacón and Ixta hurried back to the village. Nacón took Ixta to their hut and tried to convince her to stay there and rest, but Ixta didn't feel safe away from him.

"Oh, Nacón, I don't want to complicate your life at the moment because it seems to be a mess right now, but I don't feel safe here without you."

Nacón grimaced when she told him that but had to agree that it did seem to be a mess. He just hadn't wanted to admit to himself just how complicated it had gotten with the *Sin Raíces* and three assassination attempts in the matter of a few weeks. "*Mi amor (my love)*, don't worry. You are right. You are safer at my side though after Kennan's attempt in Chaac's hut, I am probably safer at your side," he laughed ruefully.

"That was just beginner's luck, and you know it," Ixta responded smiling up at him as he came and wrapped his arm around her waist. He put his other hand on her stomach protectively while he kissed her on top of her head.

"Do not discount the courage it took on your part to take action. You are a scientist, not a warrior but you behaved as any warrior would without stopping to think or call for help. Your actions were correct for that situation. I am proud to call you wife and have you at my side as the future queen of Uturax."

Ixta smiled and raised her face to his for his kiss. Then she put her head on his chest and heard his heartbeat while he wrapped his arms around her and held her close to him.

"Come, *corazón (sweetheart)*, we need to report to Chaac to tell him of our adventure and a near miss."

Once in Chaac's hut, Ixta saw Chaac express his fury in a way she had never seen as he was always so rigidly in control of his emotions. He got up and started pacing back and forth, clearly extremely agitated as he spoke to Nacón and his advisors in rapid Uturaxan. The rest of the council that had been hurriedly assembled looked grim as Chaac continued his diatribe. She couldn't follow all of what he was saying but did manage to catch words here and there in his rapid-fire speech. Ulises stepped forward when called by Chaac and gave his account and what his men had discovered about the would-be assassins who had shot the RPG at them. He looked to Nacón for understanding as he voiced what had been his concerns about the markerless ones they'd encountered in the orgy on their way to the mines.

Ixta looked over at Nacón when Ulises told Chaac that he hadn't agreed with Nacón's decision at first and saw Nacón nod to Ulises in agreement.

Apparently Nacón wasn't threatened by his first in command publicly questioning his decision. Chaac was also watching this unfold and when Ulises mentioned that he didn't agree with Nacón he broke in, "You question your prince, Ulises? What is this? Mayhap my son wishes to remove you as his first soldier. He may now have doubts as to your loyalty."

Ulises gulped and swallowed but said nothing. He did look at Nacón when the silence drew out.

"What say you, son? Does Ulises have your confidence still? How can you prepare for battle not knowing if your first in command will follow your orders because he doubts you?"

"First, before I say more, I want to know why Ulises has doubts and how deep they are. Ulises?"

"My prince. I am sorry to doubt you, but since you have married, you are different."

"More. Explain yourself, Ulises. I grow impatient."

"You think only of her it would seem and some of us have wondered if your mind still has the focus for battle. I'm sorry, my prince," Ulises finished miserably as he saw Chaac's and Nacón's looks on their faces.

"You doubt me. This is serious. My father is right, Ulises. You have been my first since we left our schooling and attained our majority. I have called you brother and felt that my life was safe in your hands and under your leadership of the guard."

Ulises hung his head first and then with jaw clenched brought his eyes up to meet Nacón's first and then Chaac's. "You need not question my loyalty, my prince and my liege lord. I will give my life for you."

Chaac continued to stare at Ulises, frowning, as he watched the scene play out.

"Er, Nacón, could I say something here?" Ixta said softly, loathe to disturb Chaac in his current frame of mind. She had never been afraid of him before but felt his controlled power strongly in the hut tonight.

Chaac looked angry still but nodded his assent and looked over at Nacón who said, "Of course, Ixta. What would you like to say?"

"I know that I know nothing about custom or history or what's expected of warriors, but I don't see that Ulises has done anything so wrong. He had doubts, Nacón, but he did what you asked. He didn't confront you in front of the others or in a way that was disrespectful. Why have a second in command at all if you don't want him to think? A thoughtful question doesn't detract from your power if done properly. If you only want someone to rubber stamp, I mean blindly agree with you, why do you have a council? Why do you even ask people what they think?

It is a good thing when people around you with knowledge and skills like his speak up to you. They either help you affirm your thinking or bring up something new to be considered. I think he has shown no disrespect and prior to this, from what I've heard, has served as your first in such a way that you've been completely happy with. Am I not right? Or are there instances of his lack of performance that I'm unaware of? Has he let you down? Has he not performed in battle to meet your expectations?" Ixta said, in a rush wondering if Chaac and Nacón would be angry at her for her interference.

Chaac and Nacón exchanged an amused look and Ulises, seeing their expressions, breathed a sigh of relief. Ulises looked at Nacón's bride with new respect. He had clearly misjudged her and apart from the fact that she had defended him in a most convincing manner in front of their furious leader, she had shown astute, critical thinking in her argument. He didn't really know anything good about off-worlders from previous encounters but realized he had a lot to learn about this one. She wasn't an uninformed frivolous female. She spoke to Chaac and the council without fear and with aplomb. And it looked like she had saved his position and rank for him if the look on both Nacón's and Chaac's faces said anything.

"You are most correct, Ixta. I have had no complaints about Ulises before and when you put it in those words, it would seem as though I should have no complaints about today. What think you, Father?"

"Agreed, my son. Once again, my daughter-by-marriage has shown her worth to our family. I like the way she thinks and I concur. Come, let us sit and plan for tomorrow and the captain's attack on our planet."

They all sat around the table and began to plan for placement of men, weapons, and resources for tomorrow. Much of the details were lost upon Ixta as her rudimentary Uturaxan language skills didn't include weapons and other resources for war. There was little discussion, mostly just a review of roles and positions on the planet to ward off the attack. Chaac stood, followed by Nacón and the rest of the council. Belatedly, Ixta got up and turned to Nacón to see what was next.

"Ixta, we will all go to our huts to sleep for a while to awaken and reassemble three hours prior to dawn. Come, let's go and rest while we can," Nacón said while extending his hand to her to lead her after him out of the hut. They met the rest of his guard outside and Ulises joined his soldiers and prepared to go to the barracks but paused a minute to speak to Ixta.

"Ixta, wife of Nacón, I would like to offer my thanks to you today for speaking for me to Chaac. You do not know me and owed me no consideration, but you offered your support and fresh eyes to view the situation. My words about you and your effect on my prince were not kind, but nevertheless, you defended me in a tense situation and brought an insightful opinion. Again, thank you."

Nacón looked at his first with approval and then at Ixta who just nodded and said, "You're welcome," and then turned to Nacón to head toward their hut. The rest of the guard fell in around them and they walked swiftly through the night to their hut, arriving without incident. Once inside, Nacón said, "Ixta, I need to talk to you about tomorrow's battle. Are you too tired now? Would you prefer we talk in the morning before I go?"

"No, Nacón. Tell me what you have to say now. I'm not sure how we're going to sleep with the anticipation of war tomorrow."

"There will be many Terran lives lost. I would protect you and the doctor by removing you from this area to a safer place. Your former crew lacks the technology to effectively overpower us, even if they had had the element of surprise. The doctor is part of our tribe now and you are my wife, and I will not see harm come to you. Traditionally, we take no prisoners when off-worlders attack our people. We show them no mercy as they would have shown none to us. Do you understand why this is necessary? Our survival depends on having no survivors to tell the story of the battle. We cultivate the impression that we are simple savages when off-worlders arrive as it tends to make them less hostile to us and then they let down their guard. If they thought us equals in strength, they would be combative from the beginning. Diplomacy is something they all talk about, but none practice. Your good doctor is one of the few who have come and put our rights as a people above the ship's needs and wants. That is why his plea for sanctuary was accepted. Plus, he saved your life that first day in our tribe. Uturaxans take this kind of pledge very seriously. *Vaya (well)*, you saw my Nana start the courting process to bring the doctor to her bed at dinner. I would say that erases any doubts about his acceptance."

As Nacón had told her more details, Ixta got quieter and quieter, the gravity of the impending situation weighing on her. Whether she liked or trusted her former crew or not, there were a few individuals that weren't greedy mercenaries she felt sure. Certainly, she hadn't misread everyone on the crew. She truly hated to think of some of them as dead. However, she saw no way out for them. If they chose to participate in the raid, they would die. She wondered at her calm acceptance of the impending death of people she knew and had worked with but could not feel sorry for them. Whether they chose to ignore the oaths they had taken when joining the crew or not was up to them. What the captain was planning was not sanctioned by any of the regulations governing space travel on any planet. They would be outlaws when they stepped out of the ship tomorrow to attack Uturax. Looking at them in that light, her expulsion from the crew hurt a little less.

She was glad not to be associated with the crew that was letting its greed overrule any sense of honor they had toward the inhabitants of this planet. She never would have participated in the raid and had she still been a crew member, she would have broken her ties with them and had no safe place to go. Perhaps everything worked out according to some grand plan after all. If she had not had sex with Nacón and subsequently become his bride as a result, she would have had no group to owe allegiance to. While the captain and some of the crew could cast aside their sense of honor to attack these people, Ixta believed completely that taking advantage of indigenous people was always wrong no matter how you tried to explain it. She hoped that Nacón's confidence in their ability to defend themselves wasn't just wishful thinking. She worried about him and the impending skirmish. He had become her best friend before becoming her husband and she didn't want to see anything happen to him. Regardless of what he said, the crew's weapons were formidable.

"Speak to me, Ixta. You're very quiet, but I know you have thoughts on this matter."

"Yes, I do. I was just thinking how glad I am that all this worked out like this: you married me, and I was forced to renounce my ship and my people. I would never have participated in the attack they are planning, and I suppose that would have been considered mutiny on my part. Shit. This whole thing is so fucked up I can hardly wrap my head around it. Ordinarily I wouldn't want to hide away from the action, but I also do not want to kill some of my former crew. The last time I saw them, some were good people. I guess I don't know now if they still are, but it would be hard to meet them in battle. I would never betray your people, but that is not the same as killing my former crewmates."

"I do not doubt your intentions and your loyalty to me and Uturax, Ixta. You have shown me your bravery. I think primarily of protecting our unborn child by not exposing you to the fighting. I do understand the complexity of your dilemma in facing former crewmates on the battlefield. You will have the doctor to keep you company. Other than the very old who lack the strength to participate fully, most Uturaxans have military training and are skilled in weapons. They are brave as you are. Thus, the majority will be participating in the conflict tomorrow in some way or another." Nacón was proud that this was true of his wife. Her loyalty and honor were immutable in all the months he had come to know her. It was something he admired greatly in her.

"Agreed. Now, let's try to get some sleep. Wake up time will be here too soon."

Nacón set their alarm for time to shower before getting ready to go. Since they hadn't had a full night's sleep and anxiety on Ixta's part and anticipation on his had made it hard to fall right asleep though they were comfortably cocooned against each other. They both started when they heard the alarm and Ixta looked over at Nacón, stifled a yawn and rubbed her eyes.

"We have time to shower before we dress. I think that will help us revive a little and wake up completely. Let's go."

Soon, they were in the elaborate shower in their hut. This time when facing each other, Nacón said nothing when Ixta reached over to shampoo his chest, not stopping her as he had the last time as her hands began to wander lower. Her sudsy hands outlined the muscles of his chest and then moved to his abs, outlining the defined muscles. Not just standing by to enjoy her ministrations, Nacón lathered up his hands and reached over to cup her breasts in his hands and then to focus on her nipples. Very quickly, their hands dropped and Nacón pulled Ixta to his body and backed up till his legs hit the edge of the shower bench. He pulled her closer, so she was straddling him, lifting one of her legs and placing it on the bench to open up her pussy to his fingers. Ixta started a little and then looked in his eyes when he placed several of his fingers inside her already moist vagina. He moved his thumb to find her clit and as he began to pleasure her, she took his already stiff penis in her hand and began to stoke it up and down. He found

her mouth and there were no slow languorous kisses
as he thrust his tongue in her mouth and began the
rhythm that he wanted to do sexually with her.
Groaning, as Ixta brought him close to climax with
her energetic stroking, he moved further back on the
shower bench and brought her closer on top of his lap
so that she was kneeling firmly astride his thighs.
Both moaned as she slipped easily and smoothly
down on top of him. He grabbed her hips to help her
establish the rhythm they both sought. The
impending danger lent an urgency to their joining
that hadn't been there before. The water rained down
on them as their bodies moved up and down
rhythmically. Previously, their urgency had stemmed
from lust alone, but now the impending battle and all
it represented made them almost frantic with their
need for each other. For Nacón, he wanted the release
of his sperm to symbolically reclaim his woman
before going into battle. Ixta's thoughts weren't so
symbolic in that moment as she neared her release;
she just wanted to come again and share that moment
of intimacy with Nacón before sending him off to
battle. Those were thoughts she had pushed aside,
however, as their bodies merged under the warm
water of the shower. Sensing that Ixta was as close to
climax as he, Nacón put his hand between them,
found her clitoris again and pushed her over the edge.
As her vagina began to spasm, he also came, and his
sperm spurted inside her again and again as she
clenched her muscles around him.

Both sat there, bodies entwined for a few more
minutes, still enjoying the afterglow of their sexual
contact as the water continued to cascade over them.

Finally, Nacón said, "We must finish and get dressed, Ixta. It is time."

"Well, I have to say I'm glad we got up early, Nacón. That was more fun than usually waking up and getting dressed."

Nacón smiled at her as he helped her to stand, and they both quickly washed away the remnants of their lovemaking and turned off the water and the blasts of warm air on to dry themselves in preparation for quickly putting on their clothes.

Chapter 8: War

Shortly after, they exited their hut hand in hand both still savoring the moment of their recent intimacy. Ulises and the guard had brought Joss with them and awaited Nacón's orders though they anticipated that Nacón would send them deep into the mountain for safety.

"Sir, women and children are already in place, and we just await your orders as to your wife and the doctor's destination."

Nacón, mentally shaking off the cocoon of sexual intimacy that had so recently occupied his mind, said, "Take them to *la base Olmeca. Supongo que ya están los otros allí, o se fueron a Monte Albán?* (Olmec base. I suppose that the others are already there, or did they go to Monte Alban?")

"Están divididos entre esos dos con unos más en Oaxaca," (They are divided among those two with some others at Oaxaca.) Ulises reported.

"Bien. Entonces, lleva a mi esposa y al doctor a Olmeca y regrésate pronto." (OK. Then, take my wife and the doctor to Olmeca and return quickly."

"A tus órdenes, mi príncipe." (As you request, my prince.)

Nacón told his wife next, *"Mi amor (my love)*, go with Ulises and several of his men now. Joss will accompany you. I know you'll have questions about where you're going but just go now. We can talk later. Yes?"

Ixta reached over and grasped his hand and then nodded her head. She was silent as the enormity of the situation quelled any urge she had for conversation. Her people were going to war with Nacón's people for greed. Not to defend themselves, not to help protect the planet, but to rape the planet of its riches to sell what they could steal to the highest bidder on the black market. She was ashamed to be human at that moment and was glad that Joss was with her. He was so above all the petty machinations of this crew, she was glad that she had left even though her decision to leave the crew had been agonizing at the time. Joss was not human, but he was a reminder of some of the good of her previous way of life. She supposed the irony in it all was that he was an alien too. Ixta looked over at Joss who looked ready to go, more ready than she as she was reluctant to leave Nacón. Her reluctance, or maybe it was the afterglow of sex, made her limbs feel like lead.

"Go!" Nacón almost shouted as Ulises and two of his men turned and began to run away from his hut. Ixta and Joss were right with them as they sped past the clearing in the village to a location within the jungle that was far to the right of the area that Ethan had come last night. Apparently, there was going to be no need for Chaac to try to sort out the problem with Ethan and his attack on Yesenia. After a quick sprint, Ulises raised his hand to call a halt to their dash through the jungle. There was a grouping of rocks off to the right and Ixta and Joss watched as Ulises took out some handheld instrument that looked similar to the one Nacón used in their hut to seal it at night. Ulises input some information and when they stepped around behind the rock formation, a door slid open, and they were met by a heavily armed guard.

"You will go with Eoin now Ixta. You too, doctor. He will take you to safety."

"Thank you, Ulises. Please take care of Nacón today. I worry about the outcome."

"Have no worries *Princesa* (Princess), Nacón will lead us to victory today. He is the best of us and will see that the battle is won."

Smiling weakly, Ixta turned to step inside the rock, and she and Joss followed Eoin into the darkness just beyond the doorway which slid closed behind them with a slight whirring sound.

"Come, please. Follow me and we will be there shortly," Eoin said as he moved quickly away as they walked ten paces and then stopped. Eoin used another handheld device like Ulises' and opened yet another doorway and they all stepped inside. It was a box that had room for perhaps six or seven people. Ixta imagined it would hold only three of Nacón's size. Almost before she had time to think, the doors slid open and then they stepped out into a large, cavernous area and walked a dozen paces and entered yet another box though this one was larger. Very soon, the doors slid open again and Ixta was met by Nana who quickly pulled her into a hug.

"Come with me, child. We need to go deeper into the mountain. Thank you, Eoin. I'll take it from here. You can go join the guard. I know you want to be in the battle. Hurry and you can still get there in time," Hattie said and smiled as she saw Eoin quickly turn and take off running.

Ixta noticed that Nana was also wearing a belt strung with various weapons that she didn't recognize and guessed that war wear was the outfit of the day. "Shit. I feel helpless here. I don't even have that primitive war club I used to bash Kennan on the head with."

Nana wasted no time in taking them along a passage that looked like it had been hewn out of the rock base of the mountain many years before as the cuts on the face of the stone were not fresh. Soon,

Nana told them to step carefully up one step and when they were all in place, Nana punched in a code of numbers on the keypad and the floor began to move out from under them. There was a railing at waist level that moved with them that Joss and Ixta grabbed to regain their balance. As they traveled yet deeper into what Nana had said was the mountain, they both looked around.

They would pass lighted areas where they heard the hum of what sounded like machinery. Ixta's thoughts were confirmed when she finally saw some shiny, sleek machines pass by in a blur. *'What the hell?! Machines? Till a few days ago I thought this was a very simple, rustic group of people. I knew something was up when Nacón finally showed me the shower, but a shower to rooms of machinery was a leap I hadn't taken mentally yet about this culture. The captain was sure right. I don't know shit about the Uturaxans. I wonder if I had then the captain wouldn't be on this mission today to try to steal from them like taking candy from a baby. Serves them right, I guess. If they had known that they had technology like this here, they surely wouldn't have decided to try to steal their wealth. Or would they?'*

After a brief trip on what Ixta decided to call the *conveyor belt* for lack of a better term, Nana turned to them and told them to step off and follow her. Ixta didn't know what to expect next but knew that she could trust Nana to take her to a place of safety, followed along without comment.

Nana stopped beside what looked like a solid rock wall and she laid her hand against the wall, a keypad appeared, and she again punched in some numbers and a door slid soundlessly open. Taken aback by the sophistication of the device, Ixta gaped at it and turned to Joss who was now beside her with a questioning look.

"Don't look at me like that for ideas. I'm in the dark as much as you."

Nana beckoned from inside the opening, and they entered to the sound of the door sliding smoothly shut behind them. "You are welcome here on the observation deck. As you can see, it's not your typical sort of observation deck, but the equipment here will allow us to follow what is happening up on the surface. You are safe now, Ixta. I'm glad that you and Dr. Joss came to be with us inside here today. There's no certainty as to how long the battle will rage nor how many will be wounded. I mean, how many of your people are, Ixta. Don't worry about Nacón. This is what he trains for and he's quite good at being a warrior.

"How did you know what I was thinking, Nana?"

"Ay, *niña (child)*. Your face tells all. I know you and Nacón have already formed a good, strong bond and you do not wish for harm to come to your husband. Am I not right?" Nana said as a huge smile lit up her face.

Ixta laughed, "It appears that you're always right, Nana."

"Now, you two, come with me over to the screens and we will look at a few vantage points topside," Nana said as she sat down on a nearby chair and indicated to Ixta and Joss that they should do the same. Ixta and Joss watched transfixed as Nana typed in a pass code that gave her access to the cameras.

She quickly went through several of them till she found the one she decided gave her the best view. "Here, let's start here. Do you see anyone out there yet?"

Ixta and Joss looked at the screen, surprised that their former ship appeared front and center in the shot. "Nana, have y'all been watching us all along from these cameras?

"Of course, mi'ja (my daughter). That's how we keep track of visitors on our planet. Most never know they're being watched though. Did you ever suspect you were on camera every time you stepped off your ship?"

"No. I hope I didn't do anything that I wouldn't want someone to watch. Oh, wait a minute. Are there cameras in the jungle area Nacón took me for the wedding celebration where we, where we er, got together that first time. That would make me cringe to think that's on tape. A sex tape of me and Nacón creeps me out."

"Speak for yourself. It sounds like an intriguing idea to me, Ixta," Joss said smiling, unruffled by the look of horror that Ixta sent him.

Laughing again, Nana said, "Not to worry, child. Yes, there are cameras there, but we turn off cameras on nights of celebration in those areas for privacy. You may know that our celebrations get a little wild once the *pulque* starts flowing."

"Oh, yes, Nana. I know all about *pulque*. Look at me now as a result of *pulque*. Thank God no one watches what goes on between couples."

"We are very concerned about security but have no wish to intrude on people's privacy. We are not a salacious culture. Did you think we were?"

"Shit. No, of course not."

"Now I've put my foot in my mouth with Nana," Ixta muttered to Joss.

Joss broke in, "Of course not. Hattie, I did have to wonder what you were thinking when you spoke with me at dinner though. All those questions about my mate, my children and the possibility of a new alliance," Joss interjected with a warm smile to let Hattie know he was not being critical, only commenting.

"Oh, doctor. You were listening. I'm glad you remember. This is not the time to pursue this line of conversation, however, because I've just seen the ship's door open."

All three sets of eyes were on the screen as the door opened a little before dawn. Ixta knew that Nacón would have positioned his men near there hours before to be sure that the ship's crew didn't get an advantage over them. She saw that the crew was heavily armed and wearing camo uniforms. *'Huh. Up to no good, clearly.'* The first mate led the phalanx of men with the captain bringing up the rear. They were carrying rucksacks that Ixta supposed were for the gems they were hoping to steal.

"Well, it doesn't look good for their intent now, does it?" Ixta said to no one in particular.

"No, *hija* (daughter) and what you do not know is that this is not the first time your crew has tried to sneak off the ship to look for gems. They have tried repeatedly to explore our planet without permission but have been rebuffed each time by our soldiers' sudden appearances that have made them turn around and run back to the ship each time."

"What? How do you know?"

"The same way we know right now what is happening, Ixta. We have had eyes and ears on them since your ship arrived, *hija (daughter)*. It is how we protect ourselves from invasion," Hattie said gently.

"Yes, of course," Ixta responded, disappointed but resigned to learn how duplicitous her former crew had been.

They watched fascinated as the crew made their way stealthily down the ramp, walking carefully, not talking. They stepped into the clearing at the bottom of the ramp and suddenly the area was flooded with light. As a one, the crew stopped and raised their weapons.

Ixta heard the click of a switch and then the crew's comments could be heard.

"Either Nacón or Chaac has turned on their mikes so you can hear what's happening," Nana explained.

"Halt. Drop your weapons. State your purpose." Nacón's voice rang out clearly.

Looking at each other in confusion, the crew started firing their weapons and milling about to take cover along the ramp's walls.

"Again. We do not want to make this a massacre. Drop your weapons and explain your purpose."

Ixta heard Wells' shout, "Those bastards are in the jungle. Open fire. Kill all those mother fuckers." The crew complied by continuing to fire at the Uturaxans, but then she heard Chaac's voice. It is time, *mi'jo (my son)*. They have chosen."

Nacon said, "Kill them now if they try to leave the ship but spare the ship if you can and drive them into it so they think they are escaping into their ship." Ixta heard the cold resolve in his voice as he sentenced her former crew to death. Given their behavior, she could not fault his decision. She was glad that Joss was here beside her and reached over and grasped his hand. Wanting to look away, but fascinated by what was coming next, Ixta stared at the screen.

"Nana, it sounds like Nacón and his men didn't get hurt when the crew fired. They're OK!"

"Yes, child. Of course. They were using shields though your captain knew none of this. He hoped to kill many Uturaxans today."

The sound of gunfire came through the screen as the Uturaxans let loose a barrage of firepower that easily cut through the minimal protection that the walls of the ship's ramp provided them. She turned away, couldn't look at the twisting bodies that were falling to the ground in rapid succession. She saw the rest of the crew members led by Wells rush the door to try to get back in the ship, but then there was a small explosion by the outer door, opening a gaping hole in the ship's door where the entry keypad used to be. There was no place left for the crew to run to except back onto the ship. Wells was still cursing and shouting at his men not to fall back when that was exactly what he was trying to do.

"Sire, this ship is of no use to us and will be easier to send skyward if we don't destroy it now. We don't want a junker like this sitting around. We can't have too many of these junkers cluttering up Uturax. It's too hard to hide them."

"Agreed. Give the order."

"Eoin, take the ship. Increase the amplitude of your weapons but keep them still set on stun."

"Yes, sir. Done."

And just as Eoin said, the ship's remaining crew that had escaped the ramp joined the other surviving members in the jungle clearing. The battle had been contained to the clearing in the jungle and then the coup was over almost as soon as it began. Ixta saw many more living crew members than she expected but couldn't tear her eyes away from the area littered with the twisted, burned bodies of some of her former crewmates. She couldn't feel sorry for them though as she had clearly seen that they were the aggressors and had intended to steal whatever they could find to fill their rucksacks with including gems and anything else of value from the planet. It was amazing that so many of them still lived. Apparently, greed overcame ethics and honor for them all.

"I am sorry, child. I know that these were your people. It is hard to watch their deaths for you."

"No, Nana. Surprisingly it's not. They made their choices and chose greed over honor. I'm sorry I thought that my former life was the best my civilization had to offer. The only one I would have mourned would have been Joss, but he's right beside me."

"Well, you know this crew wasn't the most tolerant and I wasn't afforded the opportunity to make friends while on this ship, so I have no one to mourn either. My only friend on the ship was you, Ixta. Remember I fled the ship and asked for sanctuary. I made my choice then. I had no friends there by their choice."

"It was always their loss. What I can't get over in my mind is I didn't see any of this coming. All those months of sharing my reports at weekly briefings with Wells and his first mate didn't give me any indication that they had nefarious plans like this afoot."

"Grieve not for the loss of something as base as the lives lost on this crew, child. You have a new life here as the prince's wife and you will bear his heirs. We have brought you into our village and our culture now."

"But Nana, some of you do accept me and have been really kind. You make me feel wanted and loved, but don't forget that people here are trying to kill us. That doesn't exactly make me relax when I think of my future here."

"Fear not. My Nacón will take care of you. He will teach you what you need for self-defense here, but I have to say that you've done quite well here without any teaching. Hitting Kennan on the head and knocking him out in Chaac's hut was a bold move that took courage. You have done well," Nana said with a smile and then she winked at Joss who was taken aback, not expecting to see any playful advances from Hattie on a day like today.

"I'm just playing, doctor. Do not look so fearful," Nana lightly scolded Joss with a smile on her face.

"Nana, why are we alone here? Where's the rest of the tribe?" Ixta asked with some urgency.

"We are in Chaac's personal chambers. Most of the tribe assembled to fight except for the very young and very old or nursing mothers or women in their last trimester of pregnancy. The few that remain here have access to the public viewing screens but not to the radio channel that Chaac and Nacón were broadcasting on. That was for our ears only. Now, they will be doing clean up, altering the ship's audio tape records, inserting a new final message, and preparing for a bit till liftoff, so you have time to get comfortable in Nacón's chamber which connects to here right through that small corridor. Doctor, you may stay here, go to the lounge area of the king's chambers, or come with me. What would you prefer?"

"Wait, Hattie. Did you say liftoff? What did you mean by that? The crew's not fully functional any more with the dead there on the ramp."

"Well, some of them are, but all of them, living or dead, will be loaded back onto the ship. The door has some damage but using the inner lock's door to seal it off, the ship will be airworthy shortly. Lee, one of Chaac's guard, is tampering with the computer system a little to upload a doctored message he created last night and then reprogram it to alter the ship's logs and reports and add a last Mayday Message."

"You make this sound routine. I'm thinking something like this has happened before. Why a Mayday Message? Just where is the ship going?"

"Why into our closet sun, of course. We can't have any trace of the ships that visit us here. Ixta, we take no prisoners. It is our way. Your crew needs to send distress signals back to their homes saying their navigational systems have failed and the gravitational pull of the sun is too great. That part will be real as the ship will then crash into the sun with no trace left other than the new log and distress signal explaining what happened. Lee has already spliced together a message using their voices that they will be unable to alter as they are being pulled into one of our suns."

"Take no prisoners. . .There are a lot of questions you raise in that explanation, Hattie, but I think I'll ask more another day," Ixta said, shaking her head as she tried to reconcile Hattie's description of how this primitive planet knew how to do all that she described. Given what she'd learned, it seemed impossible, but her information about Uturax was clearly woefully inadequate.

Joss and Ixta looked at each other and Ixta sighed and then headed for the corridor that would lead her to Nacón's chambers. Joss looked at Hattie with a questioning look and then said, "Lead the way, Hattie. I put myself in your hands."

Joss thought he heard a suggestive comment under her breath but wasn't sure when she looked up at him guilelessly and grabbed his arm to lead him after her to her own personal chamber. Ixta found Nacón's chamber with little difficulty and was surprised when the door opened when she placed her hand over the lighted rectangle on the side. *'Shit. That doesn't seem especially secure. We'll have to figure out how to lock this thing if we're going to be holed up here for a while. I'm sure our time here will involve sex and hot, steamy showers. Crap. I've become addicted to Nacón now. I can't be around him without wanting him inside me. I can see him thrusting and pumping his sperm inside me now if I close my eyes a little and*

*my body craves that contact with him. How did I
come to want this man so much? I feel like his sex
slave if there is such a thing in this day and age. I
would do anything to pleasure him and share another
orgasm with him. I feel like I've lost contact with
reality because I've never been so sex-obsessed
before. All my waking moments are spent fantasizing
about him and what we'll do to each other's bodies
the next time we're together. It makes me hot just
thinking about it.'*

Ixta laid down on the bed and fell asleep quickly
as the night's sleep had been short and the anxiety of
the impending battle had left her emotionally strung
out and exhausted. Her sleep was dreamless till the
end when she dreamed of Nacón's tongue on her
nipples, licking them in a circle and then gently
sucking on one. When she felt his fingers enter her
moist vagina, she opened her eyes to find Nacón
staring down at her. He bent his head, his long hair
brushing her face and then her chest as he gave her a
soft kiss. Ixta reached up to wrap her arms around his
torso.

"Sorry I woke you, Ixta. Battle makes my body
want sexual release. Once we were done at the ship,
all I could think of was getting back here and sharing
pleasures with you."

Ixta sat up and looked down at the erection poking
through his loin cloth. "I guess you really are ready. I
have to confess that I was dreaming about making
love with you too. Then my dream turned into reality
when you kissed my nipples and touched my pussy."

"Ixta, I do not want to always rush you, but you
are like my drug. I cannot get enough of you. I find I

can't even take the time to romance you and make you cry out for wanting me, for needing me like I need you."

"Nacón, enough. In case you hadn't noticed, I'm crazy for you and can't have a coherent thought that doesn't involve your dick inside my pussy. What are you waiting for?"

Nacón didn't need more of an invitation and ripped off his loincloth, moved to position himself between her thighs and then slid inside her warm, wet vagina. He felt her vagina close around him as she squeezed him and then released her muscles so that he could easily find his way inside. He buried himself completely, his shaft completely enveloped inside Ixta and began to move, the bloodlust from the battle still at the front of his thoughts. He swelled even more as he thought about the release that their coupling would bring. In and out, he built the rhythm, and Ixta lifted her hips to better accommodate him and match his rhythmic movements. For being celibate for so long, Ixta felt she'd certainly gotten back into the swing of things. She loved the way Nacón made her feel, not just the incredible sex, but his concern for her comfort and pleasure as well as his protective nature toward her. He made her feel that it was not just sex, but something more that connected them in a way that she'd never felt with another man. Looking back on her other sexual partners, they seemed like bumbling fools compared to Nacón. Even when he was in a hurry, he always took care of her.

Ixta felt her climax building and looking up at Nacón through sex-dulled eyes, forcing herself to focus on his face. She could see his jaw muscles clench, and the vein in his temple started to pound and knew he too was ready to come. He touched the entrance to her womb with his penis and it sent shockwaves through her womb and vagina as she clenched her muscles down and around him as he began pumping his sperm inside her again and again. He groaned and leaned down on his arms to keep from falling on top of her. Ixta rode the crest of her own orgasm and felt like her body was melting into the bed. She didn't have the energy to move or say anything. She closed her eyes, savoring the moment. Then she felt a soft kiss on her eyelids and then on her mouth and then Nacón withdrew from her and laid down beside her on the bed, pulling her limp body to his to cradle her. She rolled onto her side more comfortably and they lay there, spooning, saying nothing till she felt his hand cover her lower stomach protectively, she thought. He kissed her ear and then in a moment, Ixta heard his snores begin as he fell asleep. That was her last thought before she too fell asleep, tired, but happy, after a trying twenty-four hours.

They awoke a while later when they heard a tapping on the door and Nana's voice.

"What is it, Nana? Have we slept too long?"

"No, *mi'jo (my son)*. Just a few hours, but your father wants to talk to you before he convenes the war council to review the battle today. He will break his fast and wants both you and Ixta to come to his dining chamber. Can you be there in *quince minutos (fifteen minutes)*?"

"Sí (Yes), Nana. *Allí, te veo I'll see you there).*
Ixta, we have to take a fast shower and get dressed to
go see my father."

Ixta had already risen during their conversation
and was looking for the bathing room when Nacón
joined her and typed in some symbols on the lighted
panel that appeared on the wall when he placed his
hand over it. The wall opened with a bathing facility
similar to the one in Nacón's hut and they both
entered to take a quick shower after which they began
to quickly put on their clothes, mindful of Hattie's
warning about time.

"Whoa? What are you wearing? You look normal.
No kilts, no leather skins. You are wearing what we'd
wear back home? What the fuck?" Ixta said when she
saw what Nacón was pulling out of the wall closet,
thoroughly confused by the transformation in Nacón'
s attire.

"Ixta, I will speak of this more later, but these are
my regular clothes when there are no off-worlders on
my planet."

"Alright. Yes, there is a boatload to speak about
this topic later, but Nacón, I have no clothes other
than these. Will that be alright?"

"Yes, *amor*, you will find others in the storage
cabinets on the other wall for later. What you are
putting on now is fine. If there is to be a dinner
tonight, we will return here to change into more
formal clothing. I ordered clothing to be made for
you when we married, and our people have been
working non-stop to finish them, but I haven't had
the opportunity to show them to you yet. So much
has happened in such a short time."

"What? More surprises. I can't wait to check them out. There's so much I feel like I don't know and need to learn. I'm glad Joss is here to help me through this pregnancy or are there medical surprises you want to share with me?

"You know as much about this pregnancy as I do. However, I am also glad to have Joss with us to help you through your pregnancy." Nacón said as he placed a soft kiss on the top of Ixta's head and wrapped his arms gently around her.

"Let's go see your father, Nacón."

Nacón just smiled at Ixta as he guided her toward the door to see Chaac and then the war council to strategize about what would come next.

End/Fin

Glossary: Characters & Terms for Uturax Book Series

7Up-lemon-lime sweet, carbonated beverage from Earth

allí te veo- literally, there I see you, implying future tense; "I'll see you there"

Anthony- junior anthropologist from ship

atole- gruel made of corn pounded into flour and boiled in water or milk, common Uturaxan staple meal

Bekka- Chaa's wife

Camila Obregón Castillo- daughter of one of the noble families

Caray-Uturaxan exclamation meaning "wow!" "good gracious!" used to denote surprise or impatience

carumba- Uturaxan exclamation with a variety of meanings: "good heavens," "for heaven's sake!" "for crying out loud," "good gracious"

Ccaatf- Argentian swear word probably meaning . . . shit

cenote- Uturaxan word meaning rock pool with natural spring

Chaac Palenque- king of Uturax

corazón- literally "heart", term of endearment on Uturax (sweetheart)

Diego- leader of Chaac's guard

DNA markers- implanted shortly after birth, worn by ruling Uturaxans and their supporters *doña-* ma'am, title of respect for women, not girls or teenagers, usually married

Dr. Ferguson- ship's psychologist

Dr. "Joss" MsgavJoss Tvitmpr- Argentian, ship's physician

*durazno-*peach

Eoín- member of Chaac's guard

Ethan Baker-biologist

Gael- member of Nacón's guard

Hattie Castañón Lara- great aunt of Nacón, his "nana" who raised him

hijo de la chingada- "motherfucker"

hombre- literally "man, but used as an interjection meaning "wow" or "Can you believe?"

IPEC-Interstellar Planetary Exploration Consortium, company behind the ship's voyage to Uturax and other planets

Ixta Tikal (de Palenque), lead anthropologist, tall red-haired Terran female

John Paul Wells-captain of the IPEC ship

Jimmy- crew member

Justin Daniels- first officer on the ship

Kachay-member of Nacón's guard

Kennan Eisenberg Ramírez- member of *Sin Raíces*

la base Olmeca (the Olmec base), *la base Monte Albán* (the Monte Alban base), *la base Oaxaca* (the Oaxaca base)- Olmeca has the war room and quarters of the royal family; all are underground bunkers where the Uturaxan people stay during battle and especially harsh weather

lo hecho, hecho está- what's done is done

M.A.S.H.- mobile army surgical hospital, term used on spaceship

maldita- Uturaxan swear word meaning "damned"

Maysarah- Uturaxan female acquaintance of Eoin and Nacón

Melanie- crew member, friend of Ixta's

mi amor- literally, my love, term of affection expressing love

mi cielo-literally, my heaven, term of affection, expressing love

mi niña- literally my child (female), can be used as term of familiarity, can also convey affection

mi príncipe- my prince

miel de agave- literally "honey from agave", native plant, sweet, sticky substance used to sweeten food and beverages

mi'ja- slang contraction of *mi hija*, meaning my daughter, can be used as term of familiarity

Nacón Palenque -prince, son of Chaac

neodymium- rare, valuable mineral element found on Argentia

Nuxxeme- Argentian swear word

pendejo- Uturaxan swear word meaning "jerk" or "stupid fool," *"dumbass"*

pero- conjunction meaning but

Preston-crew member, acquaintance of Ixta's who wanted to date her

promethium- rare, valuable mineral element found on Argentia

pulque- native drink distilled from the maguey plant

rolag- Terran word for fleece that's been carded and rolled off the carder or handheld carding combs

Rosaura- serving woman on Uturax

Sin Raíces- rebel faction on the planet whose members look human

telóm - Uturaxan command meaning "quiet"

the markerless-look human, not furry, have no DNA markers

tlacuache- Uturaxan swear word used to mean "hell"

Ulises- Nacón's first guard, leader of the elite unit that
guards the prince
ununtrium-rare, precious radioactive Uturaxan mineral
*Uturaxan-*furry humanoid alien inhabitants of the planet
*Uturax-*unexplored planet with two suns, areas of
mountains and jungles
*vaya-*literally "go" but used as an interjection meaning
"wow" or "Can you believe?"
yajttza- Argentian word of exclamation
Yesenia Tenoch Tatanka-Iyotake- 13-year-old Uturaxan
student accosted in the jungle

www.ingramcontent.com/pod-product-compliance
Lightning Source LLC
Chambersburg PA
CBHW060534180626
46817CB00002B/572